"Exciting thriller debut with an astonishing end."
— *Westdeutsche Zeitung*

"Seldom does one get a thriller about white-collar crime, with an intelligent, independent lesbian and Asian protagonist. It's also rare to find a book with such interesting and exotic settings...Readers will find great amusement in Ava's unconventional ways and will certainly enjoy accompanying her on her travels."
— *Literaturkurier*

PRAISE FOR *THE DISCIPLE OF LAS VEGAS*

"I started to read *The Disciple of Las Vegas* at around ten at night. And I did something I have only done with two other books (Cormac McCarthy's *The Road* and Douglas Coupland's *Player One*): I read the novel in one sitting. Ava Lee is too cool. She wonderfully straddles two worlds and two identities. She does some dastardly things and still remains our hero thanks to the charm Ian Hamilton has given her on the printed page. It would take a female George Clooney to portray her in a film. The action and plot move quickly and with power. Wow. A punch to the ear, indeed."
— J. J. Lee, author of *The Measure of a Man*

"I loved *The Water Rat of Wanchai*, the first novel featuring Ava Lee. Now, Ava and Uncle make a return that's even better...Simply irresistible." — Margaret Cannon, *Globe and Mail*

"This is slick, fast-moving escapism reminiscent of Ian Fleming, with more to come in what shapes up as a high-energy, high-concept series." — *Booklist*

"Fast paced...Enough personal depth to lift this thriller above solely action-oriented fare." — *Publishers Weekly*

"Lee is a hugely original creation, and Hamilton packs his adventure with interesting facts and plenty of action." — *Irish Independent*

"Hamilton makes each page crackle with the kind of energy that could easily jump to the movie screen...This riveting read will keep you up late at night." — *Penthouse*

"Hamilton gives his reader plenty to think about...Entertaining." — *Kitchener-Waterloo Record*

PRAISE FOR *THE WILD BEASTS OF WUHAN*

"Smart and savvy Ava Lee returns in this slick mystery set in the rarefied world of high art...[A] great caper tale. Hamilton has great fun chasing villains and tossing clues about. *The Wild Beasts of Wuhan* is the best Ava Lee novel yet, and promises more and better to come." — Margaret Cannon, *Globe and Mail*

"One of my favourite new mystery series, perfect escapism." — *National Post*

"You haven't seen cold and calculating until you've double-crossed this number cruncher. Another strong entry from Arthur Ellis Award–winner Hamilton." — *Booklist*

"An intelligent kick-ass heroine anchors Canadian author Hamilton's excellent third novel featuring forensic accountant Ava Lee... Clearly conversant with the art world, Hamilton makes the intricacies of forgery as interesting as a Ponzi scheme." — *Publishers Weekly*, STARRED review

"A lively series about Ava Lee, a sexy forensic financial investigator."
— *Tampa Bay Times*

"This book is miles from the ordinary. The main character, Ava Lee, is 'the whole package.'"
— *Minneapolis Star Tribune*

"A strong heroine is challenged to discover the details of an inter-continental art scheme. Although Hamilton's star Ava Lee is technically a forensic accountant, she's more badass private investigator than desk jockey."
— *Kirkus Reviews*

"As a mystery lover, I'm devouring each book as it comes out... What I love in the novels: the constant travel, the high-stakes negotiation, and Ava's willingness to go into battle against formidable opponents, using only her martial arts skills to defend herself... If you want a great read and an education in high-level business dealings, Ian Hamilton is an author to watch."
— *Toronto Star*

"Fast-paced and very entertaining."
— *Montreal Gazette*

"Ava Lee is definitely a winner."
— *Saskatoon Star Phoenix*

"*The Wild Beasts of Wuhan* is an entertaining dip into potentially fatal worlds of artistic skulduggery."
— *Sudbury Star*

"Hamilton uses Ava's investigations as comprehensive and intriguing mechanisms for plot and character development."
— *Quill & Quire*

PRAISE FOR *THE RED POLE OF MACAU*

"Ava Lee returns as one of crime fiction's most intriguing characters. *The Red Pole of Macau* is the best page-turner of the season from the hottest writer in the business!"
— John Lawrence Reynolds, author of *Beach Strip*

"Ava Lee, that wily, wonderful hunter of nasty business brutes, is back in her best adventure ever... If you haven't yet discovered Ava Lee, start here."   — *Globe and Mail*

"The best in the series so far."   — *London Free Press*

"Ava [Lee] is a character we all could use at one time or another. Failing that, we follow her in her best adventure yet."
                              — *Hamilton Spectator*

"A romp of a story with a terrific heroine."
                              — *Saskatoon Star Phoenix*

"Fast-paced... The action unfolds like a well-oiled action flick."
                              — *Kitchener-Waterloo Record*

"A change of pace for our girl [Ava Lee]... Suspenseful."
                              — *Toronto Star*

"Hamilton packs tremendous potential in his heroine... A refreshingly relevant series. This reader will happily pay House of Anansi for the fifth instalment."   — *Canadian Literature*

PRAISE FOR *THE SCOTTISH BANKER OF SURABAYA*

"Hamilton deepens Ava's character, and imbues her with greater mettle and emotional fire, to the extent that book five is his best, most memorable, to date."   — *National Post*

"In today's crowded mystery market, it's no easy feat coming up with a protagonist who stands out from the pack. But Ian Hamilton has made a great job of it with his Ava Lee books. Young, stylish, Chinese Canadian, lesbian, and a brilliant forensic accountant, Ava is as complex a character as you could want... [A] highly addictive

series...Hamilton knows how to keep the pages turning. He eases us into the seemingly tame world of white-collar crime, then raises the stakes, bringing the action to its peak with an intensity and violence that's stomach-churning. His Ava Lee is a winner and a welcome addition to the world of strong female avengers."
— *NOW* Magazine

"Most of [the series's] success rests in Hamilton's tight plotting, attention to detail, and complex powerhouse of a heroine: strong but vulnerable, capable but not impervious...With their tight plotting and crackerjack heroine, Hamilton's novels are the sort of crowd-pleasing, narrative-focused fiction we find all too rarely in this country."
— *Quill & Quire*

"Ava is such a cool character, intelligent, Chinese-Canadian, unconventional, and original...Irresistible." — *Owen Sound Sun Times*

THE
TWO SISTERS
OF
BORNEO

Also in the Ava Lee Series

The Dragon Head of Hong Kong:
The Ava Lee Prequel (e-book)

The Water Rat of Wanchai

The Disciple of Las Vegas

The Wild Beasts of Wuhan

The Red Pole of Macau

The Scottish Banker of Surabaya

THE TWO SISTERS OF BORNEO

AN AVA LEE NOVEL

IAN HAMILTON

SPIDERLINE

DOUGLAS COLLEGE LIBRARY

This edition published in 2014 by
House of Anansi Press Inc.
110 Spadina Avenue, Suite 801
Toronto, ON, M5V 2K4
Tel. 416-363-4343
Fax 416-363-1017
www.houseofanansi.com

Distributed in Canada by
HarperCollins Canada Ltd.
1995 Markham Road
Scarborough, ON, M1B 5M8
Toll free tel. 1-800-387-0117

This is a work of fiction. Names, characters, businesses, organizations, places, and events are either a product of the author's imagination or are used fictitiously. Any resemblance to actual persons, living or dead, is purely coincidental.

19 18 17 16 15   2 3 4 5 6

Library and Archives Canada Cataloguing in Publication

Hamilton, Ian, 1946–, author
The two sisters of Borneo / Ian Hamilton.

(An Ava Lee novel)
Issued in print and electronic formats.
ISBN 978-1-77089-244-6 (pbk.).— ISBN 978-1-77089-245-3 (html)

I. Title. II. Series.

PS8615.A4423T86 2014   C813'.6   C2013-903903-1
C2013-903904-X

Jacket design: Gregg Kulick
Text design and typesetting: Alysia Shewchuk

We acknowledge for their financial support of our publishing program the Canada Council for the Arts, the Ontario Arts Council, and the Government of Canada through the Canada Book Fund.

Printed and bound in Canada

MIX
Paper from
responsible sources
FSC® C004071

For my brother, Colin, and my sister, Karen

AVA LEE SENSED SOMETHING WAS WRONG THE INSTANT she saw May Ling Wong standing alone at the entrance to the Cathedral of the Immaculate Conception.

It was the second Saturday in January, and the sky was overcast. It was cold and dank, typical weather for the middle of a Hong Kong winter. Ava was in a Bentley limousine with Amanda Yee, the bride-to-be and her future sister-in-law, and three bridesmaids when she spotted May Ling. Amanda was about to marry Ava's half-brother Michael, and Ava was the maid of honour. They had driven from Sha Tin, the town in the New Territories where Amanda's parents lived.

The five women had been up since six that morning, getting coiffed, made up, and dressed by some of the most expensive hairstylists and makeup artists in Hong Kong. Ava had resisted having her shoulder-length black hair twisted and sprayed into an elaborate updo. She had declined to have her face slathered with foundation and powder. But she had no choice about the sleek lavender silk dress that Amanda had chosen for the bridal party. The tight strapless gown fell to Ava's knees and made her feel as if she were enveloped in coloured plastic wrap.

Ava was in her mid-thirties but this was only the third wedding she had attended. The first had been her older sister Marian's, when she married a *gweilo* civil servant named Bruce. The previous August her best friend, Mimi, had married Ava's best guy friend and occasional work associate, Derek Liang, at Toronto City Hall in front of ten friends and family members. Mimi was pregnant with Derek's child, and the wedding had been little more than a formality. They had already started their life together, recently moving into a house in Leaside, one of Toronto's more affluent neighbourhoods. Afterwards Derek had treated everyone to lunch at a nearby Chinese restaurant. The Hong Kong wedding, in contrast, would be going from the splendour of the cathedral to an eight-course feast in the ballroom of the Grand Hyatt Hotel.

When the limousine arrived at Immaculate Conception, three photographers and two cameramen were waiting for the bride and her bridesmaids. Twenty or thirty of the several hundred wedding guests were huddling together on the sidewalk for a last-minute cigarette. May Ling stood to the side, apart from the others. She wore a fitted coral and pale green Chanel suit, the skirt coming to just slightly above the knee. She stared vacantly, her face impassive, her back pressed against the grey stone church wall.

"There's May," Ava said to Amanda. "She looks a bit troubled."

"Huh?" Amanda said, her attention focused on gathering up the metre-long train of her ivory Vera Wang wedding dress.

"Nothing," Ava said, knowing the word *troubled* shouldn't have escaped her lips. The wedding might be taking place in Western fashion in a Roman Catholic Church, but Chinese superstitions couldn't be that easily dismissed. Even a negative word, let alone deed, was viewed as having the potential to jinx the married couple. As the maid of honour, part of Ava's role was to make sure that Amanda stayed protected inside a happy bubble.

When Ava got out of the limo, May Ling took a step forward and waved. She smiled, but her brow was furrowed and the smile was fleeting.

Amanda slid from the car, posed for the cameras, and was then surrounded by the bridesmaids for more photos. The plan was for them to escort her to a small room just inside the main entrance, where she could make any last-minute adjustments and prepare for the walk down the aisle. As the bridal party started towards the church, Ava moved next to Amanda.

"We have about twenty minutes before the ceremony starts," Ava said. "I'm going to have quick chat with May Ling and then I'll meet you inside."

"Where is May?"

"Over there," Ava said, pointing, and realized with relief that Amanda hadn't heard her earlier comment.

Amanda glanced at May. "I'm surprised she's here."

"Why?"

"She phoned me a few days ago to say she might not make it."

"Why not?"

"She didn't say. She just said she had some issues to deal with in Wuhan."

"Well, she's here, so I guess the problem has been resolved. Now you'd better get inside."

"Don't take too long. I'm more nervous than I thought I would be," Amanda said.

"I'll be there shortly."

Ava turned and walked towards May Ling. The two women had met the previous year, when May and her husband, Changxing, had hired Ava and her partner, Uncle, to help them locate and recover the millions of dollars they had lost purchasing forged paintings. Ava and Uncle were then in the debt-recovery business. The case had not gone smoothly, and the relationship between the two women had degenerated into betrayal and mistrust when May had used and deliberately undermined Ava. But a short time later May had come to Ava's assistance in a case that involved Ava's family — specifically her half-brother Michael — and the two women had found common ground and begun to build a friendship.

May took a step forward and held out her arms. Ava slid into them and the two women hugged.

"You look absolutely gorgeous," May said.

"I spent last night and this morning with Amanda and those twenty-something friends of hers. They made me feel old, not gorgeous."

"You're only in your mid-thirties. I'm in my mid-forties, so imagine how I feel."

"May, men adore you," Ava said.

"Changxing does, anyway."

Ava took a step back. May was the same height as her — five feet three inches — and weighed maybe five pounds less. She was slim, fine-boned, and, like Ava, had an ample bosom that she didn't hesitate to show off. Her hair was straight and cut short in a fashionable bob. Physically she gave off a sense of vulnerability, but she had a sharp mind and a quick tongue that could be raw and cutting. And she could also be highly charming and subtly seductive. Uncle said that men were torn between wanting to protect her and wanting to impress her.

"Where is Changxing?" Ava asked.

"He doesn't like weddings and he hates churches. He's spending the afternoon with Uncle. He'll meet me later at the Mandarin Oriental to get dressed for the dinner."

"Uncle didn't mention anything to me about Changxing."

"He called Uncle this morning to see if he was up for a visit. He said he was, although I did tell Changxing he should have checked with you."

Uncle, like Changxing and May Ling, was from Wuhan, in Hubei province in central China. He had fled when he was a young man to escape the Communists. After he landed in Hong Kong, he had became prominent in the triad societies before retiring as its chairman and starting the debt-collection business that Ava later joined. Changxing liked to emphasize the Wuhan ties between the two men. Uncle's interest in the wealthy businessman, who was known as the "Emperor of Hubei," had always been in his *guanxi*, his connections, and in his ability to deliver favours.

Ava and May Ling's relationship stood separate from that of the men, a situation that Uncle endorsed. Though it was unsubstantiated by word or deed, Ava had a sense that Changxing didn't share Uncle's enthusiasm for the women's increasingly tight friendship, which was further emphasized by the fact that they had set up a business together. The Three Sisters was the name of their newly formed investment fund. May Ling and Ava were the majority shareholders and Amanda had a minority stake. The fund was now Amanda's full-time occupation, May Ling was splitting her time between their new venture and her business interests with Changxing, and Ava had committed herself to the business after Uncle gave her his blessing.

"I'm not Uncle's nurse or his secretary, and he hates it when I start acting like one."

"How is he?" May asked softly.

"As well as anyone can expect. The cancer has spread from his stomach to his other organs. While the doctors don't like to talk about time frames, I don't think I'll be needed in Hong Kong for much longer."

"It's been four months now?"

"We're into the fifth month. He's better than I thought he would be, though. Most days I meet him in the morning for congee, and if he's up to it, for dinner somewhere in Kowloon. The dinners are becoming rarer these days; there are only so many things he can eat. That irritates him, and not many things do. But he seems to accept what's happening, and we manage to spend our time enjoying each other's company and talking about other things. My mother flew over from Toronto for two weeks in early December. She was a blessing in terms of supporting me and taking Uncle outside himself. She makes him laugh."

"Ava, in these talks you've had with Uncle, have you kept him up to date on our business?"

"I've kept him briefed. I told him you and Amanda are running things until I'm ready to join full-time."

"Good." May hesitated, her eyes wandering past Ava

towards the church door. "I think one of the bridesmaids is looking for you," she said.

Ava turned and saw the one named Camille standing in the doorway. "I'll be right there," she shouted.

"I can't help but think how strange this situation is," May said, looking around at the guests, who were now filing into the church.

"What do you mean?" Ava asked, surprised by May's vagueness.

"Sorry. I meant your being the maid of honour," she said, and then put her hand to her mouth. "Oh, Ava, I'm sorry again. I don't mean to offend; it's just that people are talking."

"I know. This morning I met Michael's three brothers — my half-brothers — for the first time. At first they were distant, tentative. Then we chatted a bit and, truthfully, they couldn't have been nicer. But I know what some people are saying about the daughter of a second wife having such a major role in the wedding of the eldest son of the first wife."

"It is unusual."

"The way I look at it, I'm a friend and now a business partner of Amanda. Her father, Jack, was Uncle's and my client, and we even saved his life. If she had been marrying anyone else I'd have had the same role. I'm here for her."

"Ava..." Camille's voice could be heard from the church doorway.

"I have to go," Ava said to May.

"Tomorrow can we meet for breakfast? We can have dim sum at the Mandarin."

"Sure, that should be fine," Ava said, and then realized May was looking past her again. "Is there a problem?"

"No, not really. We just have some things we need to go over."

"Ava, Amanda is almost ready," Camille said, appearing at Ava's side, and reaching for her elbow.

"Tell her I think she's the most beautiful bride I have ever seen," May said.

"Yes, I will," Ava said, and then turned and walked into the church with the bridesmaid.

What a strange day, she thought. *First meeting all my half-brothers, and then May acting so anxious. And now I'm going to walk down the aisle just ahead of Amanda, knowing that most of the people in this church think it's scandalous for me even to be in the building.*

What Ava didn't know was that the day was about to become stranger still.

THE HUNDRED-YEAR-OLD IMMACULATE CONCEPTION
was a jewel of a church, with its glistening black-and-white
checkerboard floor flanked by white granite pillars and
under soaring arches. The gleaming wooden pews were
filled with guests dressed in their finest, and Amanda's
expansive silk and chiffon gown swished as she walked
down the aisle with her father, Jack Yee, by her side.

Ava had made the same walk just thirty seconds before,
keeping her eyes locked onto the altar straight ahead. She
thought she heard some whispers and murmurs, but it was
all indistinct. When she took her position, she found it a
struggle to remain calm. She couldn't help but glance at
the front pew where her father, Marcus Lee, sat next to
his first wife, Elizabeth. Ava had never seen, let alone met,
her father's first wife, but she knew it was her all the same.
Elizabeth Lee was staring at Ava, as were the other women
around her, and Ava quickly turned away.

As May Ling had implied, Amanda's choice of Ava as her
maid of honour was full of controversy and the subject of
much gossip in Hong Kong. As the daughter of a second

wife, Ava was officially considered illegitimate, so her prominent role in the wedding party was more than some people could bear. She had heard rumours that Elizabeth's four sisters were thinking of boycotting the wedding. Ava had no idea if they had, and truthfully didn't care. She was there because Amanda, backed by Jack Yee, had insisted on her presence and participation. Michael had agreed to present the idea to his father and mother. Marcus expressed no opinion; it was his wife's reputation that was at risk, so the decision was hers. To everyone's shock, she had gone along with Amanda's wishes.

Ava looked to her right. Michael and his brothers were watching Amanda as she approached. When she was about five steps away, Michael turned and looked at Ava. He raised his eyebrows ever so slightly and then smiled as if to say, *Who would have thought this day would come?* She smiled in return and felt her anxiety start to ebb.

The ceremony went off smoothly, and after the official papers were signed the wedding party walked back down the aisle to applause and cheers. Ava, her arm looped through that of her half-brother Peter, Michael's best man, kept her eyes locked straight ahead. As they left the church, the bride and groom walked under a red umbrella that was meant to symbolically ward off evil spirits. It had the added benefit of protecting them from the rice the immediate family and the rest of the wedding party were sprinkling on them. Their only concern was a light shower of confetti.

Earlier that morning, as was the custom, the groom and his party had gone to the house in Sha Tin to collect the bride. Michael and Amanda climbed into the Bentley that had brought her from Sha Tin; Ava and the bridesmaids got into one Mercedes, the groomsmen into another. The cars then drove in convoy to the Grand Hyatt, where the reception was being held.

At the hotel, Amanda and the bridesmaids went directly to their adjoining suites to freshen up. Amanda would wear a traditional red Chinese wedding dress for her initial entry into the ballroom and for the tea ceremony. After that she would change dresses several times. The dress that Amanda would wear for the early part of the evening was already laid out on the bed. The evening gown and the cheongsam she would wear later were hung in the closet. Ava wished she had something — anything — to change into, but she was stuck with the lavender dress.

The evening's activities were being held in and around the Hyatt's Grand Ballroom. When Amanda and her bridesmaids finally arrived, Michael, his brothers, and both sets of parents were standing in a casual receiving line. The instant Amanda made her appearance, the line disappeared. Michael rushed to her side and led her into the ballroom and onto the dance floor, where two chairs were placed in preparation for the tea ceremony.

Peter walked over to Ava. "We need to go inside right away as well," he said. He led her to a small table to the right of the chairs, where hotel staff had laid out teacups and pots.

"Have you done this before?" Peter asked.

"No, but I have seen it."

"Quite simple, really. Our job is to keep Michael and Amanda supplied with fresh cups of tea."

"I think I can manage that."

A crowd had gathered around the perimeter of the dance

floor. Jack Yee and his wife stepped forward to sit in the chairs. Peter poured two cups of tea and gave one to Ava, and they walked side by side over to Michael and Amanda, who were standing directly in front of the chairs. They took the cups from Ava and Peter and turned to face Amanda's parents. They knelt, bowed their heads, and held the teacups high. The Yees accepted the cups and sipped from them. Then they leaned forward with broad smiles on their faces. Jack Yee put Michael's hand on top of Amanda's, said something quietly, and then passed a red envelope to them. Ava knew this was the first of hundreds of red envelopes, or pockets, that the couple would receive that night, but she doubted that any of the others would contain quite so much money.

The tea ceremony was a traditional way for Amanda and Michael to show respect to their elder relatives and very close family friends. There was a set order. The parents of the bride would be followed by those of the groom, and then the other relatives, in descending order from the oldest, would take their places on the chairs.

Marcus and his first wife moved onto the dance floor. As they walked towards the two chairs, Ava felt discomfort at seeing her father with a woman who wasn't her own mother. It was one thing to know Elizabeth Lee existed; it was another to see her on Ava's father's arm.

Then there was Elizabeth's appearance. She was dressed in an ankle-length cheongsam of gold and green brocade. It had a vase collar, exposing a long, slender neck adorned with a green jade necklace that matched her drop earrings. The cheongsam had full-length flared sleeves that flowed over her hands. The dress was slit on one side from the ankle to the knee, exposing a slim calf. The cheongsam,

Ava had always thought, was a difficult dress to wear. It accentuated any physical shortcomings, suiting neither the too skinny nor the mildly plump. On Elizabeth Lee it looked like perfection.

Ava knew she was about sixty, but it was still a surprise to see that her grey hair was verging on white. Wealthy Chinese women did not usually succumb to nature so easily. Her hair, cut fashionably short, framed a long, slim, fine-featured face. She was about five foot four, Ava guessed, and in heels came to just above her husband's shoulder. She had a beautiful walk, slow, almost languorous, and certainly elegant. *She moves like Maggie Cheung*, Ava thought, and was startled by the comparison. Her own mother was often compared to the Hong Kong movie star, and some years ago, speaking about her father and his wives, Uncle had remarked that Marcus seemed to like one model of woman and just kept trading up for a new one.

Marcus and Elizabeth passed by Peter and Ava on their way to the chairs. Elizabeth smiled at Peter as she and Marcus took their seats, and then she glanced at Ava with dark brown eyes that were not the least unkind. Ava averted her own eyes as she stepped forward with the cup. The Lees sipped their tea, offered their words of wisdom to the bride and groom, and passed over their red pocket.

For the next half-hour a parade of aunts and uncles and friends made their way to the chairs. Ava knew none of them. Peter identified those who were associated with the Lee family, including his mother's four sisters and brother. The sisters shot Ava murderous looks when she approached with the cups of tea, and turned away when she handed them to Amanda to pass on.

After the second of his aunts snubbed Ava, Peter said, "I apologize for my aunts. They thought it was disrespectful to my mother for you to be invited to the wedding at all, and when they found out you were to be the maid of honour, well, it wasn't pretty. There was even talk of their not coming."

"I heard that rumour."

"I'm glad they were more sensible than that."

Ava saw no reason to reply.

"You do have to admit, though, that from their point of view it is a bit of an unusual situation," he went on.

"I'm not here as our father's bastard daughter. I am here as a friend of Amanda."

"I didn't mean to offend you," he said quickly.

Ava looked into his face and saw no malice. "You didn't," she said.

The end of the tea ceremony signalled the time for Amanda to change into the red dress. As Ava and Amanda left the ballroom together to go back to the suite, Ava could sense the aunts' eyes on her. She hardly knew any of the guests. Hong Kong wasn't home, and neither her mother nor Uncle ran in the social circles that filled the ballroom. The only people Ava knew, aside from the wedding party, were Simon To, Michael's business partner, his wife, Jessie, and May Ling and Changxing Wong. Ava then realized she hadn't seen May Ling since before the ceremony.

"Did you see May Ling?" she asked Amanda.

"No," Amanda said distractedly, as she applied the finishing touches to her makeup.

When they returned to the Grand Ballroom, the noise level had increased and the room was completely filled.

They made their way to the head table and settled in for a meal that had taken hours of debate to decide upon; it would cost Marcus Lee close to US$700 per person — almost $700,000 in total. And that was just the food cost. Ava had no idea what the French red and white wines they were serving or the open bar with nothing but premium alcohol brands would add to the bill. The wedding guests would have expected nothing less. They were among Hong Kong's elite and understood that Marcus Lee would never risk losing face at his eldest son's wedding.

Unlike most Western weddings, it was the parents of the groom and not the bride who bore the wedding costs. Ava knew from Amanda that Jack Yee, wealthy in his own right, had gone to Marcus and offered to pay half. She had no idea how the two men resolved the matter. The sign at the Hyatt's ballroom door welcomed the guests on behalf of both the Lee and Yee families, and the place cards at each table welcomed them to the union of the Lees and Yees. Ava suspected that Jack had increased his daughter's dowry and paid for some of the pre-wedding events, while Marcus had looked after everything else.

The men were all dressed in designer suits, most costing more than $2,000. Some were custom-made by Jay Kos in New York or H. Huntsman in London. The ties they wore were as distinctive; at one table Ava could pick out a Gucci, Fendi, Hermès, and Armani.

However well dressed the men were, the women who accompanied them were made up and coiffed to the extreme. They wore a range of luxury gowns and platinum jewellery studded with diamonds, emeralds, rubies, and jade that ranged from bright green to white and everything in between. No one dressed down. They had money, or their husbands did, and they weren't reluctant to wear it. These were first wives, mainly an older crowd, given their relationships to the Yee and Lee families, but unlike Elizabeth Lee, they didn't make any concession to age.

On the way back to the banquet, Ava and Amanda had passed Jamie and David Lee, Michael's youngest brothers, who stood by two tables decorated with pictures of the bride and groom. On each table was a box covered in white silk. As the guests filed in, they stopped to slip a red pocket into the box. Amanda guessed the couple might collect as much as HK$5 million in gifts. Whatever it was, it would be enough to give them a solid financial footing as they began their marriage.

Ava and Amanda took their seats at the head table, which was directly in front of the dance floor, the other tables spread out to the right and left. The nearest on the left was occupied by the Yee family, and to the right were the Lees: Marcus, Elizabeth, and her sisters and brother with their spouses. The sisters had their eyes fixed on the head table — fixed on Ava. She tried to ignore them, but her gaze kept drifting back to their table and her discomfort kept growing. Ava looked over their heads, searching the room for friendlier faces, but her attention was inevitably drawn back to the Lee family's table, where the aunties continued to glare. *They want me dead*, Ava thought.

Ava lowered her head, trying to shut them out of her mind. When she looked up, she saw that Elizabeth was speaking to them and motioning towards the head table. Then she stood up and walked onto the dance floor. She moved with the same measured gait with which she had approached the tea ceremony, and Ava was again struck by her elegance. Elizabeth stopped in the middle of the dance floor as if getting her bearings, and then turned and walked directly towards Ava.

A hush fell over the room. Ava thought she could hear her heart beating.

Elizabeth stopped about ten metres from the table and then said in a voice that carried, "Ava, could you come here, please."

Ava felt Amanda stiffen and heard Michael say, "Mother..."

She pushed her chair back and began to rise. Out of the corner of her eye she saw Marcus start to get out of his own seat. She looked at him and shook her head.

It was five steps from the head table to the dance floor. Ava took them slowly, trying to look casual when all she could feel was utter embarrassment. As she neared Elizabeth Lee, she could hear murmurs and whispers.

"Ava," the older woman said, extending her arms at waist height, her hands open, palms up. Ava froze. Elizabeth moved forward and grasped Ava's hands with her own. "I want to apologize for my sisters' behaviour," she said.

Ava's face flushed, and when she tried to speak, all she could muster was a slight stutter.

"None of them understand what you have done for the entire Lee family." The older woman pulled back and cocked her head to one side. "Michael told me you were pretty, and for once he understated the facts. You are a stunning young woman, perhaps a bit too much like your father for my liking, but what can we do about that?" she said, and smiled.

"You are very kind."

"Now, Ava, we are not going to be friends — I'm too old-fashioned for that. But I am pleased that you are friends with Amanda and Michael, and perhaps that can also be true for some of my other sons."

"Thank you."

"And I want you to tell your mother when you talk to her next that I think she has an absolutely marvellous daughter, and I congratulate her on a job well done."

"I will be sure to tell her."

Elizabeth leaned over and whispered in Ava's ear, "While we still have everyone's attention, why don't you give me a hug?"

Ava leaned forward. They wrapped their arms around one another, neither of them gripping tightly, the gesture more important than the feelings behind the embrace.

THE DINNER WAS NEAR PERFECTION. EIGHT DISHES were served — a number that was both traditional and lucky. Marcus Lee had insisted on making every dish something special. As the costs spiralled, Amanda and Michael had become appalled, but Marcus wouldn't be deterred. "My oldest son is getting married to Jack Yee's only child. This has to be done correctly," he said.

"This is more about your face," his son said.

"Not more…maybe as much," he conceded. "In any event, I want to make this the best wedding meal anyone has ever had."

The waiters marched in with the first course: barbecued suckling pigs on huge trays, the golden skin glistening under the overhead lights. At each table a server carved slices of crackling and laid them out on a platter. The guests placed the crackling on thin white pancakes that were almost transparent, then added hoisin sauce to finish the dish. The pig was traditional and symbolic, representing virginity.

The arrival of the abalone caused the room to buzz. Ava looked at the Lee family table and saw that Marcus had a big smile on his face. Amanda and Michael would have been content to go with ordinary sliced abalone, but Marcus had insisted on serving whole abalone, then went a step further by asking the hotel catering manager to get the Yoshihama variety from Japan. Each plate of abalone — braised for several days until it was golden brown, glittering like liquid gold and served with black mushrooms — was costing Marcus Lee more than US$100.

Next was shark-fin soup. The fin was actually from the sawfish, a shark-like ray considered by connoisseurs to be the finest raw source in the world. It was double-boiled and served with bamboo fungus. The first taste brought a smile to Ava's lips; a few minutes later, when more tables had been served, she could see heads nodding in appreciation.

A short break was scheduled after the soup to give Amanda time to change. As she and Ava walked back to the suite, Amanda asked, "What did Elizabeth say to you?"

The other bridesmaids were with them, and Ava could see they were pretending not to listen.

"She said she was pleased that I was maid of honour."

"It was a bit of a shock when she came towards you like that."

"For me as well."

"Although there was nothing to worry about. We did discuss it with her quite thoroughly, and she is...well, she is really a very good woman."

"I'm sure that's true," Ava said.

Ava hadn't been misleading Amanda when she said Elizabeth Lee's action was a shock, but the real shock had been just how gracious she was. It was one thing to agree to have Ava play such a visible role at the wedding, but it was another for her to acknowledge her husband's daughter in such a warm and public way. Until now Elizabeth had been just a name — an anonymous, important, perpetual presence. Now she was real, and Ava had to figure out how to fit Elizabeth into her perception of family.

Amanda changed quickly into an electric blue silk evening gown. Then the bridal party made their way back to the ballroom, where the waiters were hovering, waiting for their return so they could serve the fourth course.

As Ava walked into the ballroom she heard her name called. May Ling and Changxing Wong were standing just inside the doors. Ava went over to them. He gave her a tiny smile as she kissed his right cheek. May offered her arms and the women hugged. Ava looked into her friend's face and saw unfamiliar lines under eyes that seemed distracted.

"Sorry to be late," May said.

"I had a conference call to Beijing," Changxing said.

"You missed the shark-fin soup. But no matter, I'm just glad you made it."

"I'm not sure how long we will stay," Changxing said. "We're both really tired."

"It will be a hectic evening, so I'm sure no one will think it strange if you have to go."

"In case we don't see you later, I'll see you at breakfast tomorrow?" May said.

"Of course," Ava replied.

Changxing glanced nervously at his wife. "We had better find our table," he said as a line of waiters moved past them with trays of sea cucumber and shrimp. He put his arm around May's waist as if shielding her.

Ava hurried to catch up to Amanda. When she reached the head table, she could see May Ling and Changxing wending their way through the ballroom, attracting attention as they did. He was a rather ordinary-looking man, of medium height and medium build, with a small, round face and short hair combed straight back. Take away his Armani suit and Hermès tie and he could have been mistaken for any small-time Chinese businessman. But he wasn't ordinary. He was the wealthiest man in a province of more than fifty million people, which is why people called him the Emperor of Hubei. Even in Hong Kong, at an event replete with multimillionaires, he was a man who merited notice. Money spoke in Hong Kong, and the more you had, the louder it spoke. Anyone in that room who was anyone knew about Changxing Wong.

"Look at those women staring at May," Amanda said. "Even in a simple black dress she makes them jealous."

Ava hadn't paid any attention to how May was dressed when she saw her at the door. Now she looked at what was indeed a simple black dress, cut just to the middle of the knee, with spaghetti straps and a gentle V-line at her ample bosom. Her jewellery was just as plain: a pearl necklace and diamond earrings with pearl drops.

"You can't buy her bone structure," Ava said.

"Or yours," Amanda said as a plate of sea cucumber was placed in front of her.

"Let's eat," Ava said.

The sea cucumber had been stewed with shrimp, shrimp roe, and spring onions. It was another symbolic dish, one representing harmony. Michael and Amanda fed each other tiny portions, to the delight of the guests.

"I'm already getting full," Amanda said as they cleared the plates.

"The lobster and chicken are next," Ava said.

"God."

The lobster and chicken officially made one dish, the classic dragon and phoenix combination — yin and yang — representing balance in the marriage. Ava had almost had enough as well, but lobster wok-fried in ginger and garlic with applewood smoked chicken was too good to pass up.

The sixth course was steamed fish. The word *fish* in Chinese is pronounced the same as *abundance*. The caterer had wanted to use farmed fish, but Marcus had insisted it be sea-caught because it was considered luckier.

"I can't eat any more," Amanda said.

"Nibble," Ava said.

Rice was the seventh course. Despite their protestations, neither Amanda nor Ava could resist digging into the aromatic combination of rice, egg whites, shredded crabmeat, pine nuts, scallops, and shrimp.

"Just the noodles left," Ava said.

"And dessert."

They both picked at the noodles, which had been fried with a variety of exotic mushrooms.

As they waited for dessert, which did not count as one of the eight dishes, Marcus Lee came to visit with the newlyweds. He beamed. "It was wonderful, yes?"

"Dad, you couldn't have done better," Michael said.

"It was amazing," Ava added.

"I've had some people tell me it's the best wedding dinner they've ever had."

As if on cue, two men approached Marcus with words

of praise on their lips. "Wait until you try the dessert," he told them. "Double-boiled imperial bird's-nest soup with coconut cream and rock sugar."

Ava groaned. "It sounds sublime."

Full or not, Ava ate it all.

"One more trek to the room," Amanda said when the meal finally ended.

Her whole bridal party joined in to help Amanda change into her last outfit, a gold and blue cheongsam with a slit on one side that exposed her thigh.

When they returned to the ballroom, Michael was waiting by the door with May Ling and Changxing. He was holding a red pocket they had obviously just given to him. When May saw Amanda, she said, "You look stunning."

Amanda bowed her head.

"Here, this is for you. Something a little extra," May said, handing her another pocket.

"That isn't necessary."

"I know."

While the women were gone, the band had set up and were tuning their instruments.

"We have to take the first dance," Michael said to Amanda.

"And we have to go back to our hotel," May said. "It's been a long and strenuous day, and Changxing has to leave early tomorrow morning for Beijing."

There was a quick round of kisses, hugs, and handshakes.

"I'll see you at breakfast," May said to Ava. "Don't worry about the time. Just call me when you're ready."

An Andy Lau love song began to play softly in the background.

"That's our signal," Michael said.

"Let's dance," said Amanda.

The Wongs turned to leave. As they did, Ava noticed that May's lips were tightly pursed and Changxing's face was clouded. *Something has gone wrong somewhere in their world*, she thought.

The music swelled and Michael and Amanda took to the dance floor. They danced alone for the first half of the song, and then Amanda fetched her father and Michael led his mother onto the floor. The room erupted in cheers.

The rest of the evening was a blur for Ava. She had anticipated doing a lot of sitting and watching, but she ended up going from table to table with Amanda and Michael. Usually the bride and groom toasted their guests after the shark-fin soup was served, but the couple had decided to break with that tradition. Then Ava spent almost all her time on the dance floor. It started traditionally, with Peter, the best man, but then all of her half-brothers took their turn, and then her father. She hadn't expected him to dance with her.

"This must be awkward for you," she said.

"Not nearly as much as it was for you and Elizabeth," he said.

"She was so gracious," Ava said.

"I'm a lucky man."

Ava didn't ask what he meant.

As the evening progressed, Ava became the target of a very handsome man who was about her age or maybe younger. He told her he was a lawyer working for the Hong Kong government. What he didn't mention, but Amanda did, was that he was the only son of one of the wealthiest real estate barons in the New Territories. He came on to her in a polite and persistent way, asking her twice if she would join him for dinner. She was tempted to tell him she was a lesbian, but he danced so well she didn't want to lose him as a partner.

At midnight, tired in the nicest kind of way, Ava joined the rest of the wedding party at the ballroom exit to say goodbye to the guests. As they streamed past, it occurred to her that for the first time in her life she was actually part of this larger family. Before she had felt as if her mother, Marian, and she were stranded on some foreign island, her father a ship that passed from time to time, the aunties and the half-siblings distant islands. Now she had been publicly acknowledged as Marcus Lee's daughter, as a half-sister to his four sons, and she had been endorsed by Elizabeth Lee. It gave her a feeling of community, something that her family in Canada wasn't large enough to create. But here in Hong Kong, where anyone who was anyone knew everyone, and where families lived in close proximity and were constantly interacting, Ava now felt she had become a part of this wider circle.

As the last of the guests worked their way out of the ballroom, Michael spoke to the wedding party. He thanked everyone for their contribution to what had been a fantastic day. Ava listened until she became distracted by a figure just beyond Michael's shoulder. He was standing out in the corridor, leaning with his back against the wall. It was Sonny, Uncle's bodyguard and chauffeur, but it wasn't the Sonny she was accustomed to seeing.

He was wearing, as he always did, a black suit with a white shirt and black tie. He was a big man, about six foot five, massive across the shoulders and chest, and despite his bulk he was incredibly agile, quick, and ferocious. He was one of the few people in the world that Ava doubted she could overcome physically. But the man standing in the corridor didn't look like anyone to fear. His arms were crossed, his shoulders slumped, and his head hung low. He looked like a man who had crawled into himself to hide.

Without excusing herself, Ava left the group and walked towards him, her high heels clicking on the marble floor.

"Sonny," she said.

He looked up, his eyes full of confusion. Ava wondered if he recognized her.

"Uncle has just been taken to hospital. It doesn't look good," he said.

She took him by the arm, turned, and left the corridor of the Grand Hyatt without looking back.

AVA HAD SONNY DRIVE HER TO THE MANDARIN Oriental so she could change her clothes. On the way he told her that Uncle had actually seemed stronger that Saturday morning, and for the first time in weeks he had left his apartment to join Uncle Fong for lunch. Instead of the congee he'd been existing on, he ate his favourite dish: fried noodles with beef and XO sauce.

The restaurant was only a few blocks from Uncle's Kowloon apartment, and he had insisted on walking there and back. Sonny had walked with him, offering his arm for support, which Uncle had declined. The elevator in the building was being serviced, so they had to climb four flights of stairs to get to the apartment. Sonny had offered to carry Uncle, at which point Uncle angrily told him to go about his own business. But Sonny didn't leave; he followed him, a couple of steps behind, all the way up the stairs and saw him safely inside the apartment.

Lourdes had phoned Sonny just after eleven o'clock that night. Uncle had gone to the bathroom a bit earlier to throw up — not an uncommon thing for him to do. But she thought he looked particularly pale when he came out, and his eyes weren't focused. In fact it seemed to her that he didn't know where he was, or maybe even who he was. She followed him into the bedroom and tucked him in. A few minutes later she heard him vomiting and ran back into the room. There was a pool of blood on the sheets. He made a motion as if he wanted to go the bathroom, but when she tried to help him up, he collapsed. She called for an ambulance and then called Sonny. He had managed to get to the apartment before the ambulance arrived. Uncle was unconscious, breathing in whispers, his skin devoid of any colour.

Sonny had followed the ambulance to the Queen Elizabeth Hospital in southern Kowloon. After Uncle had been admitted he drove to the Grand Hyatt.

"Is he in R Block?" Ava asked. R Block was the tower where she'd visited him before and where he'd been undergoing brachytherapy.

"No, Emergency."

"Did you call Doctor Parker?"

"He should be there by now."

At the Mandarin, Ava had dithered about what to wear to the hospital. She was in shock, she realized, and not thinking clearly. It was one thing to understand what was happening to Uncle, but it was another to accept the inevitable. As long as he'd kept meeting her for their morning congee, she'd been able to shunt the horrible reality from her mind. Now she knew there would be no congee tomorrow morning. Maybe no congee ever again.

Part of her knew it made no real difference what she wore, but somewhere in the back of her mind she knew it was important to look good for him. She took out a black pencil skirt and a pink Brooks Brothers shirt with a modified Italian collar and French cuffs. She buttoned the shirt just short of the neck and joined the cuffs with green jade cufflinks. For the wedding she'd worn a pair of black stilettos; she slipped them on again and then stood and looked at herself in the mirror. Her hair was hanging loose around her face. She saw that her mascara was smeared and realized she had been crying. She brushed her hair, pulled it tightly back, and clasped it with her ivory chignon pin. She washed her face with cold water and then put on a light touch of red lipstick. She didn't trust herself enough to attempt mascara.

She had met Dr. Parker twice before, both times at the hospital when Uncle had gone in for treatment. On those occasions Ava was in her more usual dress of Adidas track pants and black Giordano T-shirt. As she walked through the entrance to the emergency department at the Queen Elizabeth, she saw him standing by the admissions desk.

"Doctor Parker," she said.

He turned and stared as if he wasn't sure he knew who she was. Then he saw Sonny and made the connection.

"Ms. Lee. I'm sorry, I didn't recognize you," Dr. Parker said.

Parker was a *gweilo*, an Englishman in his late thirties or early forties, and Ava had initially been surprised that Uncle had chosen him as his doctor. Uncle had explained that he wanted his condition kept secret and that he doubted there was a Chinese doctor in Hong Kong he could trust. Besides, Parker was young, progressive, and almost brutally honest. Uncle had come to admire that candour, since it removed any doubt about his situation and helped him prepare for what had to be.

"How is he?" she asked.

"Not well."

"Where is he?"

"I had them take him upstairs to a ward. There isn't anything they can do for him here."

"How about in R Block?"

"We're past the time for R Block."

"Is he conscious?"

"Off and on."

"Can I see him?"

He looked at Sonny. "Only one of you at a time."

She felt tightness in her chest and then a sharp pain in her stomach. "Is this the end?" she asked.

"No...not tonight. But we still need to get him stable. Then he can go home again, at least for a little while. But Ms. Lee, he has to stop eating and drinking the way he just did. It will not only shorten whatever life expectancy he has, it will cause him considerable pain."

"I will tell him."

"Please — he doesn't seem to listen to me."

And I don't expect he'll listen to me either, Ava thought. "Can I see him now?" she said.

"Of course. I'll come with you," Parker said.

They rode the elevator to the fifth floor, Sonny accompanying them. The hospital was eerily quiet, and the sound made by Ava's heels reverberated loudly throughout the hall. They checked in at the nursing station and then followed the on-duty nurse down the hallway to Uncle's room. There were two chairs outside the door. Parker motioned to Sonny to take a seat.

"Sonny, we'll take turns sitting with him," Ava said.

Parker opened the door and then stood aside to let Ava go past. Uncle lay on his back on the bed, washed by the dim glow of the equipment they had him hooked up to. The light draped over him reminded her of a shroud.

"He looks so small," she said.

"He is," Parker said.

"Being with him every day, I never noticed just how small he's become... He looks like a child."

Parker, standing behind her, placed a hand on her shoulder. She jumped.

"I'm sorry, I didn't mean to startle you," he said, and then pulled a chair towards the bed. "You can sit here with him."

"Thank you," Ava said and sat.

Parker hovered.

"Is there anything else?" she asked.

"Ms. Lee, Mr. Chow is an extraordinary man. Not many people exhibit his bravery. And not the physical kind, mind you, but the emotional courage. He was unflinching in terms of his desire to know the truth about his disease and his prospects. I have tremendous respect for him. So, please, just tell him to take better care. He doesn't have much time left. He needs to preserve it."

"The respect is mutual. He's thankful for everything you've done for him."

Parker hesitated, his discomfort obvious. "I wanted you to know how I felt."

Ava nodded. Parker smiled at her and then left the room.

She turned towards Uncle, her eyes fixed on his face. Under the bright lights, his skin had been so pale, so translucent she could see the veins that tracked across his cheeks and around his chin. Now, in the dusk-like atmosphere, it was smooth and unwrinkled. His eyes were closed, and he was breathing so lightly that she could barely hear him. Whatever trauma his body was undergoing, his face didn't reflect it. It was composed and relaxed.

Ava placed a hand on his and then rested her head on the bed. She wasn't sure how long she stayed like that, and she couldn't remember if she had fallen asleep when she felt Uncle gently pry his hand loose from hers and rest it on her head. She looked up at him and saw him smile as he lightly stroked her hair. Tears leapt into her eyes.

"No," he said.

Ava placed her head back on the bed, Uncle's hand still resting on it, as light as air.

"The doctor says you're going to be okay. He thinks you might be able to go home tomorrow," she said.

"I do not know how many more times I will be able to hear that."

"More times than you can imagine, if you look after yourself better."

"I do not put much value in buying a day here and there," he said.

"Don't talk like that."

"Ava, I have been so lucky. I tell myself that I never thought I would live to be this age, and I tell myself that I never thought I would die in a bed," he said, his voice quiet but controlled.

"But here you are, so don't make too much of what was."

"There were times…" he said, the words trailing off.

Ava, struggling to hear, lifted her head so she could see his lips.

"The worst time was when we swam from China."

"You've never told me about that in any detail."

"I thought I had," he said, and then paused, gathering his thoughts. "We were starving in Wuhan — that goddamn Cultural Revolution — but I was young, and with some other young men I decided to try to get to Hong Kong. We made it to the coast, gathered whatever strength we had left, and got into the water.

"There were twelve of us when we started. We had made a raft that could hold three. So we took turns on the raft, the others swimming alongside or clinging to it and pushing it along. We swam all night. The water was so dark and so cold. I have never been so frightened... About halfway, maybe four hours into the swim, we noticed we had lost someone. That was when I realized how dangerous and foolish we were being. But it was too late to turn back and we could not stop, so we just kept swimming. We lost three more men before we reached Hong Kong. For the last hour or two, I was convinced I was not going to make it. I was filled with complete despair. I was so young and I had done nothing with my life. I had no family. All I kept thinking was that if I died, no one would notice. That was the most terrifying thing of all, that I would be swallowed up by the sea and not one person in the world would care. Nothing I have done since has scared me so much."

Ava felt tears streaming down her face.

Uncle turned away. "I do not like to see you cry."

"I'm sorry."

He went silent and Ava wondered if he'd fallen back to sleep. Then he said, "The funeral arrangements..."

"It isn't time to go over that again. When you're at home, we can. I know you want things to be simple. No public

announcement. No elaborate ceremonies. Just a short view-
ing at the funeral home."

"This is something else."

"What's that?"

"I want you to arrange to have some monks at my
gravesite in Fanling. They do not have to be at the funeral
home, but I want them at the grave. There should be five of
them. Uncle Fong can help you contact the right person."

She must have looked surprised, because he added, "I
am not getting religious. I want Taoist monks because that
was my parents' way, and I feel I need to honour the tradition. If nothing else, it may bring me closer to my ancestors."

"Uncle, I'm sure you can tell Uncle Fong yourself, when
you see him tomorrow."

He closed his eyes and she wondered if the effort of
speaking had drained him. Then he said, "I spoke to him
about you a few days ago. He still knows a lot of the old
contacts, and I told him if you ever need help that he is to
act as if he were me."

"Uncle, I'm not going back into our old type of business.
I won't need those contacts."

His opened his eyes. "May Ling Wong has *guanxi*, I
know, but there will be times when you may need other
kinds of help. Between Sonny and Uncle Fong, they can get
you everything you need."

"Yes, Uncle."

"Good. I do not want to have to worry about you."

"You don't need to worry."

He closed his eyes. "My beautiful girl...Now, where is
Sonny?"

"He's outside."

"I need to talk to him for a moment."

"I'll get him."

Sonny had vacated his chair and was now pacing back and forth in the corridor. "Uncle wants to see you," Ava said.

He came over to her. "He's speaking?"

"Yes. Doctor Parker says he can probably go home tomorrow, but we need to keep him away from food and drink like he had tonight."

He nodded and then brushed past her into the room. Ava sat in a chair, pressed her head against the wall, and extended her legs. It didn't seem real, any of it. She knew he was ill. She had listened to Dr. Parker and had taken every word he spoke as the truth. Still, Uncle was alive and, as always, worried for her. How could that not continue?

She looked at her watch. It was just past two o'clock. She closed her eyes. When she opened them again it was ten past three and Sonny was standing over her.

"He wants to see you again," he said.

Uncle's face was turned towards the door when she entered. He tried to smile. "I just promised Sonny that I would go back on my congee diet."

"That will make everyone happy."

"I have another motive."

Ava sat by the bed, reaching for his hand. "Do I want to hear what it is?"

"I have to go to Shanghai," he said, with more energy in his voice.

"Shanghai?"

"Do not look so alarmed. I checked with Parker yesterday and he saw no reason why I could not travel. Besides, it is only a two-hour flight."

"But, Shanghai?"

"I have some business to attend to. Sonny will be travelling with me."

Ava tried to keep the surprise out of her voice. "Business?"

"It is something I cannot discuss with you. I gave my word to the other party that no one else would be involved."

"You're taking Sonny."

"To carry and drive, nothing more."

"Uncle, this is so strange," she said, bewildered.

"I am sorry for telling you like this, but it is something I have been working on for a while. It is now starting to come together, and even better than I could have hoped for. The invitation came yesterday and we did not have a chance to talk. It made me excited when I received it, so excited that I ate and drank like a fool... Ava, this does not concern any business we have ever done or people you have ever met. If it did, I would be taking you with me, so do not look so disappointed. Besides, it will give you a break. With the wedding over and me away for a few days, you can have some time to yourself."

"For how long?"

"Three or four days. They are putting me up in a suite at the Peninsula Hotel."

"And Parker said this is all right?"

"Absolutely."

"Uncle —"

"Please do not argue with me about this, Ava. My mind is made up."

"If there's any problem?"

"Someone will call you, I promise."

5

SHE SLEPT FITFULLY, WAKING EVERY FEW HOURS WITH the nagging sense that something was wrong. She looked at the message light on the hotel phone. It wasn't blinking. She checked her cellphone. No voicemails or texts. *Uncle has to be well,* she told herself. She finally woke at noon and remembered with a start that she was supposed to have met May Ling for breakfast.

Ava called her friend's cell. May answered on the second ring.

"*Wei.*"

"I'm sorry about breakfast. I just woke up. I was at the hospital until past four o'clock with Uncle. He had another attack."

"Is he okay?"

"Yes, or as okay as he can be, given the circumstances. They said they were going to let him out today."

"And are you okay?"

"I think so."

"Do you have to get him?"

"No, that's Sonny's job and he's quite territorial about it."

"So you're free to meet?"

"As soon as I've showered."

"Take your time. I'm still in my room. "

Ava did take her time. She made an instant coffee and drank it while scanning the *South China Morning Post*. The wedding hadn't received any coverage. The lawyer she'd danced with had pointed out several photographers from newspapers. She imagined they were from some of the many Hong Kong Chinese dailies.

She showered, removing the last remnants of makeup from the night before, brushed her teeth, and towel-dried her hair. She threw on a black Giordano T-shirt and her Adidas training pants, then suddenly felt at loose ends. Michael and Amanda would be in the air, on their way to a one-week honeymoon in the Seychelles Islands. Sonny would be driving to the hospital to get Uncle, and then they would be heading to Shanghai. Both of the touchstones for what had become her life in Hong Kong were gone. She phoned May Ling.

"I'm ready."

"Good. I'm upstairs in the M Bar drinking a martini."

"A martini?"

"I'll explain."

Ava rode the elevator to the twenty-fifth floor. She had no idea the M Bar opened so early, but May Ling was sitting by herself at a table overlooking Victoria Harbour. She was wearing slim black jeans and a teal turtleneck sweater. She wasn't wearing makeup, and as Ava approached her she saw small lines around the edges of her mouth and faint circles under her eyes. More surprising was that her eyes were full of worry. May Ling, in Ava's experience, was a woman who took things in stride.

"Sorry to have missed breakfast," Ava said.

May held out her arms and they hugged. Ava could feel the tension in her friend's body.

"May, what the heck is going on?"

May shrugged. "Is it that obvious?"

"You're drinking a martini at noon."

"Well, we have a problem."

"A problem?"

"A business problem."

Ava sat down at the table. When a server materialized almost instantly, she ordered a coffee.

"I thought we'd talk first and then go to Man Wah for dim sum," May said, motioning to the restaurant that made up the other half of the twenty-fifth floor.

"Sure, that sounds fine. But May, you're worrying me with all this talk about a business problem. Amanda mentioned something to me, but she thought it was a Wuhan issue."

May plucked a green olive from her drink. "It has nothing to do with Wuhan. It's a problem with the new business — our business. I've been trying to sort it out by myself. I mean, Amanda had her wedding and you had Uncle, so I thought I would leave the two of you out of it."

May Ling's eyes were like Uncle's. They were such a deep brown that in many lights they looked black, and like Uncle's, they spoke to you. Ava had seen them distressed only once before, that night in Wuhan when they had first met, when May Ling sat on Ava's bed and begged her to take their case. "Tell me what's going on."

"Ava, are you sure you're up for this conversation? I know the last few days have been really trying for you," May said.

Ava shrugged. "I've spent the past four months worrying about Uncle and worrying with Amanda about the wedding. Yesterday, between him and her, could have been the worst day since I've been here, but we got through the wedding and Uncle got through another crisis. And none of it — the past four months, I mean — has been as soul-leeching as I thought it would be. I had to get the misery out of my system with Uncle and forget about how frivolous the wedding preparations were. And I did both well enough to get by. So tell me, what's our problem?"

"It isn't officially *ours* yet," May said, biting into the olive, her eyes on the harbour below. "You haven't yet put your money into the business, and after hearing this you may not want to."

"Oh, don't give me that," Ava said. "Nothing can be that bad."

"I'm not so sure, and Changxing is most certainly sure it is."

"Why is he involved?"

May looked back at Ava. "He isn't, not directly anyway. But he does know about the problem. I couldn't disguise my distress when I found out about it, and when he asked me what was going on, I told him. I think maybe he's enjoying my discomfort. It just reinforces his idea that I can't — or, more accurately, shouldn't — do anything without him."

"I don't understand."

May drained her martini. "All the money I had was tied up in businesses I shared with him. When I went to him with this idea for our thing, he was…Well, he was somewhat understanding and tolerant, but more confused than anything else. He couldn't understand why I wanted to do something with just you and Amanda. Still, I must give him credit. He signed off on my pulling a hundred million dollars out of our joint ventures to bankroll the new company, and he didn't charge me too much interest on the fifty million I agreed to repay when your share came in. But at the core, in his heart, I think he wants me — he wants us to fail so that things can go back to the way they've always been."

"And you're trying to tell me what? That we've failed?"

"No, but we have a problem."

"That so far I know nothing about."

May slipped the last olive into her mouth and sucked on it as if she were trying to extract every last drop of gin. "Our new company has put money into three businesses in very short order. We bought Jack Yee's trading company outright, as you know, because that was the only way we could get Amanda. But it's a mature business that almost runs itself. We invested in a distribution business in Shanghai that I've had my eye on for some time. I've known the married couple who own it for years, and the wife is really the brains behind the operation. The husband died about six months ago and now she has free reign to expand the business. She came to me with a proposal; I gave it to Amanda to assess and she said it was a solid investment. We gave the woman the capital she needed to add warehouse space and to update and expand her truck fleet. It's already looking as if the returns will be very good.

"The problem investment is the only one we had no previous detailed knowledge of. It's a family business that produces fine furniture in rosewood, teak, rubberwood, and bamboo. When we looked at it, there were four equal part-ners: the two sons and two daughters of the founding fam-ily. Their parents, who started the business, have been dead for a few years." May paused as the server appeared with Ava's coffee.

"Another drink, Madam Wong?" he asked.

May Ling looked at her empty glass and then shot a small smile towards Ava. "No, thank you," she said.

Ava took a sip of her coffee. "How did these brothers and sisters find us?"

"Through Amanda. It was her project. She went to busi-ness school with the younger of the two sisters."

"No wonder you didn't want to discuss it with her before the wedding," Ava said.

"It could have ruined her day."

And might have jinxed the marriage itself, Ava thought. "But May, are you suggesting that maybe Amanda was somehow negligent?"

"No, this isn't Amanda's fault, believe me. She did thorough due diligence and I went over all the paperwork myself."

"Then why do we have a problem, and how did it happen so quickly? I mean, this investment is how old?"

"Four months."

"Good God."

"I know, I know. But the thing is, the more I look at it, the more I think we were set up from the very start."

"What do you mean? The family did this to us?"

May shook her head. "I wish it was so simple."

"Then what?"

May stared out over the harbour, her profile captured by soft overhead lighting that made her look young and vulnerable. "I think the two brothers are trying to fuck us over," she said, turning back to Ava.

Ava sipped some more coffee. Her fatigue was beginning to dissipate. "Not the sisters?"

"No."

"How have you come to that conclusion?"

"The brothers are useless, both of them."

"May, that's not telling me anything."

"Sorry, I just get so angry when I think about them."

"I'm listening."

May stared at her empty glass. "The parents built the company from scratch. They started by exporting timber overseas and then gradually eased their way into furniture production. The sons and the eldest daughter — her name is Ah-Pei — joined the company right out of high school. She was the only one who really worked at it. The brothers, Tambi and Mamat, did marketing and sales, but all that meant was that they went to trade shows, drank with buyers, and paid off enough of them to increase their sales. The actual heavy lifting in the business — anything to do with finance, administration, purchasing, or production — was managed by the parents and gradually by Ah-Pei. They all worked seven days a week, twenty-four hours a day — you know the kind of people I'm talking about. Ah-Pei never married; the business was her entire life. The two sons did marry, and then immediately became more concerned about keeping their wives happy than spending time at the company.

"As the business grew, it obviously became more complicated, and Ah-Pei and the parents decided that Chi-Tze, the youngest daughter, needed to get the education to help them deal with it. They sent her off to Melbourne, where she got a bachelor's degree with a major in business. She did so well in Australia that they sent her to the U.S. to get an MBA, and that's where she met Amanda.

"The parents died a few years ago. The four children inherited the business in equal parts. By then Chi-Tze had graduated and was working alongside her sister. Tambi and Mamat were doing what they always did: as little as possible for as much money as possible. Ah-Pei was used to it, and truthfully she seems a little old-fashioned about how she views her relationship with the male members of her family. But Chi-Tze wasn't as tolerant. She decided she wanted to take the brothers right out of the business, and with her sister's tepid approval she contacted her colleagues from business school to see if anyone would have an interest in making an investment. Amanda was on the list."

"What form did our investment take?"

"It was two-tiered. Amanda assessed the business to have a net value of just over sixty million U.S. dollars. I thought her numbers were, if anything, a little low, and I have to tell you I was pleased by her conservative approach. So we made an offer of twenty-five million for half the business, structuring the deal to buy out the brothers' shares with fifteen million, with the other ten million to be put in as working capital. So really we were offering fifteen million to buy half of a business we had assessed at sixty million.

"We assumed, of course, that the brothers would dicker with their sisters and that the women would come back to us with counter-offers, but that never happened. Amanda said she thought they were that desperate to get rid of Mamat and Tambi, and that the brothers were as desperate to get their hands on ready cash."

"On the surface it sounds like a good deal for us."

"Doesn't it."

"So what's gone wrong?"

"A customer in the Netherlands."

"One customer?"

"Yes, but the biggest by a mile, and in hindsight far too big for the health of the business."

"What's the problem with them?"

"They've declared bankruptcy," May said.

Ava, almost unaware, had finished her coffee. She felt the urge for another and looked for the waiter. He was standing to one side, his attention on their table. Everyone working in the hotel knew who May Ling was, and by now they had come to know Ava as well. Ava pointed to her cup. He nodded and then looked at May Ling. She sighed. "What the hell," she said, and signalled for another martini.

"How much do they owe?" asked Ava.

"We invoiced them for close to thirty million dollars. It cost us twenty million to make the products, so if we got that back we could break even. But as far as I'm concerned, we're out of pocket the full thirty," May said abruptly.

Ava sat back, startled. "How did that happen? I mean, why would they extend themselves that much? Weren't there at least letters of credit?"

"That's what I've spent the last week piecing together, and that's why I think the two brothers are fucking us over, either on their own or in partnership with the Dutch."

"How did they do that? I thought you had taken them out of the business."

"Some of this is supposition on my part, but let me tell you what I know and then you can tell me what you think."

The server arrived with their drinks and fussed over the table. As he did, Ava ran the numbers through her head. She didn't like the result, and that was even if they could salvage part of the thirty million.

Ava lifted her cup towards May. "Cheers," she said.

May shot her a look that implied she thought Ava was being sarcastic. Then Ava smiled, and May smiled back, but without any enthusiasm.

"I'm listening," Ava said.

May's eyes darkened. "As I said earlier, Tambi and Mamat were in charge of sales and marketing. This Dutch customer — who distributes the products all over Europe — has been buying furniture from the family for years and has always paid his bills in full and usually on time. When they first started doing business, letters of credit were always in place, but over the years a trust developed. The company started giving the customer payment terms and stopped demanding the LCs."

"The brothers were involved in the financing?"

"Not directly. Ah-Pei would have had to approve the arrangement. I can only imagine that the brothers talked her into it, and besides, the Dutch company had a good track record. But Tambi and Mamat are the ones who had the relationship with the buyer. They'd meet him in Holland or at the factory two or three times a year to put together purchase orders. But — and this a big but — this past October, after we'd done our deal with Ah-Pei and Chi-Tze but before the brothers were officially out of the business, the two of them met with the Dutch buyer and negotiated a huge purchase order. The Dutch customer bought nearly all of the existing inventory and then ordered multiple containers of new products."

"And the women didn't find that odd?"

"I think they were too excited about getting rid of their brothers, and besides, as I said, they knew the Dutch company. Or at least they thought they did."

"So Mamat and Tambi had the authority to commit the company to a deal that large?"

"They were still partners and officers in the company, but Ah-Pei's signature was required as well. The problem is that she didn't read the fine print until two weeks after the brothers were officially gone."

"Fine print...Just how bad was the deal?"

"The terms were ridiculous. Net payment wasn't due until forty-five days after the product actually arrived in the Netherlands. With thirty days thrown in for shipping, that meant it would be at least seventy-five days before any cash came back their way."

"And we actually shipped that much product that quickly?"

"They cleaned out the inventory. In a few weeks they had packed and shipped all of it."

"The women must have realized that their cash flow was going to be badly squeezed."

"Yes, they knew it, so Chi-Tze called the Netherlands and explained that they needed payment more quickly. She went as far as to offer the Dutch a two percent discount if they could pay within ten days."

"What did they say?"

"They said they'd get back to her. They didn't. The sisters called again. No one at the firm would talk to them. A month later the sisters received a registered letter from a

Dutch accounting firm telling them the importer had gone under and that they were listed as an unsecured creditor."

"Unsecured?"

"Yes, and that's not the worst of it," May said, gazing at her martini glass. With a sigh she pushed it away from her. "I shouldn't have ordered this. It doesn't help."

"How bad does this get?" Ava said.

"Well, after I heard from the women, I had my lawyer contact the accountants through a law firm he uses in the U.K. After a lot of back and forth between the U.K. and the Netherlands, the London lawyers informed mine that, under Dutch law, secured creditors are the only ones with real rights and with enough power to bypass the bankruptcy filing and seize the assets for themselves. And that's exactly what's happened. A secured creditor — a finance firm, evidently — has taken control of every liquid asset of the Dutch business. And that includes our furniture."

"All of it?"

"All of it."

"They'll sell it."

"Of course. They're doing it already, as fast as they can. All they care about is the money they're owed. The actual value of the furniture won't mean a thing to them."

"How much are the secured creditors owed?"

"According to the paperwork the trustee sent, about fifteen million euros — just over twenty million U.S."

"And we invoiced the importer for more than thirty million dollars?"

"We did."

"So they can discount the furniture and still come out well."

"Especially when you factor in the normal wholesale

markup. Chi-Tze says the Dutch importer would have sold the thirty million dollars' worth of furniture for at least forty million."

"So the secured creditor can sell it for half its wholesale value and still recover all of their money."

"They can."

"The bankruptcy trustee — the receiver, he can't do anything about this?"

"He can monitor the sales — they do have to report them — and if they raise more than twenty million dollars he can make a claim on the excess and have it distributed among the other creditors, none of whom are secured."

Ava paused. "Is there nothing we can do?"

"There's a creditors' meeting scheduled two days from now, on Tuesday, in Amsterdam. I thought I would meet with the sisters and then try to get over there to attend the meeting. I'd like to know who this finance company is and what kind of deal it had with the importer."

"Do you suspect collusion between them?"

"I can suspect all I want, but I have no proof that Mamat and Tambi did some backdoor deal with the importer, or that the importer and his financer cut a separate deal, or that all three of them planned to screw us over. All I know is that it stinks. It's just too quick and convenient for the company to go bankrupt while sitting on goods they haven't paid for yet."

"It sounds like a trip to the Netherlands is going to be necessary."

"Yes."

"But the schedule sounds way too tight. Can you meet with the sisters and still get there on time?"

May said slowly, "I'm not sure. I was actually thinking of asking you to go to Europe to represent us." She glanced quickly at Ava and then turned away. "You're the one who has the experience running things like this to ground, and you speak English far better than I do. But I know you're reluctant to leave Uncle, and I'll understand if it isn't possible."

Ava hesitated.

"I also wouldn't blame you if you were having second thoughts about jumping into the business."

Ava lowered her head and then shook it gently. "May, you're misreading me. I'm just thinking about Uncle and his schedule. As for the money, I gave you my word. Nothing you've told me changes my commitment to the partnership."

"It does from my end. I'm finding it difficult to expect you to put fifty million into the company and then lose a quarter of it the instant the ink is dry on the agreement."

"I gave you my word."

"And I'm giving you the chance to back out."

"No, I'm not backing out on the business," Ava said, sliding her hand across the table.

May took it and squeezed. "Thank you. I had to ask."

"And now you've asked twice, so please don't mention it again."

"I won't."

"I also think I might be able to go to Amsterdam."

"On such short notice? What about Uncle?"

"He and Sonny are off to Shanghai for three or four days, so I'm not needed here."

"Uncle is okay to travel?"

"That's what the doctor says."

May smiled. "This is going much better than I had imagined."

"It hasn't solved our problem, though. Tell me, what do you intend to do about the sisters and the business? The two of them must be devastated, and how is the company staying afloat when its cash flow is so crippled?"

"Hopefully I can calm the sisters."

"How about the business? Is it salvageable?"

"Maybe. We'll have to put more money into it and I need to go over the terms with them. I also think we have to send Amanda there as soon as she comes back from her honeymoon. She'll be a stabilizing influence for them, and truthfully I'll feel more comfortable knowing she's looking after our money — both the old and whatever new we have to put in."

"I don't think that will be a problem for her."

"This investment wasn't supposed to be a problem," May said, and then shook her head. "Sorry, that's my frustration about the situation talking. It's not a criticism of Amanda."

"I understand."

"One other thing. I've asked the sisters to find the meanest, toughest lawyer they can get their hands on."

"Why the lawyer?"

"I want to see if we have any grounds for suing the brothers."

"Are you serious?"

"Absolutely."

"You have no idea if they were involved in anything underhanded."

"So?"

"All you have are suspicions."

"That doesn't mean we can't sue anyway. We don't need facts to make accusations, just a plausible story. Let's see if we can scare some kind of reaction out of them. Who knows where that will lead?"

"I thought lawsuits in China took years to even surface."

May, steadier now, sipped delicately at her martini. "Who said anything about China?"

"The business isn't there?"

"No, it's in Borneo."

Ava didn't disguise her surprise. "Borneo?"

"I had the same reaction when Amanda first told me the factories were located there, but when I went to meet the sisters for the first time, I had my eyes opened. The business is just outside Kota Kinabalu, the capital of Sabah province, and the area is much more sophisticated than I ever imagined."

"It's Malaysian territory, isn't it?"

"Sabah is. The island is divided into three areas. The south side is Kalimantan and it's Indonesian. The north coast has two Malaysian provinces, Sabah and Sarawak, and Sarawak surrounds the country of Brunei."

"Borneo…" Ava said, shaking her head.

"Yes, and a Shangri-La five-star resort."

"It's never a holiday when you're chasing money."

"I guess I'm going to find that out."

"Earlier you mentioned paperwork," Ava said.

"I have it here," May said, pointing to the brown envelope that sat under her handbag on the seat beside her.

"Let me see."

May picked up the envelope and opened it. "Here — this

is the bankruptcy notification, which includes the date, time, and location of the meeting," she said, passing it to Ava.

Ava scanned it quickly.

"And this is a copy of the purchase agreement with the sisters, and a set of the company articles with you listed as an officer and director," May said. "Finally, just in case you were able to go to Amsterdam, I had our lawyer prepare a notarized statement that you are authorized to act on behalf of the corporation on all matters relating to the bankruptcy."

Ava smiled at May's presumption.

"I thought I should have something prepared in case you could go. It was a precaution, that's all. I wasn't trying to predict what you would do," May said.

"*Momentai*," Ava said. "I'll go over all of this later in detail. In the meantime, let's eat."

"Yes, before the martinis do me in."

"I think it will take more than a couple of martinis to do that."

6

DIM SUM WAS NORMALLY A CALM AFFAIR OF SIPPING jasmine tea and picking at the small dishes brought to the table in a slow parade, but no sooner had they sat down than May's cellphone rang. She answered it, her eyebrows immediately rising.

Chi-Tze, May mouthed.

Before Ava could respond, her own cellphone sounded, showing an incoming call from the Queen Elizabeth Hospital. She answered quickly, a sinking feeling in her stomach.

"Ava, it is Uncle."

"Are you okay?"

"Yes, yes. I am feeling better, but Parker will not let me out of here until later today or early tomorrow. He says that if I insist on travelling I will need more strength."

"Thank God someone is being sensible."

"I know better than to argue with him."

"Do you want me to drop by?"

"No, there is no need today. Sonny will come and get me when I can leave."

"And Shanghai?"

"Tomorrow, I would imagine."

"Uncle," Ava said slowly, "if you aren't going to be in Hong Kong, then I may take a trip as well."

"Of course, please go," he said. "But tell me, does this have anything to do with the problem in Borneo?"

"I beg your pardon?" she said, her surprise audible.

He went silent and for a second Ava thought she had offended him. Then he asked, "Have you spoken to May Ling since the wedding?"

"She's sitting right in front of me. Why do you ask?"

"Changxing."

"What about him?"

"He called me an hour ago to see how I was doing. May had told him I was in the hospital. But what he really wanted was to tell me about a business problem in Borneo."

May was still on the phone, and Ava could see she was agitated. Now Ava felt the first stirring of her own annoyance. "Why would he do that?" she asked.

"I do not know."

"Well, it's true, there is a problem, but it has nothing to do with him."

"He said there is a lot of money involved and that you and May are exposed."

"There is, and we are."

"Can you sort things out?"

"Perhaps. May is getting ready to leave for Borneo and I'm going to fly to Amsterdam tonight if I can get a flight."

"Ava, you do not have to tell me, but how much money could you personally lose?"

"Twelve to fifteen million U.S. dollars."

"No wonder Changxing was eager to tell me."

"I have the money."

"Still…"

"Uncle, I'm fine," she said.

"That may be, but I still worry about you and your future," he said. "No matter, I spoke with Peter Hutchinson today after Changxing called. I know I have gone over the basics of my will with you, but I asked him to meet with you when you are available and lay out all the details and numbers. You will have no money problems, even if the loss is double what you think it is."

"I know," she said.

"So meet with him."

"It isn't necessary."

"Do it for me. There are other provisions that I have not described, some involving Sonny and Lourdes. You need to be aware of them, and I would like to be able to answer any questions you may have."

Ava knew she couldn't say no. "I can't do it until I get back from Amsterdam, so please don't commit me to a date just yet," she said. "But I'll meet with him as soon as I return to Hong Kong."

"Thank you."

Ava looked across the table at May. She had ended her call and was now staring off into space.

"Uncle, I need to go now," she said. "If there's any change in your plans, please let me know. Otherwise I'll be leaving for Amsterdam hopefully sometime today."

"Say hello to May Ling for me, and have a safe journey."

Ava put her phone on the table. "May, what happened? You look upset."

"Chi-Tze called Amanda," she said. "She phoned to tell Amanda I was coming over. She wanted to know what to expect."

"Why would she do that?"

"She said she was nervous, she didn't know what I was going to do. She thought I might even have plans to shutter the business."

"This is the first day of Amanda's honeymoon. Surely she knows that."

"And the last, according to Chi-Tze."

"What do you mean?"

"Amanda naturally asked why I was going and why Chi-Tze was asking about what to expect. So Chi-Tze told her about the problem."

"God."

"Amanda did not take it well."

"Which part?"

"Both. She was shocked by the potential financial fallout and evidently none too pleased that I hadn't told her about it."

"The wedding—"

"Of course, and I have no doubt she will understand that's why I didn't say anything."

"So what's she going to do?"

"She plans to go to Borneo tomorrow."

"That's crazy."

May Ling shrugged. "It speaks well of her as a partner, though."

"May, you have to call Amanda and tell her to stay away."

They halted their conversation when the food began to arrive. May picked up her chopsticks and plucked a steamed baby cuttlefish from its bed of curry sauce. "Chi-Tze told her exactly the same thing," she said when the waiter had departed. "Amanda said she'd been living with Michael for a year and doubted there was anything new she would be learning on their honeymoon."

"You seem okay with this," Ava said.

"Not entirely, but I am pleased that Amanda takes her obligations to the business seriously."

"Why would Chi-Tze open her mouth?"

"She is obviously distressed and not thinking very clearly."

"When did they talk?"

"About half an hour ago."

"Amanda hasn't called either of us," Ava said.

"She might need time to digest the situation. And we can't be sure exactly how much detail Chi-Tze went into."

"Amanda also might not want us to talk her out of going."

Ava found her attention wavering as freshly fried turnip cakes stuffed with ham and onions arrived at the table. Then she thought about Amanda, and then of Changxing going behind their backs like a gossiping schoolboy, and her appetite disappeared. She thought about mentioning Uncle's conversation with Changxing, but then thought better of it. There was no point in turning into a gossip herself.

"You have to call Amanda," she said.

"I will."

"No, now," Ava said, picking up her phone and dialling Amanda's mobile. She listened as it went directly to voicemail. "It's Ava. Call me or May as soon as you can," she said. Then she tried Michael's phone. Same result. "They aren't answering," she said.

"And you aren't eating," May said.

"I can't."

"Me neither, actually," May said, delicately placing her chopsticks on top of her bowl. "I think I need to get to Borneo as soon as I can."

IT WAS ALMOST MIDNIGHT WHEN AVA WALKED OUT OF Schiphol, Amsterdam's international airport, into a cold, damp night. She shivered. The limousine pickup area was covered but a strong wind was bearing down on the terminal; it drove the rain sideways, along with the chill that was in the air. The only other time she'd been to Amsterdam it was midsummer, and she'd spent two days walking around the city in shorts and a T-shirt.

She had left Hong Kong earlier that evening after spending a hectic afternoon finding flights and a hotel and organizing the clothes she wanted to bring. After four months in one spot, her travel bags no longer packed themselves. She was surprised how long it took her to sort things out.

When she was packed, she called the hospital to let Uncle know she was leaving for Amsterdam right away. He seemed alert and his voice was strong as he again wished her a safe journey and told her he would keep in touch from Shanghai.

It was the middle of the night in Toronto, so she emailed her mother, her girlfriend Maria, and Mimi to let them know she would be travelling for a few days on a minor business matter. She emphasized that both she and Uncle were well and that no one should worry.

At four Ava had taken one of the Mandarin's limousines to the airport. She had wanted to ride with Sonny, but when she called him, he told her that Uncle was being released from the Queen Elizabeth before dinner. May had left the hotel an hour before her. Each of them had made several attempts to contact Amanda, without any success.

She had booked online a direct flight on Cathay Pacific to Amsterdam. Normally she would have used her travel agent, Gail, to make the arrangements, but Gail would be home in bed. Using travel agents these days was a bit old-fashioned, Ava knew, but she liked the idea of having someone to call, someone who actually cared if things went wrong. So she booked the first-class seat herself and copied Gail on the details.

Finding a hotel was a bit more of a challenge. Her hotel preferences were more eclectic than her airline choices, which were typically Asian-based carriers. She liked staying at the big five-star chains when she was in Asia; the Mandarin Oriental was her favourite, with the Peninsula and the Shangri-La not far behind. In North America and Europe she found the service in the larger hotels far too impersonal, so she typically opted for smaller, high-end boutique hotels in a central location. Searching online for hotels in Amsterdam, she found a room at the Dylan, a five-star hotel with only forty-one rooms and a Michelin-starred restaurant, situated on the Keizersgracht Canal, almost in the middle of the city.

The twelve-hour flight passed smoothly. Ava had two

glasses of champagne when she boarded, downed two glasses of a French white burgundy with a dinner of Dover sole, and then fell asleep watching the Chinese film *The Election*. The film chronicled the election of a chairman of the triad societies. She had seen it before but it always fascinated her, if only because Uncle had been chairman for consecutive terms. The machinations, the betrayals, and the violence that accompanied the election were horrific. It was difficult for her to accept that Uncle might have been a guiding hand in such venal events, but she knew that Hong Kong triad films were only loosely based on reality. She nodded off before the final sudden, vicious encounter between the two protagonists.

When she woke, they were still three hours from Amsterdam. She did a bathroom run, ordered a coffee, and then opened the envelope that May had given her. It contained a large volume of paper but less hard information than Ava had expected. The partnership agreement was the biggest component: thirty pages of corporate boilerplate that said nothing more than what May Ling had already explained, although Ava did find it strange to see her name affixed as a director and executive vice-president of Borneo Fine Hardwoods and Furniture. She had been a partner with Uncle for ten years without any written agreement. She could remember only one handshake. There had certainly never been any titles.

The letter from May Ling's lawyer was a simple one-page document attesting that the partnership agreement was a valid document and that Ava was fully empowered to act on any matter relating to the corporation and the bankruptcy proceedings. The bankruptcy notification itself was just that. It said, on the company's own letterhead, that

Timmerman BV had been appointed as trustee in bankruptcy to liquidate the assets of Janssen Volker NV. All secured and unsecured creditors were invited to a meeting that was scheduled for eleven a.m. the coming Tuesday at 113 Damstratt in the city of Amsterdam.

Attached to the notice were lists of creditors with the amounts they were owed. Only two were secured: a bank for a nominal amount and a company called Meijer Finance, which claimed 15 million euros as the debt owed. The list of unsecured creditors was longer: several trucking firms, a landlord, some warehouses, credit card companies, and, dwarfing them all, Borneo Fine Hardwoods and Furniture.

Ava had packed a black Moleskine notebook in her Chanel carry-on bag. She opened it now and wrote *Borneo Furniture* across the top of the first page. She had kept an individual notebook for every job she undertook for Uncle and herself. Her friends joked about her low-tech approach, but she had found that writing numbers, names, facts, questions, and theories by hand somehow enhanced her retention level and her analytical skills. And when a job was done, the notebook provided a permanent record. The notebooks for all of her jobs were stored in a safety deposit box in a bank close to her Toronto condo.

She took the details from the Timmerman document and transferred them to the Moleskine. Then she listed May Ling's suspicions about the brothers and their relationship with the Dutch company. On the surface the situation did look as if it had been contrived — everything was so damn neat. But while it was easy to make charges, it was something else entirely to prove May's assumption that there had been fraudulent collusion among three or more parties. What if it was a just a case of incompetent business management that had stumbled its way into the efficient Dutch bankruptcy system?

Ava closed her notebook and sat back. She hadn't done any work in more than five months. In the past it had taken her a while to get up to scratch after a prolonged absence. That was a luxury she didn't have this time. The bankruptcy meeting was only a day away, and the money involved wasn't someone else's to lose. As she began to contemplate the enormous sum that was $30 million, the plane banked and the flight director announced they had begun their descent into Amsterdam.

They landed at eleven thirty, and in less than thirty minutes she had walked out into the cold, damp night.

The distance from Schiphol Airport to the Dylan Hotel was only about ten kilometres. In-bound traffic at that time of night was light; in fact, Ava saw almost as many buses as cars, and by twelve thirty she was at the hotel entrance. It looked like something from another century with its stone façade interrupted by metal grilles and its metal doors crowned by a high arch. The Dylan hadn't originally been conceived as a hotel; it comprised a number of three-storey brick and stone houses surrounding a courtyard, which had been built in the 1600s.

Ava had arranged for a late check-in and her room was ready when she arrived. They called it the Kimono Room. It was entirely black and white, ultra-modern Japanese minimalism with clean, hard lines. Even the bed's four posts were thin and reed-like, more for accent than function, more symbol than decoration.

Ava unpacked her Shanghai Tang Double Happiness bag and carried her toilet kit into the bathroom. Her plan was to shower, slip into clean underwear and a T-shirt, and then sleep. As she stripped, she became aware of how dazzling the light was.

Her room was on the top floor of the hotel, and the bathroom had been built loft-style, with black wooden beams crisscrossing from wall to wall and a glass ceiling open to an overcast sky. Because of the dark contrast created by the bathroom's ceiling, the room seemed flooded with a brilliant glare when she turned on the lights, a glare that accentuated every pore of her body. Rarely had she felt more naked. Ava looked at herself in the mirror and was startled by how pale her skin seemed, even more so when she turned sideways and saw the red scar on her upper thigh where she had been shot in Macau.

Even in the harshness of the light, her body looked to be that of a younger woman. A combination of running and bak mei — the Chinese martial art she practised — had helped her maintain her physique for as long as she could remember. She was beautifully proportioned, her waist almost perfectly centred, her thighs and buttocks firm and muscular.

The bathroom, like the rest of her suite, was starkly minimalist. The immense white porcelain bathtub was completely encased in black marble. She drew water, added bubble bath, and eased herself into the tub.

As she soaked, she focused on two white pots shot through with streaks of electric blue, sitting on a ledge at the foot of the bath. They were probably Japanese pots, she thought, but they could just as easily have been Chinese.

What was she doing in Amsterdam? Then it occurred to her that not only was she away from Hong Kong for the first time in five months, she was also completely alone. She closed her eyes. The image of Uncle lying in his bed at the Queen Elizabeth leapt into her mind. She stared into his eyes. She smiled, or thought she did, but all she felt were tears running down her cheeks.

AVA SLEPT UNTIL ALMOST EIGHT O'CLOCK. SHE WOKE with a start. It took a few minutes before she realized she wasn't at the Mandarin Oriental, and that she had slept the entire night. She rolled out of bed and walked over to the window. It was still raining, and so heavily that she could barely see past the courtyard to the front entrance gate.

She brushed her teeth and hair and then dressed in a clean white T-shirt and training pants. Before going to bed she had made a mental list of the things she wanted to do that morning, but now her stomach was rumbling and had her attention. *Eat, then work*, she told herself.

She called Reception. The main restaurant, Vinkeles, was closed until dinnertime, but breakfast was being served in the Long Gallery lounge. She debated ordering room service and then decided to go downstairs.

Half an hour later, fortified by two cups of coffee and Eggs Benedict with smoked salmon, she sat at her computer and opened her emails.

She had let everyone in Toronto know that she was leaving Hong Kong for a few days. The reactions from Maria,

Mimi, and her mother were identical — worries about Uncle and about how she was holding up. She assured them that Uncle's situation hadn't changed and that she was just taking a few days after the wedding to unwind.

Two of the emails were from May Ling. There was a seven-hour time difference between Amsterdam and Borneo; the first email, sent late the night before, said that she had arrived and had been met at the airport by Ah-Pei and Chi-Tze. They had spent several hours that evening reviewing the situation. The women were devastated, but they seemed determined to keep going, whether or not they had additional support. Their attitude had pleased May.

From a preliminary look at the books and their anecdotal recap of the state of the business, it was obvious that the financial situation was dire. Their cash flow had been destroyed, and unless more funds were pumped into the business quickly, production would have to be suspended. If that happened, then their supply lines for hardwood would come under pressure. If they lost those sources of supply to another manufacturer, God knows when or whether they could ever get them back. May estimated they needed at least another $5 million to stabilize the situation.

May's second email had been sent about the same time Ava was awakening in her hotel. Amanda landed in Kota Kinabalu just before lunch and came directly to the office, May wrote. To the sisters' dismay, I sat with her alone for the first hour. She was very upset that I hadn't told her about the problems. I explained I hadn't wanted to jinx her wedding, and she began to calm down when she found out that I hadn't told you anything either. I assured her that we did not hold her responsible for the mess in Borneo, and told her that we were prepared to put in whatever money was required to keep the business viable as long as she was willing to manage the process until things were clearer. She couldn't have been more agreeable. I hope your trip was uneventful. I'm leaving my hotel with Amanda and Chi-Tze in a few minutes for a meeting with a lawyer who we think is smart and tough enough. I'll update you later tonight, she closed.

I'm in Amsterdam. Flight was fine. Call me on my cell when you finish with the lawyer. I'm going to start hunting things down at this end, Ava replied.

She closed her computer and glanced at the envelope and Moleskine notebook that sat on the desk. She reached for the book and then noticed her cellphone. *Uncle*, she thought. She punched in his number.

"*Wei*," the familiar voice said after the second ring.

"It's Ava."

"I could not tell. There is no number showing on my end."

"I'm in Amsterdam."

"And I am in Shanghai."

"Already?"

"They released me from the hospital early this morning. We caught a flight before lunch."

"And you are feeling okay?"

"I napped on the plane."

"Sonny is with you?"

"Of course."

"Are you at the hotel?"

"For an hour."

"The Peninsula, correct?"

"Yes."

"Uncle, please take it easy. Nothing good can come from overdoing things."

"Ava, stop worrying. I am not here to lift bricks."

"Still…"

"And how are things for you in Amsterdam?"

"I don't know. I just woke up and I'm about to make my first contact."

"Good luck."

"Thanks."

"If you need me, call. It appears I will be here for at least two full days."

"And you will call me, or you will instruct Sonny to call, if you need me?"

"I said I would."

"Sorry for being a pest about it," she said, sensing a touch of annoyance in his voice.

"Ava, go and look after your business. I will see you in Hong Kong in a few days," he said gently.

He's right, she thought, opening the notebook. There was nothing to be gained by worrying about what he was doing eight thousand kilometres away. Better that she focus on the problem less than five kilometres from her hotel doorway, one that started with Timmerman BV, the bankruptcy trustee. She picked up the hotel phone and made the local call.

From her previous trip to Amsterdam she knew that most Dutch people speak English, and many of them other languages as well — a testament to their trading background. So she wasn't surprised when the receptionist at Timmerman switched to English as soon as she heard Ava's voice.

"How can I help you?" she asked.

"My name is Ava Lee. I'm here for a creditors' meeting tomorrow, and I'd like to speak to the trustee who is handling the file for Janssen Volker NV."

"That would be Patrick Visser," the woman said, and then paused.

"Is there a problem?" Ava asked.

"No, I'm just checking to see if he's in the office today."

The line went silent and Ava knew she had been put on hold. Several minutes passed and she began to get impatient. Then a man's voice said, "Visser."

"Hello, my name is Ava Lee and I'm in Amsterdam for the Janssen Volker creditors' meeting."

"Really?"

"You sound surprised. The meeting is still scheduled for tomorrow, isn't it?"

"Yes, of course, but I wasn't expecting any creditors to actually show up. Just who is it you represent?"

That's strange, Ava thought, and then said, "Borneo Fine Hardwoods and Furniture."

"And you came all the way from Borneo?"

"Hong Kong, actually."

"Your English is excellent, if I may say."

"I'm Canadian."

"Ah, that explains it. But tell me, what is your relationship to this Borneo business?"

"I'm an officer and a shareholder."

"I see," he said, and then hesitated.

"Mr. Visser, I have to tell you I was somewhat surprised when I saw the list of creditors. It seemed to me rather short for such a large filing."

"It is, of course, but it's accurate. Aside from your company, Meijer Finance is the only other major one. They, of course, are secured and have already started the process of recovering as much of their funds as they can."

"Short or not, I couldn't help being even more surprised to see there were no other furniture suppliers listed."

"Janssen rid themselves of nearly all of them over the past few years. Their business appears to have become almost completely focused on your products."

"And there was only one bank involved?"

"Yes, and that was only for operational purposes — paying bills and payroll and things like that. Janssen had a very modest line of credit. It was secured, of course, but I'm told that Meijer paid it off so they could have uncontested rights to whatever assets still remained in the business."

"And what assets were those?" Ava asked, knowing already what the answer was going to be.

"Furniture."

"Just furniture?"

"It does appear to be that way."

"And all of it ours?"

"Yes."

"So Meijer has taken possession of it?"

"Yes, as they are legally entitled to do."

"And now they're selling it off."

"That is the case."

"For cents on the dollar."

"Ms. Lee, they are a secured creditor," Visser said carefully. "Under our laws, they are simply exercising their rights."

"And as the trustee, you have no power, you have no influence?"

"We have a complete record of the inventory, and Meijer is required to report any and all sales they make from that inventory. If they recover funds in excess of what they are owed, the money will be accrued to us. If they recover their funds and any inventory is left, then we are able to sell it ourselves and disperse those funds among the unsecured creditors on a pro rata basis."

"Yes, I saw there were other unsecured creditors, but aside from warehousing and transportation companies, they hardly amount to anything."

"That's correct, Ms Lee. You're talking about a landlord owed a few months' rent, and other such minor claims. The warehouse companies have already been looked after."

"What?"

"I'm told they were holding the furniture for ransom and Meijer had to pay them off to get access to it."

"So, what you're telling me," Ava said, her agitation growing, "is that there's only one unsecured creditor of any size, and that's us."

"True enough."

"And any assets in the firm happen to be tied directly to us as well."

"That is the case."

"And you don't find that strange?" Ava said.

"I don't understand your question."

"How does it come to pass that this finance company would extend that level of credit to a company that appears to have had no assets except for inventory they bought on terms from us?"

"Ms. Lee, it isn't our job to tell companies like Meijer who they can and cannot finance. Equally, it isn't our job to tell companies like yours who can they sell to and what terms they should extend to their customers. We are here to pick up the pieces when things go badly. And in this case things went badly for Janssen and Meijer, and as is their legal right, they've stepped in to protect themselves. Unfortunately — and for reasons entirely of your own doing, may I add — your company is not so well situated."

Ava had been making point-form notes as she spoke to Visser. Now as she looked down at them, all she could see was the line she had drawn between Janssen and Meijer.

"Where did the money go?" she asked abruptly.

"What do you mean?"

"If Meijer financed Janssen to the tune of more than twenty million dollars, and if the money was supposed to pay for furniture inventory but no inventory was paid for, then where the hell is the money?"

"That's a very good question," Visser said.

"Really?" Ava said.

"There's no reason to be sarcastic, and no reason for you to think we haven't done due diligence."

"Then where is the money?"

"Ms. Lee, Meijer and Janssen had a business relationship that extended over the past fifteen years. The debt in question was cumulative. In truth, Meijer could have pulled the plug on Janssen several years ago, but obviously they were hoping things would turn around with the business and so they kept it afloat."

"They told you this?"

"Yes, they did, and you need to know that we confirmed it."

"So, what? They just decided to call in their loans a month ago?"

"They did."

"Entirely coincidentally with Janssen's receiving massive shipments of goods from us?"

"I can't speak to the coincidence part."

"Of course not, although you do have to admit it was very convenient for Meijer to act when they did."

"Obviously."

"From where I stand, I have to tell you it looks like some form of collusion was at play."

"Ms. Lee —"

"It stinks, and you know it stinks," she interrupted.

"Meijer acted within their legal rights," he said.

"And what rights do we have?"

Visser paused. Ava could feel him measuring his words. "Under Dutch bankruptcy law, the secured creditors have the right to pursue recovery of their funds by any means they choose, as long as they remain within the law. I can tell you that Meijer has remained within the law. Unsecured creditors are exactly that, Ms. Lee — unsecured. They have no rights beyond filing a claim with the trustee and waiting for the trustee to collect and disperse what he can. I can assure you that we will collect what we can and we will make sure it is equitably dispersed."

"There will be nothing to collect," Ava said. "You know that already."

"There is a lot of inventory."

"Being sold at a huge discount," Ava said.

"You know, there is one avenue open to you..." Visser said carefully.

"What is it?"

"Well, you could buy back your own inventory. If it's

discounted sufficiently, perhaps you could resell it in the marketplace at its normal markup and recoup most of your funds."

"We could try to sell it into a market we don't understand, where we have no contacts, and where all the potential customers would know soon enough that our situation was desperate. What kind of sense does that make?"

"I was offering a suggestion, not making a recommendation."

Ava checked her notebook. There was no information on Meijer beyond an address. "Meijer is simply a finance company, correct?"

"Yes."

"How are they disposing of the assets? They can't be familiar with the market either."

Visser hesitated. "You would have to speak to them."

"And how would I do that? Do you have a contact name for me?"

"You can call Johann Meijer himself at his office," Visser said, and gave her a phone number.

Ava wrote it in the notebook. "It's his business?"

"Not entirely. Johann's father, who founded the company, is still active, but he's passed on most of the day-to-day operations to Johann."

She pushed her chair back from the desk and looked out the window. Rain spattered against it, driven by a wind that hadn't eased since she'd arrived. She stood and looked out towards the street. The only visible form of life was a young woman scurrying along the sidewalk, her head lowered to her chest, her umbrella turned at an angle to deflect the rain. Just watching her made Ava shiver.

"Thank you for your help, Mr. Visser. I'm not sure if I'll come to the meeting tomorrow or not. I'll probably wait until the morning to decide."

"I'll be there regardless, and if you aren't, chances are I'll be alone."

9

WHAT A MESS, AVA THOUGHT. WORSE, IT WAS A MESS she felt virtually powerless to do anything about. If everything Visser had told her was true — and she couldn't think of any reason why the bankruptcy trustee would lie to her — then her coming to Amsterdam had been a complete waste of time and money.

She looked down at the few notes she had taken. In the past she had seized goods in lieu of money as she tried to get her clients' money back. She had then proceeded to do exactly what Meijer Finance had done. She had paid off warehouses so they couldn't block access to the goods. She had identified any other creditors who might be lurking and bought them off too if it was necessary. And finally she had sold the goods at prices designed to salvage the money her clients were owed, with no concern for their real market value. Meijer's behaviour was understandable. Not that it made it any easier to accept.

She stared at the phone number Visser had given her for Johann Meijer and then picked up the phone.

"Meijer," a woman said.

"Yes, I'm calling about some furniture I understand you're selling."

"Furniture?"

"Yes, I'm told you're disposing of some inventory."

"This is Meijer Finance Company. We don't sell furniture."

"I know that isn't your main business, but I've been told you've repossessed some furniture and are selling it to recover funds."

"Just a moment," the woman said, her voice filled with doubt.

Ava waited. Had Visser lied to her?

"You need to call another number," the woman said when she came back on the line.

"Pardon?"

"You need to call a man named Jan de Groot. I'll give you his number," she said.

"This Mr. de Groot, he's selling the furniture?"

"That's what they tell me."

"Who tells you?"

"My boss."

"Can I speak to your boss?"

"Just a moment," she said again.

Ava looked at the papers strewn across her desk. Why did the name de Groot seem familiar? She flipped several pages until she came to the list of creditors. Across the top of the page was the heading ALL CREDITORS IN THE CASE OF THE BANKRUPTCY OF JANSSEN VOLKER, and underneath it were the names of the officers and directors of the firm. A Jan de Groot was identified as managing director.

"My boss says he can't help you. It's better for you to call Jan de Groot. He's the one who's responsible."

"Is this the Jan de Groot who ran Janssen Volker?"

"How would I know?"

"Then let me speak to someone who does."

"I'm sorry, no one else is available."

"You said your boss was there."

"He just left."

Ava drew a deep breath and then ate the angry retort that hovered on her tongue. "Thank you," she said.

She stared at Jan de Groot's name in her notebook. *How weird is this?* Ava thought as she dialled the number the woman had given her. The phone rang four times, and she was ready to leave a voice message when she heard, "de Groot."

"Is this Jan de Groot?"

"The same."

"I was given your name by Meijer Finance. I understand you're selling some furniture that they repossessed."

"So?"

"I have an interest in it."

"I don't recognize your voice."

"We've never spoken. My name is Ava Lee."

"And your accent isn't Dutch or English. Are you American?"

"Canadian."

"I still don't know you."

"You would have no reason to."

"Why are you calling?"

"I'm interested in meeting with you with a view to buying some of the furniture you're selling."

"No," de Groot said.

"I beg your pardon?"

"The furniture has either been sold or is committed to another party."

"If we could meet and I had a chance to go over the inventory with you, who knows, I might be able to make a better offer."

"Not interested."

"Surely Meijer Finance might be if there's more money at stake."

"Then call Meijer. If they tell me I have to meet with you, then I'll think about it."

"I find your attitude rather surprising," she said.

"Look, I was told to sell the furniture as quickly as I could. That's what I've done. It's all sold or committed to. I'm not going back on my word to the people who have bought it."

"What about the other creditors? I know the furniture is part of a bankruptcy and that Meijer is a secured creditor, but don't you feel any obligation to maximize the return from the sales? Don't you think the other creditors should be given some consideration?"

"I was hired by Meijer."

"Yes, but you were also managing director of the company that went under. You bear at least part of the responsibility for leaving the other creditors in a difficult situation."

De Groot went quiet. Ava expected the line to go dead. Instead she could hear paper rustling. "What did you say your name was?" he asked.

"Ava Lee."

"You're an officer of that company that bought into Borneo Furniture," he said.

"I am."

"Fuck off," he said.

This can't be legal, she thought. Surely the secured creditor can't hire the bankrupt company to dispose of its own inventory. She called Patrick Visser.

The receptionist made her wait again, and after close to five minutes Ava began to think he wasn't going to take her call. But he did, and the words "Ms. Lee" were hardly out of his mouth when she said, "Did you know that Jan de Groot is selling off his own inventory?"

"You sound upset."

"Why wouldn't I be?"

He sighed. "The inventory is technically and legally in the possession of Meijer Finance. They are disposing of it as best they can. In this case, not being experts in the furniture trade, they have engaged the services of someone who is, and who has an intimate knowledge of the inventory and where it might best be sold. It is a convenient and efficient arrangement and, Ms. Lee, one of which I was aware and that is not uncommon."

"When you say 'engaged,' do you mean that Janssen Volker is getting paid to do this? Because if they are, shouldn't that money flow back to you for dispersal to other creditors?"

She heard a longer, deeper sigh. "Janssen Volker is no more. My understanding is that Meijer has hired Mr. de Groot as an independent contractor. He's working, I'm told, on a commission basis."

"Why didn't you tell me this before?"

"I didn't think it was particularly relevant who was selling the furniture."

Ava could feel bile rising from her stomach. She had been away five months from the stress and anger that her business sometimes generated. Now it was back, and she wished it didn't seem so familiar. "This sounds to me like a 'let's screw over the foreigners' kind of deal, with you and Meijer and Janssen taking turns."

"Ms. Lee, I resent that accusation."

"I really don't care."

"As I said to you earlier, Meijer is perfectly within its legal rights to do what it has done, including paying Jan de Groot a commission to turn that inventory into cash," he said. "There's a creditors' meeting tomorrow morning; you know the time and place. You're welcome to attend to ask any questions you wish and to present any opinions you have. Until then, I really don't think there's any value in our continuing this conversation."

"And I don't think there's any reason for me to attend that meeting."

"The choice is yours."

10

AVA SAT AT THE DESK, LOOKING AT NAMES AND PHONE
numbers that amounted to exactly zero progress.

She walked over to the window again. Whatever thoughts she might have had about going out for a run, even a brisk walk, were immediately dashed by the sight of what she was now beginning to think was perpetual driving rain.

She shuffled back to the computer and looked up her hotel's location and then those of the Timmerman and Meijer offices. The trustee was virtually around the corner. Meijer was no more than ten blocks away. She debated the merits of visiting either of them. The trustee would probably — and maybe rightfully — tell her to come back tomorrow for the meeting. If Meijer wasn't willing to take her phone call, why would he see her in person? Besides, even if they did see her and agreed to talk to her, what exactly could she say that would make any difference to the situation?

I don't have enough information, she thought. Without thinking, she went over to the nightstand and took out a local phonebook. She started to look at it and then stopped short — it was in Dutch. Of course it was in Dutch, and she didn't read Dutch. She put the book under her arm and left the room.

The concierge was, Ava guessed, in his mid-forties. He stood a sturdy six feet, with a full head of silver hair. He didn't seem to understand her request the first time she made it.

"The police station is near the railway station," he said.

"No, I'm not looking for that kind of detective," she said. "I want to hire a private detective, someone who can gather some financial information for me. Could you look in this phonebook for me and find the proper section?"

"What should I look under?"

"Private investigators?"

He muttered something in Dutch and riffled through the pages.

"Here are some," he said. "Most of them seem to specialize in cheating spouses, divorces, insurance scams. They also seem to be ex-policemen. What appeals to you?"

"Is there anyone who even mentions the word *business*?"

"This one," he said, pointing to the name *Smits*. "He even mentions he worked for the Dutch tax administration department."

"Could you write down his name, address, and phone number for me?"

"Sure," he said, writing the name 'Jacob Smits' and his contact information on hotel stationery.

She called the detective when she got back to her room. A loud, gruff voice answered the phone with a torrent of words. The only one she understood was *Smits*.

"Do you speak English?" she asked.

"Yes."

"Thank goodness. For a second I thought I would have to get the concierge to translate."

"Concierge?"

"I'm visiting Amsterdam and I'm staying at the Dylan Hotel."

"How did you locate me?"

"The concierge found you in the phonebook."

"Ah."

"He told me you've done some work with the Dutch tax administration."

"Yes."

"What exactly did you do?"

"Chased after tax evaders."

"I see."

"And then I spent three years with the KLPD in Amsterdam, investigating white-collar crime."

"KLPD?"

"The regional police force."

"So you have a financial as well as an enforcement background?"

"I'm an accountant. The only police work I did was from behind a desk, working on a computer and going through bank and company statements."

"It sounds like you are exactly what I need."

"To do what?"

"My business finds itself caught up in bankruptcy proceedings that look to me like a put-up job. I need to understand the real financials of a couple of Dutch companies, and I want to know if there's more of a relationship between them than what's being represented. Is this something you feel you could deliver?"

He paused. "You said these are Dutch companies?"

"Yes, is that a problem?"

"No, just the opposite."

"Then why the hesitation?"

"My rate is five hundred euros a day."

"Plus expenses?"

"There are hardly ever any expenses, unless I have to travel out of the city."

"So when can you start?"

"I have a few other things I'm working on right now."

"Well, I'm here in Amsterdam right now and I don't have a lot of time to spare. Is it possible we could meet today to talk this over and see if you can fit us into your schedule?"

"Yes, I think that's possible."

"Are you available now?"

"You're staying at the Dylan?"

"Yes."

"And what's your name?"

"Ava Lee."

"Well, Ms. Lee, there's a pub called the Melancholy Miller two streets from your hotel. I can meet you there around six."

"No sooner?" Ava said, the thought of a drawn-out afternoon having no appeal.

"No."

"Okay, then six will have to do. How will I recognize you?"

"I'll be wearing a brown suit."

11

AVA CALLED DOWNSTAIRS TO THE CONCIERGE. "HOW close is the Rijksmuseum?" she asked.

"You can walk there in less than ten minutes."

"In this weather?"

"I have umbrellas here — very good umbrellas."

"Put one aside for me," she said.

Ava had visited the museum on her previous trip to Amsterdam. She had spent almost an hour staring at Rembrandt's *The Night Watch* before being hustled from the building at closing time. She figured this time she would be able to see more of Rembrandt's work and also catch the Vermeers and Van Dycks.

She checked her watch. It was just past seven o'clock in the evening in Borneo. May Ling had to be finished with the lawyer by now. Ava phoned her.

"Yes," May answered. Ava could hear the sound of clattering dishes in the background.

"It's Ava."

"I was going to call you in a little while. I'm having dinner with the sisters and Amanda."

"I got your emails."

"Good. So you're safely in Amsterdam?"

"Yes, and I've had phone conversations with all of the interested parties here — the trustee, Meijer Finance, and the charming Jan de Groot from Janssen Volker."

"How did it go?"

"Badly."

"How bad?"

"Meijer has our furniture, de Groot is selling it for them, and the trustee says there is nothing he can do to prevent it."

"De Groot? How is that possible? They let the thief sell his stolen goods?"

"According to the trustee it isn't uncommon and it's within the law."

"That is bad."

"Anyway, I still plan on going to the bankruptcy meeting tomorrow, but I'm not hopeful it will make any difference."

"Is there nothing you can do?"

"I'm going to hire a private detective."

"Why?"

"We don't know enough about anyone. I want to see what he can dig up."

"Sounds like a fishing expedition."

"It is."

"The same is true here, except that…" May paused. "Just a minute, let me move outside. It's very noisy here."

When May came back on the line, the noise level was probably greater.

"What was that about?" Ava asked.

"The sisters. I didn't want to talk in any detail in front of them. They were very reluctant, especially Ah-Pei, to agree to pursue their brothers legally. They're afraid that it's going to cause a schism in the family. And, just as bad, bring public embarrassment to the family. This is a very small community, and all the Chinese businesspeople know each other. They don't want to look like fools, and they don't want their brothers to be thought of as thieves."

"Even if they are?"

"Who knows if they are or not? The one thing I can tell you is that this lawyer is as aggressive as anyone I've ever met. Even before Amanda, Chi-Tze, and I left, he had his people working on the paperwork. He intends to serve Mamat and Tambi with a lawsuit as early as tomorrow."

"What inspired that response?"

"Money. I promised him a lot of money."

"And just what is he suing them for?"

"He's accusing them of accepting illegal commissions and is going after them for the entire sum of the Janssen contract."

"Based on what facts?"

"None. It's all supposition on his part, but he said he knows the brothers personally. He began to denigrate them so harshly I almost asked Chi-Tze to leave his office."

"But the women do know about the lawsuit."

"Of course. They just aren't happy about it and don't want to know the details."

"What does Amanda say?"

"As far as she's concerned, anything is fair. All she cares about is getting any part of our money back."

"And the lawyer actually thinks that's possible?"

"He started reading the contract they signed with the Dutch firm and said 'illegal commissions' before he even finished."

"Why was he so sure about that?" Ava asked.

"As I said, he knows Mamat and Tambi and he thinks they've always been a bit off-colour. Also, according to him, illegal commissions and other side deals are standard ways of doing business in Borneo. And, Ava, he isn't just suing them. He's sending a copy of the lawsuit to the brothers' banks, telling them what we're doing and advising them that he will be seeking full access to records of any money transfers in or out of their accounts from offshore accounts over the past five years, and putting them on notice that no large withdrawals should take place until these legal issues are resolved."

"What makes the lawyer think the bank will co-operate?"

"His brother is Superintendent of Financial Institutions for Sabah."

"Wheels within wheels."

"Big Chinese wheels within big Chinese wheels."

"Well, I'm not dealing with Chinese here."

"You'll manage."

"I wish I was so sure. I've been worrying about Uncle since I arrived and, truthfully, I was also upset for Amanda."

"I told you, Amanda is fine."

"I should speak to her."

"She said she's going to call you when she gets back to our hotel."

"Okay, but remind her that I'm seven hours behind you. It's only early afternoon here, so any time in the next three or four hours is fine. After that I'm meeting with the detective."

"I'm going to bed early tonight, and then tomorrow morning I have another session with the lawyer before he does anything official. Once that's finalized, I'm heading back to Wuhan and leaving things here in Amanda's care."

"How about the money the business needs? You said it was about five million."

"I have it organized to send tomorrow. I was waiting to make sure you agree."

"Do we have any choice?"

"Not if we want to make sure the business remains viable."

"Then send it."

Ava stood up and stretched. She could feel tension rippling through her body. The events in Borneo and Amsterdam were nothing she wasn't used to, but this time she wasn't doing a job for a stranger. And she wasn't in pursuit alone, with Uncle hovering in the background ready to lend whatever aid she needed.

"Go back to your dinner," she said to May. "I'll email you when I finish with the detective."

12

SHE PUT ON HER BLACK NYLON ADIDAS JACKET AND training pants and then slid the bankruptcy documents into her bag and headed for the lobby. The concierge nodded when he saw her, reached behind his desk, and pulled out an umbrella that looked big enough to shield a family of four.

"You said the Rijksmuseum?"

"Yes."

"When you leave the hotel, turn right at the third street, walk to the third block, and then go left," he said. "That will take you to Museum Row. The Hermitage, the Van Gogh, and the Rijksmuseum are all there."

"I want to see the Rembrandts."

"Go to the Rijksmuseum then, but if you haven't been to the Van Gogh you're missing something special. More than two hundred of his works are on display there."

"I'll see if I have time," Ava said.

Despite the umbrella she was instantly wet the minute she stepped outside. The rain was being driven sideways by the wind. She held the umbrella at an angle and started to walk.

The Rijksmuseum was the national museum of the Netherlands. More than two hundred years old, it moved into its current quarters in 1885. It was constructed in the style of a French château, with a grand central building framed by two enormous towers and flanked on either side by large and impressive wings.

Ava could see the building from several blocks away, its slanted green roofs looming through the sheets of rain. She lowered her head and plunged forward. When she got to the front entrance, she looked up and found herself confronted by construction barriers and a security guard holding an umbrella.

"Don't tell me the museum is closed," she said.

"Only the main building, for renovation."

"I wanted to see the Rembrandts. That's where they are, I think."

He pointed towards the wing to the left. "The most important pictures in the collection have been moved to the Philips Wing. You will find what you want to see there."

She took the pathway that led to the Philips. The last time she had been to the museum she had lined up for close to half an hour before getting in. As she neared the entrance this time, she couldn't see another person. *There are some benefits to wet, dreary weather,* she thought as she paid her admission. Then she stood back as the security guard examined her bag and its contents.

She was just about to climb the stairs to the first-floor exhibits when her cellphone rang. She reached into her pocket and saw Amanda's number displayed on the screen.

"No mobile devices can be used inside the museum," a voice said.

Ava turned and saw the security guard behind her. "No mobile devices," he repeated.

"Can I speak from down there?" she asked, pointing to the hallway near the front door. "I don't want to go back outside in this rain."

"Yes, that will be all right."

Ava opened her phone. "Amanda, give me a minute. I'll be right with you," she said.

She retraced her steps, and when she reached the hallway, she turned into an alcove on the left and leaned against the wall. "Sorry, I had to find a spot where I could talk," she said. "Where are you? May said you were going to call me from the hotel. I didn't expect you to be back so soon."

"I didn't want to wait. I'm in the parking lot of the restaurant."

"You should be on your honeymoon," Ava said.

"There's no way that was possible after talking to Chi-Tze."

"I'm sorry it happened this way."

"Me too, though the news is so bad I can't think of a good way to find out."

"It isn't your fault."

Ava heard Amanda sigh as if it came from her toes. "That's what May said. Logically I know I did proper due diligence, and logically I knew this business was sound. But emotionally...it was like getting kicked in the stomach. And I'm still kind of reeling."

"We'll sort it out."

"How?"

The question, quick and pointed, caught Ava off-guard. It reminded her that Amanda was not someone to be spoken to lightly or in clichés. "May thinks her lawyer will light a fire."

"He might," Amanda said.

Ava could hear the doubt in her voice. She thought about mentioning Jacob Smits and then discarded the idea. "The thing is, we won't just accept this. I'm not sure what will or will not happen; all I know is that we will pursue it until there's nothing left to chase. And there isn't much point worrying about that from your end. Just keep the sisters calm and the business in one piece."

"We meet with their bank tomorrow."

"Who are *we*?"

"Me and the sisters. May is leaving for Wuhan."

"Are you okay with that?"

"Yes. Actually, I'm glad to see she still has confidence in me."

"We have agreed to put another five million into the business."

"I know, she told us when she came back to the table after talking to you."

"How did the sisters react?"

"Relieved."

"Of course."

"They really are very capable. I mean, Ah-Pei virtually ran the business with her parents for ages, and single-handedly for a few years while Chi-Tze was finishing her degree. Then the two of them were building it very nicely until this disaster."

"Well, with the five million they can go back to building it. There's no reason for them to be distracted by this sideshow. And the same goes for you. Stay focused on the business. Let May and me worry about the other money."

"After tomorrow I think it will be easier. The bank has been leaning on them very hard. They've exhausted their lines of credit and the bank is looking for at least a partial paydown. And they haven't been able to pay some of their key suppliers, so they've have been worried sick about competitors picking them off. The five million should get everything back on track."

"That's all we want to happen."

Ava heard another deep sigh. "God, what a way to start a new business," Amanda said.

"And a marriage. Tell me, how did Michael react to your leaving the honeymoon?"

"He was okay," she said. "Actually, it surprised me just how okay he was. After the mess he and Simon got themselves into last year, he's certainly more empathetic about other people's problems. Before, he would have been dismissive. He would have said that whatever problem someone might have, they brought it down on themselves through bad judgement, or some flaw in their character. Now he understands that sometimes things happen that are beyond anyone's control."

"Good."

"And Borneo isn't that far from Hong Kong. I told him he can fly over on the weekends until I get back."

"And he will?"

"He'd better."

Ava laughed. "It sounds as if you have things organized already."

Amanda went quiet, and Ava wondered if she had somehow upset her.

"Ava, I need to tell you how much I appreciate the fact that you and May are standing by me and Ah-Pei and Chi-Tze."

"There's no need to talk about that anymore."

"Still —"

"Amanda, listen to me. I don't want to have to say this again," she said. "I was in business with Uncle for more than ten years. We never had a contract and we never had a personal disagreement. It worked because we never second-guessed one another. We each understood that both of us were doing our best, and if things didn't always work, there was no reason to point that out. There was total trust between us. We were partners in the complete sense of the term. Now, I would never have agreed to get into this business with you and May if I hadn't felt the same way, and I know those are May's feelings as well. So I don't want to hear you ever again thank us for standing by you. We are in this thing together. There will be ups and downs, but if we all carry the load, it will be bearable." She paused. "Do you understand?"

"Yes, Ava."

"Then go and calm the sisters and get this business back on track."

Ava hung up and then climbed the stairs again. The security guard stared at her cellphone. She held it up and punched the off button. He nodded and she slipped it into her pocket.

The Rembrandts occupied one large room in the centre of the Philips Wing. Ava headed there with purpose, passing some Van Dycks, Vermeers, and Hals. Vermeer's *The Milkmaid* caused her to pause for a second, but no more than that.

The Rembrandt room had paintings on three walls. The fourth was devoted to a written history of the man and his work, in ten languages. Six cushioned benches ran the length of the centre of the room. One was occupied by a Japanese couple. There was no one else in the room except for a security guard positioned at its single entrance and exit. Ava sat down. For the next ten minutes she took in the entire nineteen paintings from a distance.

Ava wasn't an art scholar. Most of what she knew technically about paintings she had learned only months before, when she was involved in running to ground some art forgers. But she loved art in general, in the same way that she appreciated good books and fine films — as the end result of creative processes she didn't understand and could never emulate. It amazed her what human beings could extract from their imaginations.

After absorbing the totality of the works on display, she stood and walked towards the nearest wall. Then, painting by painting, she worked her way around the room. She had no idea how long she spent with each, and she had no schedule. Each painting drew her in on its own merits and then released her to move on to the next.

How did he do it? she asked herself. *How could anyone use just a brush and paint to create such complicated, layered, nuanced, multihued images, so awash in light and shadow?* She got as close as she could to every painting, her neck stretched forward, her eyes searching for brushstrokes.

She circled the room once, sat on the bench to reinvigorate her senses, and then went around again. None of the paintings paled on second examination. If anything, their complexity increased. She was in front of *The Night Watch* — she had no idea for how long — when the security guard appeared at her side. His presence startled her, and for a second she wondered if she had ventured too close.

"Miss, the gallery is closing," he said.

She looked at her watch. It was ten minutes to six. "Sorry, I had no idea of the time."

"That's common enough here."

She pointed at the painting. "What a genius he was."

"I've seen tourists come here every day for a week and never leave this room," he said.

"I can understand why."

"So perhaps I'll see you tomorrow. But for now, you do have to leave."

"Of course," Ava said.

It was dark when she walked out of the Rijksmuseum, which made the wind and the rain seem even nastier. She opened her umbrella and peered into the street, trying to figure out how to get to the pub that Jacob Smits had mentioned. When she felt oriented, she held the umbrella towards the wind and started to walk.

It took more than ten minutes to get to the Melancholy Miller. The umbrella had kept her head and torso dry, but the bottoms of her pants were soaked and her running shoes were squishing. The pub was small, only ten tables spread around a horseshoe-shaped bar with six stools on each side. She looked for a man in a brown suit. There were two men at the bar, neither in a suit, and two tables were occupied by what looked like students. She sat at the table farthest from the bar. The bartender, tall and thin in a grey T-shirt and blue jeans and looking much like a student himself, yelled at her in Dutch.

"I only speak English," she said.

"What would you like to drink?" he said, switching languages.

"I'm waiting for someone. I'll order when he gets here."

A few moments later a short, squat figure burst through the door, a hooded yellow rain slicker covering him from head to knee. He stood in the doorway and stared around. When he saw Ava, he pulled back the hood.

"Ms. Lee?" he said.

"That's me."

"I'm Smits."

He pulled off the slicker over his head, scattering water in all directions, hung it on a hook, and started towards her. He was no more than five foot six but had to be well over two hundred pounds. He was almost round, his weight evenly distributed and firmly layered, with no jiggling of excess flesh. He looked surprisingly fit to Ava; she noticed how quickly he moved, his body in rhythm, and it occurred to her that he might be a very good dancer.

His head looked immense, but its size was probably exaggerated by his small, almost delicate facial features. He had tiny pink ears with lobes the size of pearls. His lips were thin and drawn. Deeply recessed blue eyes gazed at her from under light brown eyebrows that were so fine she wondered if they had been plucked and shaped. He was bald, with just a hint of fringe the same colour as his eyebrows.

"Ms. Lee," he said when he was two paces away, offering his hand.

"Mr. Smits, you should have told me about your orange tie," she said.

He looked down at his tie, loosened at the neck, its tail resting on the upper ledge of his belly. "We Dutch love our orange."

He took a seat across from Ava and made a fuss about settling in. "Sorry to be a little late."

"The weather is atrocious."

"It's typical enough."

"Do you want something to drink?"

"Of course."

Ava motioned to the bartender. "We'll order now."

"What do you want?" the bartender asked.

"I'll have a glass of Pinot Grigio," she said.

Smits looked at his watch. "I'll have a Heineken," he said and then turned back to Ava. "I'm trying to cut back. I don't drink now until after six in the evening, and even then I try to limit myself to two."

Ava didn't know if he was making a joke. "Thanks for seeing me at such short notice," she said.

"My pleasure."

"How long have you been doing this kind of work?" Ava asked.

"Six years. I was actually hired by the man who started the business, but he died eighteen months on and I found myself running it. My wife says some things are meant to be, and this is one of those things. I would never have had the courage to quit my job and start out on my own. My partner's death gave me no choice. It's worked out well, better than I could have believed."

"You're a one-man firm?"

"Yes, so I don't like to work more than a few cases at a time. Whatever jobs I have get my serious attention."

"And I could be one of those jobs?"

"If you think I'm up to it. Not everyone thinks so. I don't always make a good first impression."

"Are you always so candid?"

"Don't know any other way to be."

"Then we should get along."

He sat back in his chair, squirming as he tried to get comfortable. "Do you need references? You didn't mention anything like that on the phone, but I thought I should ask."

"Are you good at what you do?"

"I'm the best in Amsterdam," he said, and then paused. "Mind you, there aren't many other detectives who focus on money matters. Here it's all about sex and drugs and gambling and infidelity."

"So I noticed when I tried to find someone."

"I thought about advertising myself as an accountant and actually set up a separate listing, but it didn't generate any business so I got rid of it."

The bartender arrived at the table with their drinks.

Smits raised his glass. "*Proost.*"

"*Yambui.*"

"Where are you actually from? I don't recognize your accent," Smits said after draining half his beer in two immense gulps.

"I'm Canadian. Of Chinese origin, of course, but very decidedly Canadian. This business I need you to look into, though, involves a company in Borneo. My partners and I own a venture capital firm in China and we've recently made a major investment in the Borneo operation. It's gone extremely sour."

"Canada...Borneo...China...the Netherlands...that's the way all business seems to be now. The days of operating in one market are long gone."

"And will never come back."

"No," Smits said, as if he regretted it.

"In any event, I have some paperwork to leave with you," Ava said, reaching for her bag. She extracted the files that May Ling had given her and passed them to Smits. "This will give you the basic information about all the companies and people involved, and the nature of the bankruptcy."

He glanced at the paperwork. "I've heard of Meijer, but only in passing. Janssen is a new name to me. Timmerman I know. They have a decent reputation as bankruptcy trustees."

"That may be the case, and if it's true, then whatever we can dig up to prove that Meijer and Janssen colluded to defraud us of thirty million dollars should prove useful and actionable."

"I said they were decent, not saints. They'll still want to collect their fees."

"We'll be good for whatever fees they would have earned if the bankruptcy was genuine."

"That's good to know. And now there's just the small matter of proving that something underhanded went on. You seemed not quite so sure of that when we talked on the phone."

Ava sipped her wine and then noticed that Smits's glass was empty. "Another beer?"

"Please."

Ava caught the bartender's eye and motioned at Smits's glass. "Well, I'm quite certain that something funny was done. Whether it was in Borneo or here or some combination of the two, and whether it involved both Janssen and Meijer in partnership with the Borneo thieves or just

Janssen and Meijer by themselves or just Janssen and the
Borneo bunch, I don't know. We'll handle things in Borneo,
so don't worry about that. What I need you to do is bur-
row as deeply as you can into Janssen's business. I want to
see company and banking records for as far back as you
can go. I want to see the details of how they were financed,
and just how entwined Meijer and Janssen were, and I want
to understand the relationship between these two companies — personal and business. And when you've got all that
information, I want you to analyze it and give me your best
assessment as to what happened."

"You said you'd look after Borneo. What you find there
could help me, no?"

"Yes, of course. I'll pass everything along to you."

His second beer arrived. He eyed it lovingly and this
time half-emptied it with only one gulp. He wiped his
mouth with the back of his hand. "If you don't mind me
saying, it sounds like you've been involved in this kind of
investigation before."

"Once or twice."

"Good. Then you'll know I need some time. I can't make
bank records and the like just materialize overnight."

"How much time are we talking about?"

"Maybe a week."

Ava nodded. "That's fine. It may take us that long to start
shaking out things in Borneo."

Smits eyed his beer. "I'm not having any problems sticking to my six-o'clock rule, but the two-beer limit is still a bit
of a challenge."

"You aren't driving, are you?"

"I am."

"Don't you think—" Ava began.

He smiled. "I live about two kilometres from here. My bicycle is parked out front."

"Can you manage the files and the bicycle?"

"I'm very high-tech. I have a carrier basket."

"Indeed," Ava said. "Now, what kind of retainer do you want?"

"A thousand euros?"

"That's fine. Is there an ATM near here?"

"Just around the corner," he said, pointing.

"Finish your beer. I'll be back."

She had to use two bank cards to get the cash. When she returned to the pub, Smits had a full glass in front of him. "I'm getting worried about that bicycle," she said.

"I have a low centre of gravity."

"I'm not sure what that means," Ava said, the wad of cash in her hand.

Smits looked at the money and shrugged. "I didn't bring a contract with me."

Ava counted out the thousand euros and passed it to him. "Just give me your business card. I'll email you tomorrow with a summary of our understanding. You can sign it and send it back."

"And how do I contact you?"

"Email is best," Ava said, and then thought about how often she was away from her computer these days. "But just in case, here is my cell number. You can call or text me."

"I won't be in touch unless it's important."

"That's best. I don't need updates, so if I don't hear from you for a day or two, I won't worry about it. I know how disruptive to investigative work anxious clients can be."

He had his glass in his hand, poised to meet his mouth, and now he glanced at her over its top. She saw a question forming in his eyes and turned her head.

"I won't bother you," he said. "But if there's been any funny stuff going on, I'll find out. I may ride a bicycle to work but I know my away around a computer. I couldn't spend as many years as I did with the Dutch Tax and Customs Administration and the KLPD without making a lot of contacts, which I've been careful to maintain."

"Tell you what," Ava said. "You bring me the information I need to prove that Janssen screwed us over, and I'll make sure there's a nice bonus in it for you."

"That's not necessary. My daily rate is enough to ensure you're going to get my best efforts."

"Mr. Smits, I have to say that I'm really pleased I've hired you," Ava said with a smile.

13

AVA ATE DINNER IN HER ROOM AT THE HOTEL. THE once-familiar feeling of jet lag was seeping through her system. It had been a long time between trips, and she had forgotten how fatiguing this kind of travel could be. It was barely nine o'clock when she finished eating, but her eyes kept closing. She crawled into bed with the idea of watching television for an hour or so. She had barely turned on the set before she fell asleep.

It was semi-light outside when Ava woke. She glanced at the bedside clock and saw that it was already eight o'clock. She walked to the window. The morning sun was draped in heavy black clouds that continued to unleash rain; it had been constant for more than twenty-four hours.

After a bathroom run she made a coffee and turned on her computer. Both May and Amanda had sent emails.

May wrote, I reviewed and signed off on the lawsuit this morning. It is attached. As you will see, the lawyer is accusing Mamat and Tambi of every corporate crime you could possibly imagine. They will be served later today. I'm leaving for Hong Kong at one and then connecting to

Wuhan. Call me after the bankruptcy hearing. I should be mobile-accessible by then.

Amanda was even blunter. We sued the brothers' asses off today. Ah-Pei and Chi-Tze are nervous. I told them it was the brothers or the business. They chose the business. Not that they really had a choice. May Ling was determined to go ahead, with them or without them.

Ava opened the attachment from May and skimmed over it. The basic thrust was that Mamat and Tambi had either assisted in or executed a scheme to defraud the company. It named Janssen Volker as a co-conspirator. They were suing the brothers for the $25 million that had been taken, plus another $10 million in damages and costs. A covering letter made mention that a copy of the lawsuit had been sent to the Commercial Fraud Division of the Royal Malaysian Police in Sabah, requesting a criminal investigation. Another copy had gone to the brothers' bank, asking that their accounts be frozen until the matter was adjudicated or otherwise settled.

Ava replied to both of them. Let's hope the suit gets the reaction we want. It would certainly help our credibility with the Dutch bankruptcy trustee if either the police or the bank takes any action.

She then transferred the documents to a memory stick. The bankruptcy meeting was in less than two hours. She had just enough time to shower, dress, eat a light breakfast, and print copies of the documents to take to Timmerman.

At a quarter to ten she left the hotel with a golf umbrella in one hand and the concierge's written directions to Timmerman in the other. Although the offices were only a ten-minute walk from the hotel, getting there involved a number of rights and lefts that Ava wouldn't trust to memory.

The constantly shifting wind at times drove the rain right into her. She wore only a white button-down shirt, abandoning her nylon jacket in favour of a more professional look. *That was a mistake,* she thought more than once, feeling the chill down to her bones. It was with a sense of relief that she finally found the two-storey red-brick building that housed the Timmerman offices.

She twisted and tugged at the solid brass doorknobs with no success before she saw the intercom to one side of the entrance. She pushed the button.

A woman's voice spoke in Dutch.

"I'm here to attend a bankruptcy meeting that Timmerman is having at ten o'clock," she said.

"Just a moment, please," the voice replied.

The entrance was open to the sky and the rain continued to pelt down. Ava tried to position her umbrella to deflect it and in the process blocked her view of the front door. She heard it open, walked directly inside, and closed the umbrella.

"You must be Ava Lee," a man said. "I'm Patrick Visser."

He was at least six foot six, Ava guessed, a skeleton of a man whose vertically striped grey suit made him look taller, thinner, and even more frail. His face was as long and bony, but his blue eyes were lively, almost gay, as he stared down at her.

"I am."

"I know you said you were coming, but I rather hoped you wouldn't."

"Why not?"

"No one else has come — or will come, I wager — and I was in the middle of some other work. Now I will have to put it on hold."

"Given the situation my company is in, I don't see any need to apologize."

"Of course not. Despite the circumstances, it is nice to meet you," he said, offering his hand. "But since you're the only attendee, do you mind if we meet in our small boardroom rather than the meeting room we reserve for hearings?"

"That would be fine."

"Then follow me."

He led her down a hallway whose walls were decorated with photos of Amsterdam illuminated by pot lights. Every office door they passed was closed. He opened the last one on the right and stood back so she could enter a small room with a single round wooden table and four aluminum and leather chairs.

"I need to get the file," he said. "Shall I bring you back a coffee or tea? Perhaps some water?"

"No, thank you."

When he left, she sat down at the table and took from her bag the two copies of the lawsuit and its accompanying letters that she had printed at the hotel. She placed both sets in front of her.

The file Visser had under his arm when he came back into the office was a good four inches thick. He tossed it onto the table. "I wasn't sure how much detail you wanted."

"As much as possible."

He nodded and then sat. "I made duplicates of everything I have for you to take away."

"Thank you."

"The information won't be much different from the notice we sent, or from what I told you over the telephone."

"Janssen is bankrupt, Meijer is the only secured creditor, and the rest of us are screwed?"

"More or less."

Ava slid one set of her papers across the table to him. "I thought you should see this," she said. "We've launched civil legal action in Sabah against Janssen and two former officers of our company. We are also seeking criminal indictments."

"Here in the Netherlands?"

"Not yet."

"I don't believe that anything you do in Sabah will have any bearing on our course of action here."

"I've also hired a private detective in Amsterdam. He specializes in commercial fraud. He's looking into the bankruptcy for us, focusing on Janssen and Meijer and their relationship."

"Ms. Lee, after we spoke yesterday I revisited all of our documentation. It is, as you will see, quite complete, and it indicates nothing improper in that relationship."

Ava shrugged. "We think there was something going on, and between our course of action in Sabah and the detective here, we're going to find out. In the meantime, there's the matter of our money disappearing," she said. "The lawsuit in Borneo has been copied to the bank involved. We've asked them to freeze account activity until we get to the bottom of this. We would like you to do the same."

"I beg your pardon?" Visser said.

"Meijer is selling off our furniture and pocketing the

money and the money is going God knows where. Isn't there some way you can force them to transfer the funds to you in trust, to hold until all these issues are resolved?"

His head rolled back, his chin pointing straight at her like the tip of a spear. "Ms. Lee, please don't make me go over all this again."

"We have taken legal action —"

"In Sabah, not in the Netherlands," he said. "And even if you had taken legal action here, I doubt it would interfere with Meijer's rights as a secured creditor. Please understand, I am not being capricious or nasty, but we have not a scintilla of evidence that anything the least bit underhanded is connected to this bankruptcy file. All I have are your assertions, and they are so far unsupported by any documentation."

"Read the papers I've given you."

"I will, I promise you I will. But tell me, what is in them that materially supports your claims? Show me now, if you can."

"There is a pattern. We need to get to the bottom of it," Ava said.

"That's terribly weak, wouldn't you agree?"

"Yes, but that doesn't mean it isn't or can't be true."

"Well, when you find something substantive, come back and talk to me. For now, and for good reason, I'm treating this as a normal bankruptcy and I'm giving Meijer the benefit of their status as a secured creditor with millions at risk. I will, as my responsibility entails, monitor their progress as they dispose of assets with a view to eventually aiding some of the unsecured creditors."

"Mr. Visser —"

He stood. "If there's anything in that file I've given you that you specifically want to discuss, then I will stay. Otherwise, I intend to see you to the front door and then go back to my office to register the bankruptcy as officially filed, with no actionable objections from any of the creditors."

"I have objections."

"They are noted, and I will make your lawsuit an addendum to the official file, but that is all I am prepared to do. If you do uncover information that you think could change or reverse my decision, I will be pleased to look at it."

"That might be too late. Our money could have disappeared by then."

"Technically, Ms. Lee, it isn't your money."

He looked down at her from what seemed an impossible height. She stared into his eyes. He didn't blink or turn away. She couldn't find a shred of doubt or cynicism in them.

"I'll be in touch," she said.

"I sincerely hope you have a valid reason for doing so. Now I need to get back to work."

He walked Ava to the front door, both of them silent. He opened it for her and then, as he had before, stood aside to let her pass. She took her umbrella from the stand by the door and stepped into the dreary morning. The rain smashed into her before she could get the umbrella open. When she finally did, she turned back towards Visser, but he had already closed the door.

She peered from under the umbrella at the sky. It was like looking up at a concrete ceiling. She checked her watch; it was just past ten thirty. *I've had enough of Amsterdam and its rain and its bankruptcy trustees*, she thought. She had an entire day in front of her; more than enough time to catch a flight to somewhere else.

14

IT HAD BEEN THAT AWKWARD PERIOD BETWEEN THE end of summer and the beginning of fall when Ava left Toronto five months before. Now the weather wasn't in any doubt. As the plane approached Pearson International Airport, Ava looked down on ribbons of illuminated black highway surrounded by white. The pilot announced that it was minus eighteen degrees Celsius and snow flurries were in the forecast. Ava had never thought she'd miss the cold and the snow, so she was surprised to find the prospect of winter weather almost comforting. *I'm home*, she thought.

After her meeting with Patrick Visser she had returned to the Dylan Hotel to figure out where she wanted to go. Uncle had just arrived in Shanghai and was going to be there for at least a few more days, so there was no compelling reason for her to be in Hong Kong. The business in Sabah was in Amanda's care, and Ava's appearance there would make it look as if didn't trust her sister-in-law. She felt no need for a holiday, but she did feel the need for some love, and the best place for that in her world was Toronto.

She booked a business-class seat on the afternoon Air Canada flight, let May Ling know the meeting with Timmerman hadn't changed anything and that she was headed to Toronto for a few days, and then emailed her flight schedule to her girlfriend, Maria. Seven hours later, just before local dinnertime, Ava walked through Immigration and Customs and into the cavernous Terminal 1 arrivals hall. She looked out into the sea of faces. Maria hadn't said she'd be there, but since their first meeting — in that same hall — she had always met Ava at the airport.

Ava actually saw the sweater before she saw Maria. It was a Jóhanna av Steinum creation, a hand-knit combination of wild colours and shapes that was in direct contrast to the perpetually damp and gloomy Faroe Islands, where Ava had bought the sweater. She had also bought one for herself, and to her dismay Maria was holding that second sweater above her head. Ava loved it, and it was certainly cold enough to wear it, but she had always been appalled by the tendency of some couples — lesbian or straight — to dress almost identically.

The two women hugged. Maria was five inches taller, and Ava's head fit snugly into the nook of her neck. Maria thrust the sweater at her.

"Do we have a limo?" Ava asked, knowing that Maria left her car in the garage at even the hint of a little snow.

Maria nodded, "It's parked just outside."

"Then I won't need the sweater," Ava said, stroking her arm.

Maria stared at the garment in her hand but said nothing.

It was only about twenty steps from the terminal to the idling limo, but the biting north wind cut through Ava's

Adidas jacket and made her catch her breath. She shuddered from the cold as she scampered into the back seat.

The limo driver told them there had been an accident on Highway 427 and asked if they minded if he took the longer route down the Don Valley Parkway southbound and then along the Gardiner Expressway to the city centre, where Ava lived.

"Whatever is quickest," Ava said.

The two women sat silently for the first ten minutes of the drive, not so much lost in their own thoughts as confused about where to start a conversation about the events of the past week. Finally Maria asked how many people had attended the wedding.

Ava said, "More than you could count." And then her words flowed. She talked about the morning preparations, the church service, the dinner, and Elizabeth Lee's dramatic gesture. Ava's voice caught a little when she explained how they met on the ballroom floor and hugged. When she glanced at Maria, she saw that her eyes were moist.

"How did the night end?" Maria asked.

Ava turned away to look at Lake Ontario, its white-capped winter water crashing against the rocks that lined the shore near Gzowski Park. "At the hospital with Uncle, actually," Ava said, and then proceeded to describe Sonny's arrival at the Grand Hyatt and her time at the Queen Elizabeth.

"None of your emails mentioned that."

"I didn't want to alarm you. As it happens, he's all right — at least, as all right as he can be — and now he's in Shanghai with Sonny for a few days. That's why I felt I could go to Amsterdam on business and come home to see you."

"I've missed you."

"I know you have. And I've missed you too."

"I feel guilty sometimes when I wish you were here with me instead of with Uncle."

"It's a very...complicated time," Ava said slowly.

Maria squeezed her hand. "Tell me more about the wedding," she said.

Ava started to talk about the music and the dancing as the limo left the Gardiner Expressway and worked its way north on University Avenue towards Yorkville. She was describing the young lawyer's dinner invitations when they turned right onto Cumberland Avenue and stopped in front of her condo.

"Perfect timing," she said.

Her body was still working on Hong Kong time. Ava slept fitfully and finally pulled herself out of bed at six a.m. Gently closing the bedroom door behind her so as not to wake Maria, she went to the bathroom to brush her teeth and hair and splash cold water on her face.

Maria had her own small house about six kilometres east of Ava's condo, but when they stayed together, it was nearly always at Ava's. It was a matter of convenience, Ava said. Everything they needed in terms of shops, grocery stores, and restaurants was within walking distance. Maria didn't argue, even though her house was only one block north of shop-laden Danforth Avenue; while her neighbourhood wasn't as upscale as Yorkville, it was equally well provisioned. They each had keys for the other's home, but Maria was the only one who used both. She had let herself in after receiving Ava's email about her arrival from Amsterdam. The sinks and the toilet were freshly cleaned, the fridge was full, and a supply of Starbuck's VIA instant coffee sat next to the hot-water Thermos in the kitchen.

Did she remember to restart delivery of the Globe and Mail? Ava wondered as she opened the condo's front door. The paper lay at her feet.

She sat in the kitchen at a round table pressed against the window. She closed her eyes, lowered her head, and said a small prayer to Saint Jude to thank him for her safe arrival. When she opened her eyes, she looked out onto Cumberland Avenue and then west to Avenue Road. More snow had fallen during the night, and the snowploughs hadn't caught up to it. There were few cars on the roads that early in the morning. Ava thought about her Audi A6 in the garage downstairs. The car would remain sheltered until the ploughs and sanders and salters had done their work.

She made herself a coffee and opened the newspaper. It was her morning ritual regardless of where she was, but this time it was different. This wasn't the *South China Morning Post* or the *International Herald Tribune* she was reading; she wasn't looking out onto Victoria Harbour; and the next person she would see was not Uncle, sitting at the rear of the Kowloon restaurant where she met him for congee, but Maria, emerging from the bedroom. *My life is back to normal*, she thought, and just as quickly wondered for how long. *Read the paper*, she told herself. *You're home for now.*

Ava made slow work of the newspaper, and it was past eight o'clock when she finally pushed it aside and turned on her computer and cellphone. Nothing from Uncle. There was an email from May Ling saying she was back in

Wuhan and that she hoped Ava's flight had been fine. She asked Ava to call when she could.

Ava called May's cell number, which rang five times before going to voicemail. "I'm in Toronto and everything is fine. The Amsterdam trustee thinks we're screwed. He barely looked at the lawsuit. The thing is, he came across as honest and professional, and I think if he had a reason to move against Janssen and Meijer, he would. On the other hand, he isn't going to bend the rules, even in the slightest. So either we're going to need that detective I hired or your lawsuit will have to generate some heat. I'm going to spend probably one or two days here before going back to Hong Kong. Call me whenever," Ava said.

It was probably too early to call her mother in Richmond Hill, but Mimi should be up with her baby by now. She was beginning to call her friend when she heard Maria's voice. Ava turned and saw her framed in the doorway, slipping her arms into the sleeves of a red silk blouse.

"I have to go to work," Maria said. "I've been lying in bed trying to figure out how to avoid it, but the day is full of meetings, so I can't."

Maria was assistant trade commissioner at the Colombian consulate in Toronto. It was usually a job that wasn't inflexible when it came to getting out of the office.

"There's no way you can meet me for lunch?" Ava asked.

"We have a delegation from Bogotá that includes the deputy minister of trade and economic development. We're scheduled from morning to late afternoon. Besides, I need to make a good impression."

"Well, I would like to see Mimi, and my mother will be upset if I don't see her as well. If it all works out I can have lunch with one of them and perhaps see the other in the afternoon. Then you and I can have dinner together. By tonight I should know if I can stay another day."

"Oh, I hope you can," Maria said, then turned and went back into the bedroom.

Ava picked up the phone and this time completed dialling Mimi's number. Her phone also went to voicemail, but the greeting was different from the last time Ava had encountered it. "You have reached Mimi, Derek, and Amber. We can't come to the phone right now. If you leave a message we'll get back to you as soon possible."

Ava smiled. Mimi and Derek were only recently married, and the baby had arrived three months after the wedding. Derek was Chinese, a bak mei expert like her, and she had used him as backup on some particularly dangerous jobs. Mimi was German Canadian, a tall blonde with a terrific sense of humour. They were both her friends but hadn't known each other until Ava quite accidently brought them together about a year ago. Ava hadn't been happy at first. She didn't think the relationship would work and had worried about the fallout. She had also been annoyed initially that she had lost the use of Derek's martial arts skills, since there was no way she could ask him to assist her — and put himself at risk — now that he and Mimi were married and parents. The annoyance had passed quickly, and now her only concern was for their happiness and for her godchild's health.

"This is Ava. I'm in Toronto for a few days. I'd love to see all three of you. Call me when you can."

She hung up and contemplated the phone. In all likelihood her mother would have been up late playing mah-jong.

What the hell, Ava thought. *If she's really tired she probably won't even hear the phone.*

"*Wei,*" the familiar voice said.

"Mummy, it's Ava."

"Where are you?"

"I'm in Toronto. I flew in last night."

"What a nice surprise," she said.

"I'm just as surprised — that you answered the phone so early in the morning."

"I was in bed by ten. I have a mah-jong game with Auntie Kimmie and Auntie Grace that begins late this afternoon. I needed my rest."

Ava knew the aunties well, and knew that any game with them would be for large stakes and had the potential to run all night. "Does that mean you're free for dim sum?"

"I am."

"Lucky Season at twelve?"

"Perfect," Jennie Lee said, and then paused. "Ava, forgive me, I should have asked...Are you home because something has happened to Uncle?"

"Nothing new to report on that front, Mummy. How about we get caught up at lunch?"

"Okay, see you then."

Maria walked into the kitchen as Ava put down the phone. She was now fully dressed and made up, and Ava's heart skipped a beat when she looked at her. Maria was five foot eight and slim, with a generous bust and a way of walking that made it seem her feet weren't actually touching the ground.

"You look glorious," Ava said.

Maria smiled. "Is your day set?"

"I had no luck getting Mimi, but I have my mother for dim sum."

Maria came to her side and wrapped her arms around Ava's shoulders. "That should leave you some time to relax."

"That's all I've been doing for months."

"Go for a run."

Ava waved at the window. "Have you looked outside?"

"It's stopped snowing."

Ava looked out onto the street. The weather did seem to have improved, and she could see people walking about with open coats. But the sidewalks were still covered in pools of slush, and she knew that underneath would be patches of ice. "Maybe I'll go see Grandmaster Tang."

"Say hello for me," Maria said. She had met him only once but, like Ava's mother, she regarded every associate and friend of Ava's as her own.

"Call me when you know when you're coming home," Ava said.

"I will," Maria said and then bent over to kiss her, her tongue flirting with Ava's.

"Don't go too far or I'll drag you back to bed," Ava said.

Maria laughed and pulled back. "Don't worry, I'm going. Now wish me good luck. If I do well today, chances are very good that my appointment will be extended."

Ava watched her leave, made herself another coffee, and then headed for the bathroom to shower and change. The thought of seeing her bak mai instructor had come to her unexpectedly. Now that it had, it seemed almost perfect.

Ava had started training in martial arts when she was a girl and had progressed very quickly. She had speed, flexibility, imagination, a desire to learn, and the willingness to practise hard. After several years at a school in Richmond Hill, her instructor asked if she had ever heard of bak mei. She hadn't. He explained that it was one of the oldest martial arts, almost a secret form, and that it was always taught one-on-one, father to son, mentor to student. He told her she was the only one of his students he thought capable of learning it and asked if she was willing to try. She said she was and asked when they could start. He had smiled. "I can't teach you. You would have to go downtown to see Grandmaster Tang. I've already spoken to him about you, and he's prepared to take you on as a student if you pass the assessment test."

Grandmaster Tang worked from a small two-storey brick house on a side street that ran west from Avenue Road, no more than a ten-minute walk from where Ava now lived. There were no notices or signs on the house. The Grandmaster didn't need to advertise and he didn't take walk-in business. If you were serious about martial arts in Toronto, you knew where to find him.

Her Richmond Hill instructor drove her there, took her to the door, and then left, bowing as he did so, when Tang opened it. He looked to be in his early forties, was about five foot six, Ava guessed, and had a slight build and gentle brown eyes. A smile played on his lips as he greeted her. His long, silky black hair was brushed back and fixed with a red rubber band.

"You're smaller than I expected," he said in Cantonese.

Ava didn't know how to respond to a remark about something she couldn't change. So she said nothing.

"Do you speak Cantonese?" he asked.

"Yes, and Mandarin."

"Good. I would have difficulty explaining bak mei in English."

"Use the language that makes it easiest."

He nodded. "What do you know about bak mei?" he asked, continuing in Cantonese.

"Nothing."

"Then I will tell you. Come into my house," he said, stepping aside so she could pass.

The room he directed her to would have been the living room in a normal home. This one was bare, with plain white walls and a hardwood floor that looked worn in places. The windows were covered with black curtains. Ava took off her jacket and her sneakers.

"First, show me what you've been taught," he said.

For fifteen minutes, and then fifteen minutes more, at Tang's urging, Ava went through the routine her teacher in Richmond Hill had choreographed. When she was done, Tang said, "You're agile and quick...but are you agile and quick enough?"

Before Ava could answer, the middle knuckle of Tang's right forefinger was one inch from her forehead. She hadn't seen him move. One second she was looking at him, the next all she could see was his hand in front of her face.

"That is called the phoenix-eye fist," he said. "It is central to bak mei. You will need to learn how to take all the power you can generate from your entire body — from the movement of your hips, from the muscles in your shoulders and arms, from the speed in your legs — and focus that energy and power into a single knuckle."

"I understand," she said.

"Bak mei is initially defensive. It is fought at close range. The objective is to first block any attacking blow and then counter with deadly force," he said, stepping back, his hands flowing to his sides. "We use our hands primarily; the only kicking we do is below the waist."

"Yes, Grandmaster."

His hand shot out again, but this time Ava tilted her head slightly to one side and blocked its path with her arm.

He smiled. "You will need to learn to move with the grace of a tiger, but also with the power of a dragon."

"Yes, Grandmaster."

For five years she had made the trek to his house once a week for their sessions. That ended when she started university, but she worked out two or three times a week on her own, and during the summer and holidays she went to visit the Grandmaster more often. By the time she was in her mid-twenties and his hair was beginning to streak with grey, he said to her, "You are my equal now."

Ava left her condo an hour after Maria's departure. She walked to Tang's house bundled up in the Steinum sweater and her Adidas jacket, with a woollen tuque on her head. During the week, Tang taught classes from four in the afternoon until ten in the evening. Ava had always gone in the morning, and in recent years without an appointment. There was a bell at the front door. If he was at home and available, he would answer and Ava would be admitted. If he wasn't, then she would turn around and walk back to her condo. She could think of only a handful of times she hadn't been welcomed.

He opened the door after the first ring and greeted her as if he had seen her the day before.

"Come in," he said.

She exercised by herself for half an hour, working out the kinks and feeling her way back into her body. He joined her then, gradually increasing the speed and intensity of his attacks, becoming her foe. She parried and counterattacked, trying to rid her mind of any thought processes, relying simply on reflexes and instinct and the core technique he had implanted in her over so many years.

Twice he penetrated her defences. Both times he stepped back and smiled. "You haven't been practising," he said.

"Not enough," she said. "I'd like to do another session right now. And then I want to come back tomorrow, and the day after."

"I will be here."

It was just after eleven when Ava got back to the condo. She made herself a coffee, then spooned out a bowl of rice from the cooker that sat next to the hot-water Thermos. She took the mug and bowl to the kitchen table, opened her computer, and went online.

Amanda had emailed her and May Ling from Borneo with a report. The $5 million had arrived from China and been deposited in Borneo Furniture's bank. She and Chi-Tze had met with bank officials and had been assured that they had the bank's full and continuing support. Then she and the two sisters met with several of their key raw-material suppliers to calm their concerns about payment and to reactivate the supply lines. Her final meeting of the day was with the lawyer May Ling had hired; neither of the sisters attended. The brothers had responded to the accusations through their own lawyer and were threatening to countersue for libel.

Amanda attached a story that had run that afternoon in the *Daily Express* in English and was repeated almost word for word in the *Overseas Daily Chinese News*. Their lawyer, who had a nephew working at the *Express* and a cousin at the *News*, had planted both the stories. The stories state quite boldly that the brothers are being sued for large-scale fraud, and mentioned that their banks have been asked to freeze their accounts. They also say, thank goodness, that the company is not at any risk and intends to operate as usual, Amanda wrote. Our lawyer is very good.

Ava replied, I'm just glad you're there. I'm in Toronto for a day or two. You can reach me by email or phone.

As she went to close her computer, a new email popped into her inbox. The name *Smits* was attached to it.

I spent most of today looking into your problem. I think I've found some information and a contact that look promising. Without going into detail, it may cost some money for me to acquire certain files. 10 000 euros should be enough. Do I have your permission to spend the money? Let me know as soon as you can. I find that snitches get nervous if they have to wait too long. Sincerely, Jacob.

Ava paused. He had moved much more quickly than she'd expected, and his request was suspicious. Did she trust him enough to send 10,000 euros? She reread the email and realized that he hadn't actually asked her to send the money. Good news. How will I send you the money? she wrote.

Don't worry about that. If you agree to spend it, I'll front it. It will save time, was his instant reply.

Ava stared at her computer screen. She tried to remember a time when a hired hand had financed any part of a job she and Uncle were on. She couldn't think of a single case. Spend whatever you think is necessary. We need to get to the truth. By the way, I've left Amsterdam and I'm back in Canada. Phone or text me if anything breaks, she wrote.

Her initial impression of Jacob Smits as a capable man strengthened. The only thing she couldn't help wondering was whether he was too good to be true.

15

IT WAS A HALF-HOUR DRIVE FROM AVA'S DOWNTOWN condo to the dim sum restaurant her mother had chosen in the northern suburb of Richmond Hill. For years her mother's restaurant of choice had been the Lucky Season in Times Square. There had to be at least five hundred Chinese restaurants in the Richmond Hill–Thornhill–Markham corridor that housed at least half of Toronto's population of more than half a million Chinese. Ava had once counted thirty restaurants in one mall. So her mother's choice of Lucky Season wasn't because of lack of options. The food had to be good for the restaurant to survive, and she knew it had been around for more than fifteen years.

She had to circle the parking lot twice before finding a spot for her Audi A6. As she walked through the restaurant doors she saw her mother at the hostess stand, chatting with a woman in a blue suit with a name tag pinned to the lapel. Jennie Lee spoke to everyone. Every sales associate and server in every store and restaurant she frequented was asked his or her name. And if Jennie went back to the establishment more than once, she soon knew about their husbands and kids too. It was a trait that had bypassed both Ava and her sister, Marian; they had no interest in casual acquaintances. They also didn't get the preferential treatment that seemed to follow their mother wherever she went.

The hostess's name was Anne, and she was smiling and nodding as Jennie spoke. Ava looked at her mother and felt a surge of pride. Her jet-black hair was cut short, shaved at the nape of her neck. From a distance she looked like a well-maintained woman in her early to mid-forties, but she was dressed a little younger, in black Donna Karan jeans, a red cashmere sweater, and black Gucci leather slip-ons.

Ava was dressed in her black Adidas tracksuit. She wore no makeup, and her hair was tied back with a brown scrunchie. When Jennie saw her, she frowned. Ava smiled and reached towards her for a hug and a kiss.

"I didn't have time to change after my workout," she lied.

Behind Ava a large crowd had gathered, waiting for a table. Jennie turned to Anne. "This is my daughter Ava, the one I was telling you about. We can go in now."

"Right this way," Anne said, leading them past the throng.

They were seated at a table near a window that looked out onto the mall's parking lot. Ava could see six cars circling as they looked for a spot.

Jennie leaned across the table and took Ava's hand in her own. "I'm so happy you're here. Do you know how long you're staying? This mah-jong game is the only thing I have on my schedule for the next few days."

"Uncle is in Shanghai with Sonny on business. I'll probably head back to Hong Kong late tomorrow or the day after."

"How is he?"

"I don't know how he can get any thinner."

"I mean his spirits."

"On the surface he seems content enough. He tells me he's come to terms with the situation, though there are times when I sense there are things he can't come to grips with. He becomes quite withdrawn."

"Would we be any different?" Jennie asked, reaching for the dim sum list.

"No, of course not, and I doubt that I would ever have his level of composure."

"Me neither. I have to tell you that I enjoyed his company when I was in Hong Kong in December. There is something almost serene about him. We don't know what's going on inside him, of course, but he has this ability to make everyone around him feel calm in his presence."

"He enjoyed your company as well."

"Really?"

"Yes, he said so quite specifically," Ava said. "But don't ask me to go into detail. You don't need more compliments."

Jennie looked pleased enough. "I'm hungry. Shall we order?"

"Let's."

"Hot and sour soup?"

"Please."

"The fried octopus is really good, and I think the chicken feet are the best in the city."

"Order what you want."

Jennie ticked off various boxes and then held the list in the air. Within seconds a server had taken it and placed their order, leaving a copy on the table so that each dish could be marked off as delivered.

"When I was spending that time alone with him in Hong Kong, he spoke about you," Jennie said. "He said he thought of you as his daughter and asked me to forgive him if he was being presumptuous."

"Well, I am closer to him than any man I've ever known, including Daddy."

A pot of tea was placed on the table. Jennie reached for it and poured for both of them. "Speaking of Daddy, how was the wedding?"

"It was wonderful," Ava said, tapping the middle finger of her right hand on the table in thanks.

"And how was Elizabeth?"

Ava paused. She knew her mother would be acutely sensitive about anything she might say about her father's first wife. "She was gracious," she said finally.

"She couldn't have been happy that you had such a prominent role."

"Her sisters weren't pleased, that's certain, but she was quite polite."

"She does have class."

"Uncle said that was something you have in common with her."

Jennie glanced at Ava, her eyes saying that she wasn't quite sure Ava was being truthful. "How did she look?" she finally asked.

"Distinguished."

"Did she speak to you?"

"Yes, and she told me to tell you that you have done a wonderful job raising your children."

"After what you did for her son — and for that family — what else could she say?"

"She could have said nothing," Ava said as the hot and sour soup arrived.

Jennie spooned soup into both of their bowls. Just as Ava was taking her first sip, her cellphone rang. She looked at the incoming number and saw the country code for China, but the rest of the numbers were unfamiliar. She let it go to voicemail.

"You aren't answering your phone these days?" her mother asked.

"Some things don't seem quite as urgent as they used to."

"What are you going to do when Uncle is gone? Stay in that business?"

"No. I've entered into a partnership with May Ling Wong and Amanda. We're investing in some companies together, including one that's having a few problems."

"In Asia?"

"Yes."

"Is it wise to invest your money in places so far away?"

"Are you asking me if I can trust May Ling?"

Jennie started to reply but stopped as plates of chicken feet and fried octopus were placed on the table. She let the subject drop and reached for the octopus with her chopsticks.

They were starting in on two new dishes — har gow and radish cake — when Ava's phone rang again. It was the same Chinese number.

"Answer that, please," her mother said.

She did with a brisk "*Wei.*" The caller began to speak, the words tumbling together. Ava thought the voice sounded vaguely familiar, but it was breaking up so much that she could barely make out what the person was saying above the background noise of the restaurant.

"Just a minute," she said loudly. "I have to go outside to hear you properly."

A group of smokers was standing outside the entrance, chatting loudly in Cantonese. Ava moved down the sidewalk until the only competing noise came from traffic in the parking lot.

"Okay, I can hear you now."

"Ava, this is May Ling."

"I didn't recognize the phone number."

"I'm calling from my hotel room in Guangzhou. I'm here on business. I flew in late this evening," she said.

The line was clear. It was May Ling's voice that was breaking. "You sound terrible," Ava said.

"It's Borneo."

"What about Borneo?" Ava heard May Ling draw a deep breath, then another. "May, what's happened?"

"It's Amanda and Chi-Tze... They've been hurt."

"What? How?"

"I don't have all the details," she said slowly, her voice catching again. "I've been back and forth on the phone with Ah-Pei for the past half-hour. She's at the hospital, and she's so emotional that I had trouble making sense of everything she said."

"What has she told you?" Ava pressed.

"After work, Amanda and Chi-Tze went out for dinner together downtown. When they were leaving the restaurant, they were attacked in the parking lot. According to Ah-Pei, at least eight people saw what happened. None of them went to help."

"How does she know that?"

"She found out about the attack from the restaurant's owner. He knows the sisters well, and he called Ah-Pei as soon as it happened. Right after that he called for the police and an ambulance."

"How badly are they hurt?"

"I don't know," May said, her voice cracking.

"Was it an attempted robbery?" Ava asked.

"No," May Ling said. "It was a beating."

"That's what Ah-Pei told you?"

"Yes."

"How can she be so sure?"

"The restaurant owner spoke to the people who saw it happen. He told Ah-Pei that two men were hitting them with bats, shouting obscenities at them."

Ava leaned back against the wall and shivered in her nylon jacket. "And Ah-Pei has no idea how hurt they are?" she asked.

"Ah-Pei hasn't seen them, so she really doesn't know. The restaurant owner made it sound like there had to be broken bones, and there was certainly blood. He thought Amanda was unconscious when they put her in the ambulance," May Ling said, her voice quavering.

"May, don't cry."

"That's all I've been doing every time Ah-Pei calls. She's very upset, but she's still calmer than I am."

"We need to find out how the girls are."

"All I can get out of Ah-Pei is that they're in surgery."

"Is she at the hospital by herself?"

"No, she has a cousin with her, who's just as vague."

"Where are her brothers?"

May paused. "Ah-Pei says she tried to reach them and couldn't. Those sons of bitches."

"Let's not go there, May. Let's not leap to that conclusion."

"Well, who else could it be?"

"I don't know, and right now it doesn't matter. Look, I

know it's late there but can you reach the lawyer you hired?"

"I have his home number."

"Then call him. Tell him to get over to the hospital — he needs to take control of the situation. He needs to calm Ah-Pei, he needs to find out exactly how the girls are, and he needs to stay there and keep communicating with you until there is nothing new to learn."

"I'll do that right away."

"Good."

"Ava, I've booked a flight out of here first thing tomorrow morning. I'll be in Kota Kinabalu by mid-afternoon."

"And I'll get there as soon as I can."

"Christ, what a mess," May groaned.

"Who else knows about this?"

"What do you mean?"

"Michael? Jack Yee?"

"God, I forgot about them."

"So they don't know?"

"Not unless the police or someone from the hospital called them."

"On second thought, I can't imagine they would know anything. Otherwise I'm quite sure that one of them would have phoned me by now."

"Are you going to call them?"

Ava paused. "Yes, I will, but not until we know what state Amanda is in. So call that lawyer and keep in touch with me. I want to know everything."

16

"WHAT'S THE MATTER?" JENNIE LEE ASKED WHEN AVA came back into the restaurant.

"Nothing."

"Don't tell me that. You have that look in your eyes that means you're upset about something."

"It's nothing for you to worry about."

"Does it have anything to do with Maria?"

"Mummy, please. It's a business problem."

"Then it must be a serious one."

"Let's just eat, okay? It isn't worth discussing and I'm not that worried," Ava said, putting the phone next to her bowl.

"I don't believe you."

Ava shrugged. "I feel like having some sticky rice. Will you share?"

Her mother stared at her. "Just tell me it isn't a problem with the girl."

"It isn't."

"Good. I like her."

"Sticky rice?"

"I'll have some."

They ate slowly, their conversation returning to stories about Marian, Jennie's recent run of very good luck at the mah-jong tables, and her inability to transport that luck north to Casino Rama's baccarat tables. It was past two o'clock when they finished, almost an hour since May Ling's call, and Ava's phone hadn't rung again. She said goodbye to her mother outside the restaurant in a flurry of hugs and kisses and then darted towards her car.

As soon as Ava was inside the Audi, she checked the phone to see if she had somehow missed an incoming call. She hadn't. She calculated the time it would take for May Ling to reach the lawyer and for him to rouse himself from bed and get to the hospital. *Calm down*, she thought. *You'll find out soon enough.*

In the meantime, she had to get herself organized, so she called Gail. "I need to get to Kota Kinabalu as soon as possible. It's in Borneo and I know there are direct flights from Hong Kong, Singapore, and Kuala Lumpur. I don't care which airline I fly or how you get me there. Please call me or email me when you have the flight information."

She put the phone in the coffee-cup holder. *Ring*, she thought.

The Don Valley Parkway going south towards the city was clogged. Her estimated half-hour drive ran close to an hour. Her phone rang once. She leapt at it and then saw that the incoming number was Gail's. She had booked Ava on the Cathay Pacific flight that evening to Hong Kong, where she would connect with an Air Asia plane flying nonstop to Kota Kinabalu. She would be in transit for less than twenty-four hours.

It was mid-afternoon when she reached the condo, the

middle of the night in Borneo. She went into the bedroom and took her Shanghai Tang Double Happiness black leather bag out of the closet. She tossed it onto the bed and began to methodically pack it with clothes that were associated with work: two pairs of black slacks, a grey pencil skirt, Cole Haan pumps, four Brooks Brothers shirts — two white button-downs and a light blue and a pink with modified Italian collar, all of them with French cuffs — and bras and underwear. She checked her jewellery case and took out her favourite set of green jade cufflinks, which she had bought in Beijing, and a set of Shanghai Tang blue enamel links. She transferred them to a smaller kid-leather pouch and then added her Cartier Tank Française watch and the ivory chignon pin, which had become fixed in her mind as a good-luck token. Her cosmetics went into a separate bag: black mascara, red lipstick, and a bottle of Annick Goutal perfume.

Ava zipped the bag and went back to the closet for the Chanel bag she used for her running gear and her computer and notebooks. She placed her shoes in the bottom and then tossed in two pairs of shorts, a sports bra, and three black Giordano T-shirts. The laptop, still sitting on her kitchen table, would go in last.

She carried the Chanel bag into the kitchen. She packed enough sachets of Starbucks VIA instant coffee to last for a week, then spotted the notebook she had started in Amsterdam lying next to the computer. She picked it up and put it in the bag. Was there a link between what had transpired in Borneo and what was going on in Amsterdam? The thought came to her as a question but was almost instantly transformed by her mind into a fact.

She stood at the kitchen window and looked out on the grey, overcast day. It was beginning to snow again. She hardly noticed. Her imagination was now cementing the connections between the brothers and the Dutch companies. *This attack has to be a reaction to the lawsuit*, Ava thought. Tambi and Mamat had paid, directly or indirectly, to have the women beaten. There was no other explanation for what had happened. Men with bats in restaurant parking lots don't occur at random. Men with bats are paid to wield them. The women were targeted. And who else had a motive?

Her mind was fixed on Borneo. She had told May Ling not to speculate about what had happened. Now what was she doing? Not speculating, she thought; it was all too certain. Uncle often said that if something looked like a bowl of white rice, smelled like white rice, and tasted like white rice, you could call it Emperor's Treasure Feast all you wanted, but it wouldn't change the fact that it was plain white rice.

Her cellphone rang in the bedroom. Ava ran to it and saw May Ling's number.

"Yes, May," Ava said.

"I just heard from the lawyer."

The apprehension that had been floating around Ava like an aura now settled on her like a shroud. "Did he get to the hospital?" she asked.

"He did."

"How bad is it?"

"Chi-Tze has just come out of surgery. She has four broken ribs, her right arm is broken in two places, and her right shin bone is badly damaged. The doctor said she was fortunate not to have been struck on the kneecap."

"And Amanda?" Ava asked.

"They don't know yet," May said.

"Why?"

"She's still being attended to."

"Why?"

"Ava...they struck her on the head," May said.

Ava sat down on the bed, the phone almost slipping from her hand.

"The policeman the lawyer spoke to said Chi-Tze was lucky because she held her arm in front of her face. That's why it was broken in two places."

"The bastards," Ava whispered.

"They have no idea when we'll know any more about Amanda."

Ava felt sweat gathering on her upper lip. "The lawyer is going to stay at the hospital?" she asked.

"Of course."

"And report to you if anything happens?"

"I told him to call me every half-hour, even if it is only to tell me there's no change."

"Good."

"When are you arriving?"

"I leave Toronto tonight at around eleven. I'll be in Borneo the day after tomorrow, around lunchtime."

"Thank God. I don't think I can handle this by myself."

"Keep the lawyer or one of his people at the hospital until we get things sorted."

May Ling took a deep breath. "Ava, they've been asking about notifying Amanda's family. The police are quite anxious to let them know what's happened."

"I'm not going to call Michael or Jack until we know

for certain how she is," Ava said, more harshly than she meant. "If they insist on speaking to someone, give them my number."

"Okay. I'll keep in touch."

Ava closed the phone and walked back towards the kitchen. She looked out the window and watched the wind whip the snow into swirling eddies. She went to her computer and logged on to the Pearson International website. So far it looked as if most of the flights from the airport were leaving on time. She switched over to her email account. She wrote to Uncle, copying Sonny in case Uncle wasn't checking his mail — a not infrequent occurrence.

I'm leaving Toronto tonight for Hong Kong, where I'm connecting with an Asia Air flight to Kota Kinabalu at 11 a.m. I may need your help. Let me know where you are and how I can reach you.

She checked the time. It was the middle of the night in Shanghai. She called Uncle's mobile and repeated the message she had emailed to him.

Ava pushed her chair back from the table. She needed to call Maria and her mother to let them know she was travelling again. She reached for her phone, but it rang before she could pick it up. She stared at an unfamiliar country code.

"Yes, this is Ava Lee," she said.

"Jacob Smits here."

Again, and so soon, she thought. Then she said, "Mr. Smits, we communicated just a few hours ago. Was anything unclear?"

"No, not at all, but I've met with my contact. I spent the last hour going through the paperwork he gave me. I was going to email you but I thought a phone call might be better, because the situation's a bit complicated and I thought you would have questions."

She heard eagerness in his voice. "You've found something?"

"I have."

"Good or bad?"

"I think *great* is the right word."

"Let me get my notebook," Ava said, reaching into her Chanel bag to retrieve it. She opened it and sat at the table. "Tell me what you have."

"Well, earlier today I went over the documents you gave me that relate to the bankruptcy filing. As you told me, Meijer supposedly advanced money and made loans to Janssen that went sour — thus their secured creditor position. There were seventeen different transactions, adding up to the twenty million dollars or so Meijer claims they are owed. Every transaction is papered and on the surface appears completely genuine. I can't fault Timmerman for taking them at face value."

"So far, Mr. Smits, you haven't told me anything I don't know."

She heard the sound of Smits taking a drink. She looked at the time: eight in the evening in Amsterdam. She wondered if he was sticking to his two-beer rule.

"I said the transactions *appear* genuine. In fact, they are not."

"How can you be so certain?" she asked.

"I couldn't find the money."

"What do you mean?"

"What Timmerman has in its bankruptcy files are various loan documents and company financial statements that support the transactions. I decided to dig a bit deeper. I wanted to know what Janssen did with all that money Meijer supposedly gave to them."

"And?"

"They didn't spend a euro of it."

Ava stopped writing. "How can you know that?" she asked.

"Fortunately I know the accountant for Meijer. I know him from my days on the police force, when he was a naughty boy and it was my decision whether or not to prosecute him. It seems I made the right decision, because he's still quite grateful and very willing to help. He didn't come right out and tell me what they did, but he said it might be instructive to look at the actual banking records for both companies, which happened—good for us—to use the same bank. You can invent company accounts but a bank can't handle imaginary cash. The bank's records show that none of the money related to those seventeen transactions found its way into the Janssen account."

"Couldn't the money have gone offshore?" Ava asked.

"There was no money," he said, his voice triumphant. "Meijer's bank records show that not a single euro was ever taken from their account and transferred to Janssen, here in the Netherlands or anywhere else. All the transaction records the trustee has are bogus. The companies' financial statements were produced after the fact."

"And you have the actual bank records?"

"That's what cost me fifteen thousand euros, and even then I had to be very persuasive. Our Dutch bankers consider themselves to be morally superior to even our Protestant churchmen. Ms. Lee, I know I told you it would be ten thousand, but my contact needed a lot more coaxing."

"Your snitch is a banker?"

"Exactly."

"And you have the bank records?" she pressed.

"I have them in front of me, in a nice neat pile."

"Mr. Smits—"

"Please, call me Jacob," he said.

"This is very good work, Jacob."

"Thank you."

"What I don't understand is why the trustee couldn't fig-ure this out."

"Ms. Lee—"

"Call me Ava."

"Ava, they process the paperwork they're given. This was a clean, well-documented bankruptcy. They had no reason to start digging into bank records—assuming they'd ever gotten to see them in the first place."

"You haven't told me why Meijer and Janssen would do this. Trying to pull off a scam like this presumes some strong connections between the companies, and obviously some strong motivation."

"My contact at Meijer told me that Johann Meijer and Jan de Groot are old university roommates. They're also brothers-in-law."

"Ah."

"Janssen did have financial problems. Nowhere close to as large as the money involved in your situation—they were about two million dollars in the hole—but they were being squeezed. And from what I saw in Meijer's records, while they weren't in any financial difficulty, they had hardly made a dollar over the past three years. My opinion is that these two old friends and relations saw the chance to scoop you and grabbed it. And if you don't mind me saying, they obviously weren't afraid of any consequences from your side."

"No, they weren't. We — that is to say, the previous management of our company — gave them a sweetheart deal with some ridiculously advantageous payment terms. It's as if they were setting the table for us to be taken. But that's another issue," she said. "So now what?"

"What do you mean?"

"What do we do?"

"Ava, you hired me to find out if there was any fire behind the smoke you sensed. I've found one that's blazing."

"Well, now I'm asking you for advice. Can we take this information to the trustee and get him to put the brakes on the bankruptcy process and seize whatever inventory is left, as well as the cash that sales have generated thus far? Or do we have to go see Meijer and threaten them with God knows what we can threaten them with under Dutch law?"

She heard him slurp.

"I hope that's only your second beer," she said.

"It is."

"Then your advice should be coming from a clear head."

"Suing Meijer and Janssen would take forever, and by then, who knows how much money would be left and where it would be?"

"That isn't my first preference anyway. How about going to the trustee and getting him to intervene in the current process?"

"There are some problems here — I mean, with the questions you're asking. They aren't so simple to answer."

"Why not?"

"The bank records, for a start. They're a problem."

"How?"

"I told the guy I bought them from that I'd keep them confidential, that I'd protect his identity, and I want to keep my word."

"I see."

"And on top of that, I have doubts that the trustee would take too kindly to me showing up at his office with stolen records. And in this country, Ava, these documents would be considered stolen. Knowing Timmerman, they'd be as likely to turn me in as go after Meijer and Janssen."

"There has to be a way —"

"Lastly, there is something really curious about the bank information that I think we need to clarify before you start making decisions about what to do," he interrupted, and then paused.

"I'm listening."

"Well, the records are completely up to date. For Janssen that doesn't matter, because the bank account was shuttered more than a month ago. But Meijer's account is still fully active, as it should be. The thing is, I don't see any recent deposits from or through Janssen, or any other deposits that look to be outside their normal business pattern. In other words, if furniture has been sold — and you were told it has been — then where the hell is that money? These kinds of distress sales don't lend themselves to terms. Normally immediate payment is made via certified cheque or a wire transfer, but nothing has shown up in the Meijer account."

"The money has gone offshore?"

"That's my guess, and I think it would be wise for us to find out where it actually is before we approach Timmerman or Meijer."

"Do you think you can do that?"

"Why not? There can't be that many furniture dealers in the Netherlands. I'm sure I can find one who did a deal with Janssen, and with the right enticement I'm sure I can convince them to show me his invoices and how they paid for the goods. Once we have a copy of the cheque or wire transfer, we'll know where the money is."

"By 'enticement,' do you mean pay them off?"

"We should assume we'll have to."

"Yes, we should. I have no issue with that."

"I'll keep the outlay as small as possible."

"Just get the information," Ava said. "Now, I already owe you fifteen thousand euros. Email me your bank information. I'll send you a wire for thirty thousand. Deduct what you've spent and use the rest as you see fit."

"I have to tell you that I don't have receipts for what I've spent already, and I can't imagine getting them from anyone else I have to pay."

"I don't think that's a problem."

"You are trusting."

"You trusted me to repay the fifteen thousand you advanced."

Smits grunted. "And you're taking my word that I actually paid someone fifteen thousand."

"Well, there we are. We're either at the start of a solid relationship or one of us is a completely naive fool. Frankly, I'm prepared to take my chances with you. If that makes me a fool, I'll live with it."

"Okay, I'll email you my bank information. I'll get on the job first thing in the morning. With any luck I'll find us a dealer who'll co-operate."

"Don't rush," Ava said. "I'm going to be out of touch for at least the next twenty-four hours. I'm dealing with another situation right now that may occupy my time and energy for well past that. So take the time to be thorough, and if you find something, email me. If I don't respond right away, don't worry. It doesn't mean I'm not interested."

"Okay."

"So send me the bank information. Until we talk again, thanks," Ava said, and closed her phone.

She sighed. Suddenly she felt exhausted. Normally Smits's call would have had her pumped. Instead she felt disengaged, and the situation in the Netherlands felt like a distraction. All she could think about was Amanda.

At three thirty, Ava checked her email on her cellphone and saw that Smits had sent the bank information. She got up and headed downstairs to walk to her bank branch, which was only two blocks way. She was standing in line waiting to see a teller when her phone rang. She grabbed for it, certain it was May.

"I just wanted to let you know that I won't be free until at least eight or nine," Maria said, talking in a whisper as she always did when discussing personal matters on the consulate line.

"Shit."

"What's the matter?"

"I have to leave Toronto tonight for Hong Kong."

"Uncle?"

"No. Something's happened with Amanda and I need to

get over there."

"Can you tell me about it?"

"I'm standing in line at the bank. I'd rather not right now."

"But it's bad?"

"Yes. I'll call you later to explain."

"I could try to get out of these meetings."

"I thought you said they were important."

"Not as important as you."

"Has your day gone badly?" Ava said.

"Not at all. The deputy minister keeps smiling at me when I'm talking, and his two assistants have been nodding in agreement. I think I've made the impression I wanted."

"Good. That's the best news I've had today."

"You do remember that I've applied for a two-year extension?"

"Maria, why would you ask me that question? You know I do."

"I need the woman I love to tell me more often that she loves me and wants me to stick with her," she said, laughing.

"I love you, and I want you here and nowhere else," Ava said.

"Good. So do you want me to leave the office?"

"This really can't be about us right now. I have to get a limo to the airport. And besides, I don't think I would be the best company."

"But you'll call?"

"Of course, and for goodness' sake, stop worrying." She closed the phone and turned back to the bank teller, who was waiting for her to sign the transfer. "Sorry."

"Do you want us to create a template for this?" the teller asked.

"You might as well. I'm not sure I'll be sending money to this account again, but you never know, so let's save the information."

She phoned her mother as soon as she got back to the condo and got voicemail. The mah-jong game had begun, she figured. "I have to go back to Hong Kong tonight on a business matter. Nothing to do with Uncle. I'll call you when I can," she said in her message.

She checked her emails. Nothing from Uncle or Sonny.

She had spent four months in Hong Kong doing nothing much but waiting. She thought she had become good at it. She hadn't.

17

AVA ARRIVED AT THE AIRPORT WITH A LITTLE MORE than an hour to spare. She checked in, cleared security, and walked to the business-class lounge that Cathay Pacific shared with British Airways. She poured herself a glass of Pinot Grigio and found a quiet corner to sit. There was no way, she decided, she was getting on the plane without talking to May Ling and without reaching out to Michael and Jack Yee. She couldn't spend sixteen hours on a plane and risk having someone else contact her half-brother and Amanda's father. She would never forgive herself if that happened, and she was sure they would not be forgiving either.

She called the number at May Ling's hotel and was told that Madam Wong had checked out. Ava groaned and phoned May's cell. It rang four times before she picked up, a cauldron of noise in the background.

"I've just walked into the Guangzhou airport," she said.

"Can you find a quiet place to talk?" Ava said, so loudly that the other lounge guests looked in her direction, disapproval etching their faces.

"Give me ten minutes."

"I'm at the Toronto airport and we have to board soon. Don't take too long. Please."

"Ten minutes."

Ava finished her wine and poured another glass. She sat down again, her eyes on her watch. At the nine-minute mark her phone rang.

"May, how is Amanda?" she said.

"I was speaking to the lawyer just as I arrived at the airport. I didn't have a chance to call you."

"What did he say?"

"The orbital bone around her eye is broken, but beyond that they're not exactly sure how she is. She goes in and out of consciousness and is not really aware."

"Any other damage?"

"Like Chi-Tze, some broken bones."

"What can they do for her head?"

"They're running tests to figure out if she was concussed. Other than that, it's a matter of waiting."

"Shit."

"They're trying to keep her awake for now, just to be safe. They're really worried she'll lapse into a coma."

"Has she said anything?"

"No."

"How about Chi-Tze?"

"She spoke to our lawyer and then to the police. He was with her when she did."

"What did she tell them?"

"She said two men were waiting in a car when she and Amanda left the restaurant. The men climbed out as soon as they saw them and ran at them with bats. All she can remember is that they were large and wore masks."

"You told me earlier that the men yelled at them. What did they say?"

"They just cursed at them, called them 'fucking bitches' over and over again."

"It makes me want to vomit."

"Me too."

"What did the lawyer say about the hospital and the kind of medical treatment they're receiving?"

"He has a lot of confidence in them."

"Can we move Amanda?"

"What are you thinking?"

"Can we fly her to Hong Kong? There must be some kind of air ambulance service we can use."

"Are you sure that's a good idea?"

"Have the lawyer talk to the doctors. If they think it's okay, then let's do it. She'll be somewhere familiar, somewhere where her family and friends can look after her. Can you reach him now?"

"I think so."

"I'm boarding in about fifteen minutes. Leave me a voicemail once you know what's possible."

"I will."

"I have to call Michael and Jack."

"What will you tell them?"

"I'd like to be able to say that she's well enough to be flown to Hong Kong."

"You can't."

"May, I have to call Michael and tell him what's happened, and then I'm getting on a plane for sixteen hours. If the doctors there say Amanda can be moved, I need you to call Michael directly and let him know."

"Yes, that I can do."

"Good. I'll tell him what we're trying to do, without making any promises, and ask him to stay put in Hong Kong until we know what the story is."

"That works."

Almost absently, Ava sipped at her wine. It had no taste. "And how is Chi-Tze? I keep forgetting about her, and I know I shouldn't."

"They have tended to the breaks. They'll keep her in hospital until they can send her home. No one knows how long that will be."

"And then how long will she have to be at home?"

"I have no idea, and in the meantime I'm worried about the business. I know it isn't our priority this minute, but we can't ignore it."

"What do you mean?"

"With Amanda and Chi-Tze incapacitated, that leaves only Ah-Pei to represent our interests. She seems composed enough, but who knows what kind of emotional upheaval she's experiencing. She didn't want me to hire the lawyer to go after her brothers, and now I keep waiting for her to say, 'See what damage you've caused.'"

"But she hasn't?"

"Not yet."

"What do you think we should do?"

"We need to provide more support for the business. I have a couple of bright young people in Wuhan I could fly over. They aren't terribly experienced, but they speak English and they have solid academic backgrounds in management and accounting, and they're loyal to me. We can trust them."

"Send them."

"I will."

"Though I don't know how I really feel about hanging on to this business. There's some kind of bad luck attached to it," Ava said.

"That's a longer-term decision, and this isn't the time to discuss it," May said. "I'm not arguing with you, Ava. But we need to look after the here-and-now. When things settle, let's talk about whether or not to keep it."

"I know, I know. And the crazy thing is, right after you called me about the girls, the guy I hired in Amsterdam came up with some very interesting material. Under normal circumstances I would have yipped with glee. He must have found my reaction a bit muted."

"What did he find?"

"As we thought, we were set up. We're being cheated. He found out how it was done — at least, how it was done so it would satisfy the bankruptcy trustee. The importer and a company that was supposedly lending him money set up phony financing deals and then created two sets of books. The investigator got into their bank accounts, though, and found that no money ever changed hands."

"That's a ray of sunshine on this miserable day. What are we doing about it?"

"So far we aren't doing anything."

"Couldn't we go to the trustee?"

"No, that would be premature," Ava said, not wanting to get into the details of Smits's report. "The furniture is being sold; most of it is probably gone already and converted to cash. The proceeds aren't going into any regular bank accounts. We want to find out where the money is before we alert anyone — and that includes those fucking thieves — that we're on to them. The investigator is trying to track where the proceeds are going, and I have to tell you that, from my experience with him so far, he'll probably find out."

"Then?"

"We'll get our money back."

"How?"

"Let me worry about that."

May Ling was quiet, and for a second Ava thought she was going to press her about the money. Instead she said, "Ava, you said we were set up. Does it look as if the brothers were involved?"

"I don't know for certain, but it does seem logical."

"And this attack on Amanda and Chi-Tze?"

"Who else had a reason?"

"What are we going to do about that?"

It was Ava's turn to be silent.

"Ava, what are we going to do?" May pressed.

"Look, I have to call Michael and Jack Yee. I'm going to be boarding soon here and I can't put off telling them what happened. We'll talk about Mamat and Tambi when we meet in Kota Kinabalu."

"All right. I'll meet you at the airport or arrange for you to be met. We're staying at the Méridien Hotel, right in the city centre. It's closest to Queen Elizabeth General Hospital."

"Another Queen Elizabeth?"

"What do you mean?"

"That's the name of the hospital in Hong Kong where Uncle goes."

"I didn't know."

"No matter. A name is just a name."

While Ava was on the phone, the lounge had slowly filled to capacity. There was still about ten minutes to go before boarding but now there was no chance of her making a call and keeping it private. She picked up her bags and left. It was a long walk to the gate; about halfway there she found a stretch between the restrooms and the shops that was quiet. She put down her bags, leaned against the wall, and called her brother's cellphone.

"Hello," he answered.

"Michael, it's Ava."

"Ava, I'm in a meeting. Can I call you back in a few hours?"

"No, we need to talk right now. It's about Amanda."

She heard a chair creaking and imagined it being pushed back from a table. Michael's voice sounded as if it was coming from the bottom of a barrel as he told whoever he was with that he had to leave the meeting to take an urgent call. She took deep breaths.

"I haven't been able to reach her since last night," he said in a nervous voice.

Ava breathed deeply one more time and then began to speak. He didn't interrupt until she had repeated for the third time, "I'm told that she's in good hands and in stable condition."

"Oh, my God," he said. "I had this horrible feeling that something was wrong, but I couldn't imagine anything like this. It's crazy. Who would have reason to hurt her?"

"We don't know."

"My God," he repeated.

Ava could sense that he was on the verge of tears. "Michael, she's going to be all right."

"I need to get to Borneo."

"Don't do that right away. May is trying to arrange an air ambulance to fly her to Hong Kong. She'll be calling you in the next few hours to tell you if that's possible."

"Ava, I'm going to Borneo, as soon as I can get there."

"Okay, I understand."

"Where are you?" he asked.

"I'm at Pearson Airport in Toronto. I'm leaving in about five minutes for Hong Kong, and from there I'm heading to Borneo myself. May Ling is already en route."

He went quiet. All Ava could hear was laboured breathing. "Michael?" she said.

"I should have insisted that she not leave our honeymoon."

"Michael, this is not the time for hindsight. We need to rally together so that she has all the support she needs."

"What did her father say?"

The question caught Ava off-guard. "Nothing — I haven't spoken to him yet. You're the first person I called. But I need to talk to him before I leave here."

"No, I'll do it."

"Michael, are you sure?"

"Do you know it's been only four days since we were married?"

"I know," Ava said.

18

AVA COULDN'T REMEMBER SLEEPING SO BADLY ON A late-night long-haul flight. Even three glasses of wine, a fully reclined seat, earplugs, an eyeshade, and the repetitive slow-motion bak mei moves she played over in her head couldn't overcome her mental images of Amanda and Chi-Tze being beaten by bats in the parking lot of a restaurant. She knew the damage that bats could inflict. She knew the sound they made when they struck bone. She could see the girls' faces contorted in fear and pain. It roiled her stomach, first with pity, but that swiftly moved on to anger, and then to rage.

She pulled herself out of her seat several times to pace up and down the aisle. That didn't help calm her. She turned the entertainment system on and off, looking for anything that could distract her. But whatever she watched was soon crowded out by thoughts of Amanda and Chi-Tze. She finally fell asleep from sheer exhaustion when the plane began to cross Japan, about six hours out from Hong Kong. They woke her four hours later for a breakfast she didn't want.

The flight landed on schedule, and she opened her phone the instant she walked into the terminal. There were single messages from Uncle and Maria, and three from May. Uncle and Maria said to call back when she could. May's were a progression, detailing her arrival in Kota Kinabalu and at the Queen Elizabeth Hospital, her unsuccessful negotiations with the doctors to allow Amanda to fly to Hong Kong, and finally — only an hour before Ava had landed — her news that Amanda was being ambulanced to the airport for the trip to Hong Kong, with Michael and Jack Yee by her side. They had arrived in KK late the day before, and over the objections of the local doctors they had insisted on moving Amanda, signing a release to do so. Ava called May. Her phone went directly to voicemail.

"I'm in Hong Kong. I got your messages. Call me. If I don't hear from you, I'll see you in three or four hours," Ava said.

She leaned against a wall, out of the path of the early-morning airport crush. She decided to make her other calls from the quiet of Cathay Pacific's Wing Lounge. It took twenty minutes to clear the customs and immigration checkpoint for in-transit passengers and to reach the entrance to the Wing, one of Cathay's business-class lounges. She still had a one-hour wait before the Air Asia flight was scheduled to leave.

She laid claim to a Balzac armchair and then went to the coffee bar and ordered a double espresso. She drank half of it on the way back to her seat.

She called Uncle first. His phone rang three times; she was about to curse the fourth ring and the inevitable voicemail prompt when she heard the familiar "*Wei.*"

"It's Ava."

"Where are you?"

"Hong Kong."

"So soon?"

"Where are you?"

"Still in Shanghai."

"How are you feeling?"

"I am well enough. I think we will be here for one more day at least, maybe even two. You did not have to rush back."

"I didn't come back for you," she said, and then instantly felt a rush of shame when she realized how her words must have sounded. "Oh, but that's not what I meant, not what I meant at all."

"I would never think any different, so do not be so concerned about my feelings. But you — you sounded distressed when you left me that message, and now again you seem upset. Something else has happened?"

"We have a problem in Kota Kinabalu, in Borneo — May and I — the same one that put me on the plane to Amsterdam. Except this time Amanda has been caught up in it."

"How?"

"She and one of the young women we partner with in Borneo were attacked in the parking lot of a restaurant. They were beaten with baseball bats."

"Robbed? Molested?"

"No, just attacked. We think it was planned, premeditated."

"Why?"

"It's the money issue that Changxing alluded to, but it's too complicated to explain over the phone."

"Then you know who did it?"

"Well, we think we know who was behind it, but we have no proof. I was hoping you could help me answer that question," Ava said. "I think that the men who attacked them were hired to do the job, and you don't just find men like that on the street, especially on short notice. So if I wanted to hire someone in Kota Kinabalu, who would I talk to?"

"I do not know."

"But you can find out?"

"Perhaps."

"All I need is a starting point. If not the exact person, then the name of someone who can at least point me in the right direction."

"I will speak with some people. I will get you a name."

"Thank you."

"Ava, I find that I have been able to manage quite well here, and my hosts have been extremely supportive. Sonny has not been absolutely necessary —"

She knew what he was going to say next. "I want Sonny to stay in Shanghai with you," she interrupted. "It would be more of a worry for me knowing that you were alone."

"You might need help."

"If I do, I'll let you know. Right now I just want to get there, get things resolved, and get back to Hong Kong by the time you do."

She heard him sigh and felt the worry in it. She almost wished she hadn't called him. The last thing he needed was concerns about her to add to his load.

"Sonny is only a few hours away if you require him," he said.

"I know."

He paused. She thought he was going to persist about

Sonny, but instead he said, "I will try to get your information before you leave Hong Kong. Leave your phone on."

Ava laid her head against the back of the chair and closed her eyes. Speaking to Uncle had helped calm her, as it always had in the past. She could remember time after time, when jobs had gone bad, when she was beginning to feel things slipping away, when a single phone call to him was enough to change her perspective, to make her feel that maybe things would work out if they just stayed the course. His belief in her abilities was absolute, to the point of being unrealistic. The thing was, she couldn't help but be buoyed by it.

She sat up, finished her espresso, and picked up her phone again. It was evening in Toronto and Maria should be home.

"Hi, sweetheart," Maria said.

"Hi. I just landed in Hong Kong. I'm sorry again that I had to leave in such a rush."

"Me too, and I'm sorry I was tied up in those damn meetings. This thing, wherever you have to go, it sounds serious."

"A little bit."

"I thought those days were behind you. I thought I didn't have to worry every time you left."

"Maria, this is a business problem, not much more than that. Amanda got caught up in something stupid. I'll deal with it, and then I'm coming back to Hong Kong and Uncle. I would have ended up in Hong Kong under any circumstance."

"I know, but—"

"But nothing. I will deal with the problem and then come back to Hong Kong as I would have done."

Maria was quiet. Ava could almost hear her pouting.

"Now I need to go," Ava said gently. "I want to shower and change before getting my next flight. I'll email you with my hotel information once I know what it is."

She found an empty stall in the women's washroom and took a quick shower. Then she slipped into a pair of black slacks and white shirt. As she walked back into the lounge she had only twenty minutes to spare before her flight. She left and headed for the gate. Her phone rang just as she reached it; Uncle's cell number lit the screen.

"That was fast," she said.

"His name is Wan," Uncle said. "He runs KK, according to my sources."

"Is he triad?"

"It is not so easy to characterize. He has an affiliation with 14K, but my sources emphasize that it is an affiliation only. He is not officially 14K."

"What does that mean?"

"He works with them on a deal-to-deal basis."

"But there is a relationship?"

"Of course. What is more difficult is determining how it is valued."

"By them?"

"No, by him."

"He is that independent?"

"None of us are, but KK is not exactly the centre of attention for anyone not living there."

"Still—"

"Here is his phone number. They told me not to expect him to answer and not to expect him to return messages unless they are from someone he knows. They said that he conducts much of his business from the Fa Pang restaurant downtown. He is there most nights."

"Thank you."

"Ava, it is a big gang."

"How big can it be in a place like that?"

"I am told it has about thirty members in Kota, but it casts its shadow far wider than the city and can pull in other men as needed."

"I don't understand."

"I was told that in Borneo there are two Malaysian provinces, each with its own operations. In Sabah, which is where Kota is, Wan is the boss. In the other province, Sarawak, things are controlled by a guy named Yeung. Evidently they have some kind of territorial agreement and a loose working relationship. They are both Hakka, though Wan has Sichuan roots and Yeung's family is from Fujian."

"I didn't realize the Chinese presence was so strong there."

"Sabah is at least fifty percent Chinese origin, and my source said you can get by there just speaking Mandarin."

"That should make doing business that much easier," Ava said.

"I am told he can be a difficult man."

"And who doesn't have that capacity?"

"No, I am told that it is his nature to be difficult. You should expect that."

"I'll manage."

"Ava, it worries me. In fact, from everything I have heard, I think you should accept my offer to send Sonny."

The gate was almost empty, the last few stragglers getting their passports and boarding passes checked. "Uncle, let me meet with this Wan before you do anything. Even a difficult man can be reasonable if he's offered the right incentives. Let me see if I can find a way to accommodate him and get what I want."

"I cannot help but feel uncomfortable."

"Uncle, I promise I'll be careful. And I promise if I need help I won't hesitate to ask for it. Now I need to board the plane. I'll be in touch."

19

THE PLANE WAS ONLY HALF FULL, AND ONLY AVA AND what looked like a family of five occupied business class. She pushed back her seat as soon as they reached cruising altitude and closed her eyes to try to catch up on the sleep she had lost on the flight to Hong Kong. May's news about Amanda had lifted a weight from her, and the thought of having to construct a deal with the man named Wan wasn't any cause for worry. How many deals had she done? How many men had she outmanoeuvred? She was just drifting off when she heard the family begin to talk excitedly about Borneo.

They were on a two-week vacation from Australia. The first week had been spent in Bali—a more traditional Australian vacation choice. Now they were looking forward to a less crowded, more tranquil destination. Sabah was evidently ecotourist friendly. They had planned trips into the rainforest to see orangutans and proboscis monkeys, and to go whitewater rafting. The mother was less enthusiastic about climbing Mount Kinabalu. It was a two-day venture, with a stopover at a lodge during the ascent. The mountain was evidently the tallest in Southeast Asia, more than four thousand metres, but it was a relatively easy trek and didn't require any mountain-climbing experience or equipment. The father was trying to convince his wife that the view of the sunset and sunrise from the peak would be worth the effort. Back and forth they went, the conversation penetrating Ava's earplugs. By the time the plane landed, Ava had gotten no sleep but now knew more about the tourist attractions of Sabah than those of Toronto.

She glided through Immigration and walked into an arrivals hall that was virtually deserted. May Ling was standing directly in front of the exit door. Ava hadn't taken more than five steps when she found herself wrapped in her friend's arms. She could feel the tension in May's body. When they separated, Ava looked into her face and saw that it was drawn, her skin almost translucent, with tiny blue veins visible below her eyes.

"You look exhausted," Ava said.

"This is my third trip to the airport today. My two people from Wuhan arrived early this morning and I had to take them to the offices and get them settled. Then I met your brother and Jack at the hospital, followed them here, and waited until Amanda was transferred from the ambulance to the plane. Then I went back to the hospital to sit with Chi-Tze for a while. It's been a brutal twenty-four hours."

"I'm sorry I couldn't get here any faster. That's one thing I've always hated about the trip from Toronto to anywhere in Asia. Your entire world could collapse while you're in mid-air and there wouldn't be a damn thing you could do about it."

"Well, you're here now, thank God."

They began to walk side by side towards the exit, May Ling's arm hooked tightly through Ava's. The instant they left the terminal, Ava felt the heat. It almost startled her. After months of Hong Kong winter weather and the cold and damp of Amsterdam and Toronto, she had forgotten what tropical heat felt like. It had to be at least thirty degrees, she guessed, and the air was heavy with humidity. She felt sweat beading on her brow, and by the time they reached a black Mercedes S-Class idling by the curb, it had begun to trickle into her eyes.

A driver dressed in black slacks and a white shirt stood by the Mercedes' open back door. Ava dropped her bag on the curb and climbed in. The air conditioning was on full blast. She shivered. The worst colds she'd had in her life had come from moving back and forth between outside heat and the air conditioning indoors.

"I leased the car, with the driver, for the week," May said as she slid in beside her. "He can drive everyone back and forth from the hospital, and the Wuhan staff to the office. I have him on twenty-four-hour call. He speaks Mandarin," she added. "It's only a ten-minute drive to the hotel. I thought we'd go there first and get you checked in."

"Could you ask him to turn down the air con a bit?" Ava said. "That's fine. Now tell me, how was Amanda?"

"If it had been up to the doctors she would never have travelled. She's still lapsing in and out of consciousness. But Michael and Jack were insistent and the doctors gave in. The air ambulance staff didn't seem that concerned about taking her, so that eased my worries. But Ava, you should see her — she's not the Amanda we know."

"I don't want a description."

"No . . . I understand."

"How about her other injuries?"

"She has two broken ribs and a fracture in her shin bone."

"Those fuckers."

"Your brother's words exactly."

The car pulled away from the curb. When the plane had landed, Ava had noticed that the airport faced the South China Sea coastline; now she saw that the other side was connected directly to the city.

"When did he and Jack arrive?"

"Late yesterday afternoon."

"Did they stay at the hotel?"

"No, they bunked at the hospital."

"How were they?"

"Very emotional. I'm not used to seeing men cry."

"I should call Michael."

"He asked that we don't. He said he would call us the moment he had any news."

Ava turned her head and looked out the window at the passing city. She had seen Michael distressed before and could imagine just how visible his reaction had been to his wife's suffering. She did not want to pursue a discussion about her brother's fragility. "That mosque is magnificent," she said, pointing to a brown-gold building with four minarets rising high in the sky, its bright blue dome glistening under the sun.

"That's the City Mosque. The dome is made of enamel," May said. "I've been past this part of KK so often I could almost be a tour guide. The driver must be tired of my questions."

"The hospital is close?"

"Yes, it's also right in the middle of the city, only a five-minute drive from the hotel. We'll go there to see Chi-Tze after you check in. Then we'll head to the office and see how my people — Peter and Grace — are doing. I also have the lawyer on standby in case we need him."

Ava was still looking out the window. The South China Sea was on their left and they were driving parallel to it. On their right was a mountain range that seemed to encircle and close in on the entire city. Between the sea and the mountains was a landscape awash in cranes. "Lots of construction."

"The place is booming. It's evidently one of the fastest-growing cities in Malaysia."

"What's the population?"

"About a million people, and growing."

"None of the buildings seem very tall, though, do they."

"Most of this is reclaimed land and there are height restrictions," May Ling said. "The mountainside is too steep for construction, so flat land is at a premium. That makes the city very compact and easy to get around in. Our hotel is almost right on the harbour, along with the main shopping and restaurant area, and anywhere else we need to get to is minutes away, more or less."

"I see," Ava said.

"And there's the hotel," May said.

Like the rest of central Kota Kinabalu, the Méridien was in a low-rise building, but it had enough land to accommodate a sweeping circular driveway. When the driver pulled up at the entrance, a doorman and two bellhops leapt towards the car.

"I've been tipping well," May said.

Ten minutes later they were back in the car, and five minutes after that they were walking through the front doors of Queen Elizabeth General Hospital.

Ava was never comfortable in hospitals. Her longest stay had been a single day in a private clinic in Macau, where the bullet had been removed from her leg. Apart from that, there had only been visits to emergency wards for treatment of various second-party-inflicted injuries. Those short exposures had been enough to instil a permanent image of black-and-white tile floors, green walls, acoustic-panelled ceilings, rows of wheelchairs, gurneys in hallways, and stale, heavy air redolent with disinfectant.

Uncle had been in and out of the Queen Elizabeth in Hong Kong over the past three months, sometimes for several days but most often for a check-up. She had accompanied him on every trip, and it didn't matter if he was there overnight or just in and out — every single time she stepped through the doors and her feet touched the tiles, a feeling of unease cloaked her. *This is where people come to die*, she always thought. She knew that was irrational. Logic said it was where people came to heal. But there was something about the smell, about the nurses with their rubber-soled shoes, about the open doors exposing visitors at the bedsides of loved ones, holding their hands as they whispered to them, that rattled Ava's sense of order. Hospitals were not a world she knew, or ever wanted to know.

"Chi-Tze is on the fourth floor. We're paying for a private room," May Ling said as they entered the main lobby.

The area was thick with people. Two long lines had formed at the reception desk, and every chair around the perimeter was occupied. They walked to a bank of elevators and joined a throng that included two wheelchairs and a gurney. The elderly woman on the gurney was covered to the chin by a blanket. She moaned, her eyes closed, her head rocking from side to side. The elevator door opened and the gurney was rolled in, followed by the wheelchairs.

"There's room for you if you squeeze," the orderly with the gurney said to May Ling.

"I'll wait," Ava said.

May stepped back from the door. She looked quizzically at Ava.

"I feel as if I've been living in a hospital," Ava said.

"I understand. I've only been doing it for a day and a half and I've already had enough of it. I can imagine how it's been with Uncle," said May.

"He isn't in hospital all that often — not for long periods, anyway — but even when he isn't, the idea that he's heading back there weighs on me. He sees how uncomfortable I get and says that I don't like being reminded of my own mortality."

"There is some truth in that," May said.

Another elevator arrived and they rode it to the fourth floor. May led Ava along the corridor, their high heels sounding like castanets on the tile floor. The only difference between the Queen Elizabeth in KK and the one in Hong Kong was that the walls were grey instead of green.

They reached the end of the corridor to find a closed door. May knocked. The door opened and Ava found herself looking at a tiny woman. She wasn't more than five feet tall, and in flat sandals she barely reached Ava's shoulders. She was wearing blue jeans and a plain short-sleeved black silk shirt. If it weren't for her hair and the slightest touch of red lipstick, she might have passed for a young boy.

"Ava, this is Ah-Pei," May said.

Ah-Pei gave Ava a slight smile. "Thank you for coming."

Ava leaned forward, grasped her hands, and squeezed. "I'm so sorry we have to meet like this."

"It's a terrible situation for everyone," Ah-Pei said.

"How is she doing?" May asked.

"Sleeping," Ah-Pei said, stepping aside.

The room had two beds. Chi-Tze occupied the one farthest from the door. She seemed to be as small and slim as Ah-Pei, dwarfed by the metal rack that held the bags of intravenous solution pumping into her system. Her left arm, encased in plaster, lay at an awkward angle. Her right leg was suspended in mid-air and was also in plaster.

Ava walked over to her. She knew she was about Amanda's age — in her late twenties — but she could have passed for sixteen.

"We were fortunate that she wasn't struck on the head," Ah-Pei said from behind her.

"Yes, of course," Ava said.

"We're scared for Amanda," Ah-Pei continued. "There was so much blood. Chi-Tze was awake when they reached the hospital, but they put her to sleep quite quickly and she had no idea how much of damage had been done to Amanda. When she woke, it was the first thing she asked. I think she was afraid that the blow to Amanda's head had actually killed her."

"You know that Amanda's husband flew her back to Hong Kong this morning?" Ava said.

"May told me."

"She'll be better off surrounded by family."

"How is she, though?"

"No one is sure about the extent of the damage."

"Why would anyone do this?"

"I don't know, and we need to find out."

May glanced at Ava as if to say *No more talk on this subject.*

Ah-Pei stared at her sister. "They're telling me she can come home in about a week. I'm going to hire some nurses to look after her while I'm at work."

"Ah-Pei has been back and forth between here and the office," May said. "I told her, now that Grace and Peter are here, she can spend more time with Chi-Tze."

"The business isn't that simple," Ah-Pei said.

"No, but once they have their bearings they can help maintain the day-to-day business. We understand how valuable you and your sister are, and we're as anxious to have both of you back at work, but your sister needs to mend, and you need to spend time with her without feeling guilty about it."

Ah-Pei looked doubtful but nodded slowly.

"Now I want to take Ava over to see the offices and the factory and to meet Peter and Grace. I'll be back later this afternoon, and then tonight we can all have dinner."

"I would like that," Ah-Pei said.

"Speaking of dinner," Ava said, "what was the name of the restaurant where the incident took place?"

"Lu Ying Seafood."

"Where is it?"

"Across from the esplanade that runs along the harbour."

"May told me the attackers cursed the girls."

"It was horrible stuff, so demeaning."

"That's usually the way men do things like that. Not many of them are silent when they're hitting a woman."

"How would you know that?"

Ava shrugged. "Did the men say anything else?"

"What do you mean?"

"Did they give any clue as to why they were attacking them?"

"No, they just swore at them."

Ava felt May fidgeting beside her and knew she was uncomfortable with the conversation. "Thanks. I'm sorry to ask you these questions."

Ah-Pei lowered her head.

May and Ava turned to leave the room, only to be caught by Ah-Pei's voice. "I want to thank you for standing by us," she said in a rush.

The two women turned. Ah-Pei's head was still slightly lowered and tears filled her eyes. Ava saw that her hands were trembling.

May walked towards Ah-Pei and embraced her. "We're partners. This is what being a partner means. Chi-Tze is going to recover. And so is our business," she said.

As Ava and May left the room and started back down the hallway, May said, "She's actually getting stronger."

"I notice she didn't mention her brothers," Ava said. "Does she really believe they had nothing to do with this?"

"No, she just can't bear to think that they did. She hasn't mentioned their names once since I've been here. I've decided to follow the same policy. You should do the same, at least in her presence."

"I will."

They waited for the elevator to take them to the main floor, Ava's eyes fixed on the doors.

"You said you needed to find out who did this to the girls. Do you have a way of doing that?" May asked.

"I have the name of someone who might help me."

"He lives here?"

"Yes."

"Have you spoken to him?"

"No. I'm told he doesn't take phone calls."

"So how will you get to him?"

"Evidently he uses a restaurant in the city as his office. He's there most evenings, I'm told. I'm going to go there tonight, so don't count on me for dinner."

"How did you get the name?"

"Uncle."

"So this guy, he is…"

"Not exactly, but probably close enough," Ava said.

The elevator doors opened.

"Ava, if you want me to go with you —"

"No, let's stick to the plans you told Ah-Pei. We'll go the factory this afternoon and then you can take Peter and Grace and her out to dinner tonight."

20

THE BORNEO FINE HARDWOODS AND FURNITURE COM-
pany was located near an industrial park in Spanggar, an
area to the south of KK about a twenty-minute drive away.

"That is one huge operation," Ava said, eyeing the complex of buildings from the car. "It's so damn big."

"Not really. We have larger operations in Wuhan, and the
Shanghai warehouse and distribution business we bought
in to is at least twice this size."

"The biggest thing I've ever owned is my condo."

The buildings were surrounded by concrete-block walls
topped by razor wire, and the entrance was guarded by
a steel gate. As the Mercedes approached, the gate rolled
open slowly. A security guard stood to one side, pressed his
heels together, and gave a very smart salute.

"I can't get used to that," May said.

As they drove into the courtyard, Ava saw a three-storey
wood-frame structure directly in front of them. On either
side were five-storey buildings made of corrugated steel.
None of them had windows, and up close they weren't as
impressive as they had been when they filled the horizon.

"Warehouses?" Ava said.

"This is a business that needs lots of space," May said. "We have two buildings where we actually manufacture the furniture, four where we store the lumber, and six where we keep the finished goods. It costs a fortune to transport furniture because in weight terms it takes so little to fill a truck or a container."

The wooden structure was where the office was located. May led Ava inside, nodded at the receptionist, and took a sharp left. The air conditioning was so cold it almost took Ava's breath away. At the end of the hall she could see a glass-enclosed boardroom with five people sitting around a table.

"Peter Chik is the young man in the grey suit and Grace Chik is in the red dress. They aren't related," May said as they drew near. "Peter is an accountant; Grace has her MBA and works for us in sales and marketing. Those others work here. They've been getting Peter and Grace up to speed."

When the people in the boardroom saw May and Ava, they stood up. The young man May had identified as Peter Chik came to the door and opened it.

"Ms. Wong," he said, bowing his head.

"This is Ms. Ava Lee. She is my partner in this business, and others," May said. "Peter, why don't you introduce us to everyone here, please."

In addition to Grace Chik there were two financial people, both men, and one marketing person, a woman, attached to the firm. Ava could see that they looked apprehensive, and she wondered how much they had been told about the Netherlands and about Amanda and Chi-Tze. May sat and motioned for Ava to sit next to her. The others sat too.

"Are things going well?" May asked.

"Well enough. We spoke with the bank an hour ago and there shouldn't be any problems maintaining the business at its current level of production for the foreseeable future," Peter Chik said. "I've gone over the numbers with the staff here, and things are very well organized. They have excellent systems."

"Great. And Grace, how are you doing on the marketing side?" May said.

"We've been reviewing accounts. Dorothy and I have made a list of current customers that we're going to start calling to see if we can increase their order rate. I brought with me a list of our key importers and trading partners from the Wuhan side. We'll start calling them tomorrow to let them know we're now in the furniture business and that we want them to become clients."

"I want to know who is supportive and who isn't," May said. "I'll personally call anyone who's reluctant to help us with this new venture."

"Yes, ma'am," Grace said.

Ava looked at the group around the table. They were all young, probably still in their twenties. The three locals were dressed casually in jeans and shirts, while Peter and Grace looked the part of young professionals. There was also a difference in their demeanour. The Borneo Furniture employees looked nervous, their eyes darting from face to face. The Chiks seemed calm, completely in control. On her most recent trips to China Ava had noticed this self-confidence among the new young cadre of university graduates.

"Do you have any questions for me, any of you?" May asked.

"How is Ms. Chi-Tze?" Dorothy asked.

"She's recovering, and we think she'll be going home in a week or so. Ms. Ah-Pei will be back and forth between here and the hospital and their house," May said. "Anything else? If not, then I think Ms. Lee would like to take a tour of the facilities. Dorothy, will you show her around?"

For the next two hours Ava was guided from building to building, learning about the availability and costs of various hardwoods as Dorothy pointed to stack after stack. Ava could hardly tell one wood from another. Her interest was piqued when they walked into the first of the actual manufacturing centres, but after being taken through the assembly of a dining-room set, there wasn't anything more she actually wanted to know. By the time they had left the last building, Ava was exhausted from a combination of jet lag and information overload. She was also hot and sweaty again. The factory buildings had no central air conditioning, just huge overhead fans for circulating air and fans built into the walls to expel the dust the processing operations generated.

May was locked in deep conversation with Peter Chik and the other financial people when Ava and Dorothy returned to the boardroom. The table was covered with spreadsheets streaked with red and black marker, and May held the black marker in her hand. Ava had never actually seen her in full business mode before.

"How was the tour?" May asked.

"Just great," Ava said.

"We're just verifying the cash-flow projections," May said, waving a hand over the papers. "Do you want to sit in?"

"Under normal circumstances I would, but truthfully

I'm feeling really jet-lagged and wouldn't mind going back to the hotel and having a rest. It could be a long evening."

"We'll get the driver."

"Thanks."

"What time do you think you'll leave the hotel for your meeting?"

"About seven."

"We're planning on dinner around the same time."

"I'll call you when I'm done or if there are any changes in my plans," Ava said, and turned to leave.

"Wait a second," May said. "Jack Yee gave me this note for you. I put it in my purse and entirely forgot about it."

It was a single folded piece of paper. Ava opened it as she walked to the car. It had two words written on it: GET THEM.

21

AVA HAD TO FIGHT TO KEEP HER EYES OPEN ON THE drive to the hotel. When she arrived there, she barely had the presence of mind to confirm with the concierge that the Fa Pang did indeed exist and was within walking distance. As soon as she got to her room she stripped and crawled into bed. The jet lag was overpowering, and she needed to sleep if she was going to be alert when she met with Wan. She was just dozing off when she realized she hadn't set an alarm. She set the bedside clock to wake her at six thirty and flopped back onto the pillows. The next thing she knew the alarm was buzzing and two and a half hours had passed in what felt like an instant.

She showered, brushed her hair, and fixed it with the ivory chignon pin. She debated whether to wear a skirt or slacks, and opted for the skirt. This wasn't any accountant she was meeting, and looking conservative wouldn't necessarily be a plus. She put on a light touch of red lipstick, some mascara, and her Annick Goutal perfume.

At ten to seven she walked into the hotel lobby. The Méridien was right on Sutera Harbour, and from its doorway

Ava could see what she presumed was the esplanade, running along beside the water and all lit up. The doorman pointed towards it. "The restaurant you want is on the left, just past the swordfish monument."

She started along the esplanade on a wooden boardwalk edged by a weather-beaten wooden railing that overlooked the sea and an unending row of metal street lamps that looked as if they belonged in Victorian London. The sea was on the right, and on the left were shops and restaurants. The sun had set but the tropical climate still bore down on her. She hadn't gone fifty metres before she began to sweat, and by the time she reached the giant blue and silver leaping swordfish statue, her armpits and the waistband of her skirt were wet.

Fa Pang was about twenty metres past the swordfish, directly facing the harbour and the South China Sea. It was fronted by two banks of fish tanks three tiers high, angled from front to back. It was an impressive live display of spiny lobsters, crabs, several species of shrimp, squid, clams, *garoupa*, and flatfish. Ava stepped inside. The restaurant was small; there were fewer than twenty tables, and half of them set for two diners. The place was plain, with white tile floors, white walls, unadorned wooden tables, and aluminum chairs with plastic seats. There were only ten customers in the place, a family of six at one table and couples at two others.

A small, bald man in a dirty apron emerged from the back of the restaurant. "Sit wherever you want," he said.

"I'm actually looking for a Mr. Wan," she said. "I don't see anyone here who looks like it might be him."

"Is he expecting you?"

"No, but I was told I could find him here."

"Sometimes that is true. But it's always true that he doesn't like surprise visitors."

"I was also told that he doesn't answer phone calls, so how else was I to get hold of him?"

"Anyway, he isn't here," the man said, staring intently into Ava's eyes.

"Do you expect him?"

He shrugged. "He doesn't fill me in on his schedule."

"But he's here most nights?"

"What's your name?"

"Ava Lee."

"And who told you about Wan?"

"People who know him, who may have worked with him. People who live in Hong Kong."

"If he does come in, and he does want to talk to you, how can he reach you?"

"My cellphone number is on this card," Ava said. "I'm staying in KK and I can be here in ten minutes."

"If I see him I'll tell him."

"Thanks."

"Now, excuse me. I have a business to run."

Ava hovered. "I haven't had dinner."

"And you aren't going to have it here," he said. "If Wan wants to talk to you, he'll call. I don't want you hanging around."

"I've heard of another seafood restaurant called Lu Ying. Would you recommend it?"

"Not bad."

"Where is it?"

"Go out the door and turn left. It's a two-minute walk."

"Is it a safe place for a woman who's on her own? I heard that two young women were attacked in their parking lot a few nights ago."

The man looked away, reached for the hem of his apron, and wiped his hands on it. "I don't know anything about that."

"I find that rather strange."

"I don't care if you do."

"I see. Well, please let Mr. Wan know that I'm waiting for his call."

"If he comes."

"Of course. If he comes."

Ava went back onto the esplanade, where some people were strolling and even more were leaning against the railing, looking out at the South China Sea and Sutera Harbour. She thought about waiting at the railing herself to watch the front door of Fa Pang, and then dismissed the idea. She didn't know what Wan looked like. Besides, she was hungry. She turned left and started towards Lu Ying. She would have dinner there and wait for his phone call. If it didn't come by the time she finished, she'd revisit Fa Pang.

22

LU YING WAS FARTHER ALONG THE ESPLANADE THAN she had been told. In fact it was almost at the most westerly end, and she was sweating by the time she got there. Like Fa Pang, its entire façade was obscured by fish tanks, but Ava's attention was drawn to the parking lot beside the restaurant. It was completely exposed: no walls, no fences, and open to plain view from both the esplanade and the street. It was dimly lit, the only illumination coming from a corner street lamp and the headlights of passing cars. But the lot was only big enough to hold about twenty cars in two rows. She figured that Amanda and Chi-Tze would have been clearly visible. Any car or pedestrian passing on either side of the lot was sure to have seen them.

She walked onto the lot and glanced to the right, towards the restaurant, which had a glass door and a large picture window. She could see at least ten tables from where she was standing. May had said that the restaurant owner saw the attack and reported it. She knew enough about how people react to violence to understand why no one had tried to intervene. There would have been initial shock, followed by confusion about what to do. By the time any decision had been made, the thugs would have been able to escape. What really bothered Ava was how brazen the attack had been.

The restaurant was at least ten times larger than Fa Pang, and the man who greeted her wasn't dressed like someone who had been killing fish in the back room. He was tall and slim, with a thick head of black hair, and dressed in a loose short-sleeved white shirt over lightweight grey slacks. Behind him Ava saw two young women in pale blue cheongsams.

"Do you have a table for one?" she asked in Mandarin.

"Certainly," he said with a smile.

"My name is Ava Lee. I'm a friend of Amanda Yee and a colleague of Chi-Tze and Ah-Pei, who I understand are known to you."

"My name is Yip," he said, his easy manner replaced by a frown. "And yes, I know the women, and I also met your friend. It is a terrible thing that happened to them. How are they?"

"Amanda is in Hong Kong; she was flown there this morning. Chi-Tze is at the Queen Elizabeth Hospital here. Both of them will recover physically, but it will take time. Emotionally, I'm not so sure."

"I'm so sorry that we couldn't have done more...moved faster, you know."

"I know, though I don't think there is much anyone could have done to prevent what happened. From all accounts it was premeditated."

Yip nodded, his eyes flitting around the room. "Are you actually here to eat?" he asked.

"Oh yes. I didn't come specifically to talk about the attack, although I did want to see where it occurred and find out all I could about what people actually saw."

"I was the one who saw it first," he said quickly. "Truthfully, I heard it first — men swearing outside. I went to the window and there they were, in the middle of the parking lot, swinging bats at two women on the ground. The men wore black T-shirts and blue jeans and had masks pulled over their faces. I yelled at one of my hostesses to call the police, and then I ran to the door. When I opened it, I think they saw me. In fact, I know they did, because one of them stared at me. Then he turned away and hit one of the women again. That was the last blow. They swore at the women, screamed at me to mind my own fucking business, and then went east along the esplanade on foot."

"They just walked away?" Ava asked, surprised by how eager Yip seemed to be to talk about it.

"Yes."

"No rush?"

"No, they were almost casual about the whole thing."

"And no one pursued them?"

"I was the only other person in the parking lot by then, and I ran to the women. Maybe I should have run after the men, but the women seemed more important."

"Yes, of course."

"Your friend, Amanda...her head was quite bloody."

"Yes, I know."

"And Chi-Tze was in great pain when the paramedics moved her."

"Broken ribs, and breaks in her arm and leg."

Yip sighed. "Please send them my best wishes."

"I will."

"And now let me find you a table."

The restaurant was almost full, and Ava found herself near the back, next to a swinging kitchen door. Every time it opened, aromas wafted through, and she could hear the sizzle of what she knew would be at least twenty giant woks being put to hard and good use. She placed her cellphone on the table so she wouldn't miss its ring. A waitress in the same blue cheongsam she'd seen at the entrance appeared with a menu.

Ava waved it away. "All I want is steamed fish with some white rice."

"*Garoupa*?"

"Perfect."

"Soy sauce, cilantro, chives?"

"Also perfect."

"And to drink?"

"Jasmine tea."

When the waitress left, Ava saw Yip looking at her from across the room. She waved at him and motioned for him to come to her table. "I didn't mean to ask so many questions before," she said when he was standing next to her. "I hope it didn't upset you."

"No, it was actually good to get it out of my system."

"The police didn't interview you?"

"All they asked was if I recognized the men, and when I said they were wearing masks, they didn't ask me anything else."

"They didn't want a physical description?"

"I think I might have said something about the T-shirts and jeans, and mentioned that they were average size."

"What do you mean by average?"

"Not thin, not fat, medium height."

"I see. Tell me, Mr. Yip, does this kind of thing happen often around here?"

"No, it was quite unusual."

"So don't you find it a bit strange that the police weren't more aggressive with their questioning?"

"I assumed they'd spent more time talking to the women."

The waitress arrived with Ava's pot of tea. As she poured the first cup, Yip started to move away from the table. "Mr. Yip, do you know of a man named Wan?" Ava asked.

"Why do you ask?"

Ava noticed the waitress glance in her boss's direction. There was confusion, and maybe a touch of concern, on her face.

"I've been told he is the man I should speak to about this attack."

"Speak to?"

"I want to find out who did it. I've been told he can help."

"That is possible," Yip said. "He is a man who has very broad business interests. He is a man who knows a lot of people."

"You say that very carefully."

"He can also be a difficult man."

"A dangerous man?"

"He isn't someone you want for an enemy."

"Do you do business with him?"

"Only indirectly."

"Protection money?"

Yip looked down at Ava as if he was trying to memorize her face. "Are you police?"

"No, I told you, I'm in business with Chi-Tze and Ah-Pei."

"Then ask them about Wan. They know who he is."

The kitchen door opened and a server appeared with a silver *garoupa* nestled in a bed of spring onions.

"That was quick, and it looks fantastic," Ava said.

"Thank you," Yip said, backing away from the table.

Ava sipped tea while the server used a fork and spoon to separate flesh from bone. Just as he was finishing, her cellphone rang.

"Hello," she said.

"It's May."

"Oh."

"You sound disappointed."

"I'm waiting for the man I want to meet to call me."

"Where are you?"

"In a restaurant."

"You should have let me know. We're at the hotel just sitting down for dinner. You could have joined us."

"Better that I didn't. How did the day end?"

"Well enough, I think. On the financial side, things are under control and in capable hands. The salespeople have more work to do. You don't lose a piece of business as big as that Dutch contract and replace it in a heartbeat. Luckily our trading base is big enough that Grace should be able to find some immediate takers. And then, just before I left the office, I spoke to Michael."

"He called you?"

"No, I couldn't help myself. But he didn't sound angry that I called. The trip was uneventful. Amanda was no worse for it and now she's in a private room at the Queen Elizabeth. Michael plans to sleep there until they know exactly what the damage is."

"That's not where he imagined he'd spend part of his honeymoon."

"No, but he was in good enough spirits. I think getting back to Hong Kong improved everyone's mood. He said he would call you when he had the chance. The last time you spoke, he said, he was a bit abrupt. He knows what happened isn't anyone's fault."

"That's not true."'

"No, but you know what he means."

"Look, May, I'm sitting here with a plate of steamed *garoupa* that's getting cold. You have your dinner and then we'll talk when I get back to the hotel. If my contact doesn't call me in the next half-hour, I'm going back to the place where he's supposed to hang out."

"Keep in touch."

"I will."

"I don't like the idea of your being alone."

"You do remember what I did for a living?"

"Yes, and I also remember you with a bullet in your leg."

"I'll be careful," Ava said.

She ate slowly, finishing the body flesh before turning her efforts to the head. She plucked the meat from the fish's cheeks and then snapped the bones in the head and sucked on them. Uncle and her mother always ate the eyes. It was one of the few things in Chinese cuisine that Ava wouldn't eat. When she was done, the eyes and a pile of bones were all that was left on the plate.

She looked at her watch — almost eight o'clock. She waved at her waitress for the bill.

The waitress came to the table empty-handed. "Mr. Yip said the meal is on the house," she said.

Ava glanced around the restaurant. There was no sign of Yip. She reached into her bag. "Tell him thanks, and give him this and tell him to spread it around any way he chooses," she said, handing the woman a U.S. hundred-dollar bill.

As she left Lu Ying she noticed there had been a change in the night air. What had been hot, heavy, and oppressive now had some life in it. The air was infused with a light aroma of brine that a newly arrived breeze carried in from the sea. She crossed the esplanade so she could walk along the harbour's edge. The tide was edging in, lapping against stone walls. She walked for more than a kilometre, passing Fa Pang, and then turned and walked back. The harbour was surrounded by a number of small islands, close enough that she could see lights glinting from them. She passed a ferry terminal and thought how very casual it all was. Unlike Hong Kong's harbour, where the sea was constantly being churned by propellers, there was hardly a boat in sight.

She stopped directly across from the restaurant, leaning against the railing. The fish tanks blocked the view of the interior. She looked at her watch again and then double-checked her phone to make sure it was on. Waiting had never been her strong suit. She was more of a charge-right-in kind of woman, except in this case she had no one to charge at. She felt frustration gnawing at her. She would give it until nine, she decided, before heading across the street again to the restaurant.

Fa Pang was busier now, a steady stream of customers coming and going, nearly all families and couples. The one male she saw enter by himself looked as if he was barely out of high school. She checked the time every five minutes, and by ten to nine she had had enough. She put her phone in her bag and stepped off the sidewalk. Just as she did, her cell rang.

"Ava Lee," she said.

"Jacob Smits here."

"Your timing—"

"Sorry. Do you want me to call back?"

"No, I have a few minutes," she said, moving back onto the sidewalk.

"I'm in Rotterdam. I found a dealer here who was prepared to be co-operative. I've just left him."

"And?"

"He spent three hundred thousand euros for furniture he guesses is worth a million. He said the sellers were eager to do a quick deal. A 'quick deal' meant fast payment."

"Exactly what you thought."

"He sent a wire transfer."

"To where?"

"Aruba."

"Do you have the account information?"

"I have an actual copy of the wire."

"How soon can you email it to me?"

"I'll find an Internet café here. Give me an hour."

"Jacob, this is good, really good."

"Thanks."

"And I'm sorry if I sounded a bit annoyed when you called. It's nine in the evening here and I've been waiting for a phone call to confirm a meeting. I thought that was the other party."

"No bother. By the way, where is 'here'?"

"I'm in Borneo, where the furniture is made."

"So you're how many hours ahead of us?"

"Seven."

"I'll keep that in mind."

"How difficult was it to persuade the buyer to help?"

"Ten thousand euros difficult."

"Still worth it."

"I thought so."

"Whose name is on the bank account?"

"It's a numbered company."

"Which bank?"

"Barrett's, an English bank."

"I know them."

"Is that good?"

"It could very well be."

"So now what?"

As Ava was speaking, her eyes had never left the other side of the esplanade. Now she saw four men emerge from the corner where the statue of the swordfish stood and turn in the direction of Fa Pang. The smallest walked in front, talking on his cellphone as he did. The others trailed, one on either side, one straight behind. From a distance they were a cluster, but as they drew closer they became distinct.

The one in front, the leader — and in Ava's mind Wan — was wearing a loose-fitting short-sleeved black silk shirt over a pair of black jeans and sandals. His head was round, and made even rounder by long hair that was parted in the middle and fell over both ears.

The others were all in T-shirts, blue jeans, and running shoes. One wore his hair long like Wan's, but combed straight back. The other two had buzz cuts. All of them had spectacular tattoos covering both arms, and while only one had designs that extended above the collar of his shirt, Ava guessed his friends would have close to the same coverage.

"Jacob, I need to think about this," she said. "Send me the wire copy and then do some thinking yourself. We'll get caught up tomorrow."

"I have to tell you," he said slowly, "I don't think this will change much with the trustee."

"Perhaps not."

"So?"

Her four men reached Fa Pang and walked through the restaurant's doors. "Jacob, I'll call you tomorrow," she said.

She closed her phone and strained to see past the fish tanks. It was hopeless. *Ten minutes*, she thought. *I'll give Wan ten minutes to call me.*

The sea breeze intensified behind her, and she turned to feel it touch her face.

23

FIVE MINUTES HAD PASSED. SHE KEPT STARING AT THE restaurant, willing him to call. At the nine-minute mark her phone rang. She glanced at the screen, which read PRIVATE CALLER.

"Hello," she said.

"Your name is Ava Lee?"

"Yes. Is this Wan?" she said.

"Who gave you my name?"

"Does that matter?"

"Where are you?"

"I'm on the esplanade, directly across from the restaurant."

"Come," he said.

She walked as slowly as she could. When she was halfway there, she saw the restaurant door open. The man in the apron she had talked to earlier looked at her and then to her right and left, as if he was trying to confirm she was alone.

"Thank you for giving him my message," she said as she neared.

"It means nothing," he said as he turned back into the restaurant.

Ava walked into the entrance and was immediately immersed in a cloud of steam that smelled of ginger, fried garlic, and coriander. "You've been busy," she said.

"No more than usual," he said. "There — see that door at the back of the restaurant, the one with the copper dragon fixed to it? He's in there."

When she reached the door, she paused. Knock or just enter? She knocked, waited for a few seconds, and then turned the handle.

The man she had seen on the street, the one she assumed was Wan, sat at a round restaurant table that looked big enough to accommodate twelve people. The table was positioned near the far wall. Wan sat facing the door, his back against the wall. The man with the long combed-back hair sat next to Wan. The other two leaned against opposite walls, their eyes fixed on Ava.

"What do you want?" Wan said, his head down, his fingers flicking through a pile of paper in front of him.

"I was told you could help me."

"With what?"

"Information."

"I'm not the tourist board."

"Not that kind of information."

"I'm also not the police."

"I understand."

"Who gave you my name?"

"Does that matter?"

"I've asked you twice. I won't ask a third time."

"Uncle Chow Tung."

He looked up. She saw that his head was not as round close up, its shape distorted by sagging flesh around his chin, earlobes that looked swollen and distended, and a deeply etched brow that was partially hidden by layers of fat, making his forehead look like a window blind. His eyes were small, dark, and narrow.

"I haven't heard that name in a long time," he said.

"So you do know of him."

"I know he is retired and out of our business. I thought he would be dead by now."

"He's not."

"I don't really care."

Ava felt her face flush. She started to speak, then stopped.

"What did the old man tell you about me?" Wan asked, his attention turning back to his paperwork.

"He said you run Sabah."

"Why would he tell you that?"

"I asked."

"And why would you do that?"

"Two young women were attacked a few nights ago in the parking lot of Lu Ying restaurant. I want to know who did it and who paid them to do it. Uncle referred me to you."

"Sabah is a long way from Hong Kong. He should stick to his own turf. I don't like my name being used by people I don't know."

"He was trying to help me."

"Why? What are you to him?"

"A friend."

Wan raised his head. "The only young women-friends a man his age has are there to keep his bones warm."

"Or suck his bone," the other man at the table said.

One of the men leaning against the wall snickered. Ava glanced at him. He nudged his companion with his elbow.

Both of them smiled at her.

"Let's keep this to business, shall we?" Ava said. "I'm here about the two young women who were attacked. I'm prepared to pay to get the information I want."

Wan tilted back his chair until it reached the wall. He put his hands behind his head, his feet dangling in mid-air. "What two women? What attack?" he said.

"Okay, let's assume that you don't already know what happened. I'll pay you to find out."

"I told you, I'm not the police."

"I wouldn't offer to pay the police."

"Then you don't know Sabah," he said.

Ava closed her eyes, trying to will away the anger that was growing inside her. "How much money do I have to pay you to get the information I need?"

"What are these women to you?"

"Partners in a business."

"What business?"

"Borneo Fine Hardwoods and Furniture."

"I know it. I don't know them."

"Chi-Tze is local. Amanda Yee is from Hong Kong."

"And you own part of the business?"

"I do."

Wan turned towards the other man seated at the table. "What do you think, Yu Fei? Could we find out what this woman wants to know?"

"It's possible," he said, his eyes locked on Ava.

"And if we could, do you think we should ask for a fee?"

"A hundred thousand ringgit?"

"No, we would need more," Wan said. "Maybe double."

"How much is that in U.S. dollars?" Ava asked.

"Three for one, so sixty or seventy thousand."

"I'll pay," she said.

Wan twisted his head from side to side as if he was trying to unlock his neck. "The problem is, from my side, I don't know what you would do with the information… assuming I could get it."

"I wouldn't go to the police."

"I wouldn't care if you did, but that isn't what I asked you."

"If I pay you the money, why should it matter what I do?"

The chair rocked back and forth and then slammed onto the floor. Wan's open palm followed it onto the tabletop with a crack. "Get out of here!" he yelled.

Ava didn't move. She saw Yu Fei nod at the two men leaning against the walls and knew she had almost run out of time. "Chi-Tze has two brothers," she said. "We think they've stolen money from the company and we've taken legal action against them. It seems to us that this attack could have been organized by them as a way of calling us off."

"So?"

"If we can prove that, it will strengthen our legal position. It will give us even more ammunition to go after them."

"That would involve the police."

"Not necessarily. There are a lot of things we can do through civil action."

"How much money did they steal?"

"Enough."

"Stop fucking around with me," Wan said.

Ava spun the numbers in her head, trying to find one

that would justify spending seventy thousand U.S. but wouldn't encourage Wan to get even greedier. "About a million U.S.," she said.

Yu and Wan exchanged glances. *They know I'm lying about the amount*, Ava thought.

"You're willing to spend all that money to get back a million?"

"I also want to make sure the brothers are punished, one way or another."

"What if it wasn't them? What if it was just some random attack?"

"As long as you can identify who did it and I can verify that, I'll pay the money."

"What do you think?" Wan said to Yu.

"We can make some phone calls," Yu said.

"Maybe, but I don't want to spend much time on this."

"I don't think it would take very long."

Wan looked at Ava. "If we get you the information, how fast can you get us the money?"

"One day."

"Who knows you're here?"

"Uncle."

He nodded. "Give us a couple of hours. Come back here around eleven."

"Thanks."

"I'm only doing it because of the old man."

"Does that mean you don't want the money?"

"Don't be so fucking stupid," Wan said.

"I was joking."

"So was I. About the old man, I mean."

24

AVA LEFT THE RESTAURANT WITH MIXED FEELINGS about the way the meeting had gone. Wan had become annoyed the second she'd mentioned Uncle's name. She shouldn't have been so tight-lipped; there was nothing to be gained by it. She hadn't provoked him, but she had irked him. She would be more careful the second time around, she decided. She had known men like Wan before. They ran a little fiefdom in some backwater, where they were lord of their own realm, and they didn't like to be reminded there was a bigger world outside, where other men were kings.

The breeze coming off the South China Sea swirled around her, enveloping her in a salted perfume. She stood on the esplanade, trying to decide how to spend the next few hours. Then she remembered Jacob Smits and his news, and started walking back to her hotel. If Wan came through for her the way Jacob had, an evening that had began hot, muggy, and disjointed would end as cool and pleasing.

The Méridien lobby was empty except for the staff. Ava went to the concierge to ask if he had seen Madam Wong.

"She went to the Circle Restaurant around seven," the concierge said, pointing across the lobby. "I didn't see her leave, but I was on break about half an hour ago."

Ava went to the restaurant and peeked inside. There was no sign of May Ling. She thought about calling her room and then shunted the idea aside; she had nothing definitive to tell her. She would wait until she had seen Wan again.

The maid had been to her room during her absence. The bed was freshly made and a purple orchid and a small box of chocolates lay on her pillow. She went to her laptop and opened her email, expecting to find the scanned copy of the wire transfer from Smits, but there was nothing from him. She looked at her watch. It had been only half an hour since he had called. Impatient, she reached for her cellphone.

"Smits."

"You were going to send me a copy of that wire transfer."

"I just had a quick lunch. I'm going to do it now."

"Don't bother. I'm back in my room and can take notes. Read the details to me."

"Wait a second while I pull it from my folder... Yes, here it is. It's a numbered company registered in Aruba, which isn't surprising, given the Dutch connection. It's registered as 7793579 Aruba Inc., and the address is Box 459, 12 Willem Street, Oranjestad."

"Bank account number?"

"022-1098-652377."

"You said Barrett's Bank?"

"Yes, at Caya G.F. — I guess that means ground floor — Betico Croes 47, Oranjestad."

"This is most helpful, Jacob."

"Do you want the phone and fax numbers?"

"I might as well have them, though I don't intend to call them directly. Not yet, anyway."

"You mentioned you have a bank contact?" Jacob said after he read her the numbers.

"Yes, a while ago I had a job that took me to the British Virgin Islands and the Barrett's Bank branch there. Let's hope the guy I dealt with is still there and that he remembers me — actually, that he remembers me in a positive way."

"He might not?"

"Unfortunately there is that possibility. I left a bit of a mess behind, and I'm not sure if he's aware of that now."

"A job in the British Virgin Islands? A mess?"

"This is not the time to get into it. I need to phone my man and see what I can do about that numbered company's bank account."

"What makes you think you can do anything?"

"Well, if the Aruba branch is anything like the one in BVI, it will be quite strict about how it conducts its business. My understanding is that Barrett's is absolutely paranoid about being used to launder money. I'm going to make the case that this is exactly what's going on in Aruba. If I can get my guy worried enough, he'll call his Aruban counterpart and we'll take it from there."

"That won't get you your money back."

"No, and that's not the intent. All I want to do is spread enough doubt to make them freeze the account. That will keep our money in one place while we work out all the legal and bankruptcy issues."

"I see."

"Jacob, I'd also like you to call Timmerman when you get back to Amsterdam. I'll email the guy there and tell him

I've hired you to work with us on this matter. I'll tell him that you speak for us and that you have some information you want to share with him."

"How much do you want me to say?"

"Tell him about the accounting and banking irregularities you've come across. Tell him about the offshore bank account. Tell him that we expect him to do nothing — at least, nothing just yet — but that on our end we intend to talk to the bank in Aruba."

"What do you hope to gain?"

"An ally," Ava said finally. "The best I can do with the bank is freeze the account. I won't be able to get the money released to us and the other creditors without a court order or instructions from the trustee, so I want the trustee on side. I want to lay the groundwork to make him willing to go to the bank and lay claim to the funds."

"Have you thought of hiring a lawyer here?"

"Why do you ask that?"

"From my experience, regardless of what you tell them, Timmerman is not going to be that willing to listen to me. I'm a bit too…ex officio. A lawyer, on the other hand, would get their attention."

"Do you have someone in mind?"

"I do."

"Then hire them."

"It will be done as soon as I get back."

"Thanks, Jacob."

Ava closed her phone and turned to the computer. She punched in "Barrett's Bank, British Virgin Islands" and then wrote down the phone number listed on the website. There was no mention of Jeremy Bates on the site. He had been the branch manager when Ava had last visited for a job. Things had gone relatively well between them, but Ava had not only stood him up for a dinner date but also left behind two bodies — live, if slightly damaged — in the apartment she had been renting. Her hope was that he hadn't heard about the bodies, one of whom was a customer of his bank, a customer she had drugged and taped up and then forged his signature to get funds released from Barrett's back to her client. *There are so many reasons for Bates not to take my call*, she thought.

"Barrett's," a woman's voice answered.

"Jeremy Bates, please."

"And who shall I say is calling?"

"Ava Lee."

"Just one second."

The second became a minute and the minute became three. Whatever optimism she had began to fade. Then she heard, "Is this Ava Lee from Hong Kong?"

"It is. Thank you for taking my call, Jeremy."

"I have to say I'm surprised to hear from you again. You left us quite suddenly the last time you were here."

"Yes, I'm sorry about that," she said, struggling to detect disapproval in his voice. "It wasn't my choice."

"Are you here in Road Town?"

"No, I'm in Asia."

"Then this is business."

"Yes, unfortunately it is."

"Involving the bank?"

"Only in the most peripheral manner. It's a little bit complicated."

"Like everything else to do with you." He laughed.

Ava found herself smiling. "At least I'm never boring."

"You are most certainly not. Now this matter you're calling about, it concerns my branch?"

"No, the one in Aruba," she said. "I didn't want to call them directly, as I have no contacts there."

"So you're looking for an introduction?"

"I would actually prefer if you could call them for me."

"Really? That's a rather unusual request."

"This is a rather unusual situation."

"You obviously have some questions or some information you want me to pass along. Am I guessing correctly?"

"That's the general idea, but of course only if you think it's advisable. I do have to tell you, though, that if they exercise the same degree of prudence that I saw at your branch, I think they will appreciate having the information that has come to my attention."

"Another client playing games?"

"Not a client, but games certainly. One of our businesses has been a victim of fraud, and that's something I know Barrett's would not appreciate being implicated in, even at second or third hand."

"Explain, please."

"Well, my business partners and I are part-owners of a company in Sabah, Borneo, that manufactures furniture. We sold millions of dollars' worth to a Dutch firm that promptly declared bankruptcy and left us with nothing. The Dutch firm, we've discovered, was in league with a finance company in the Netherlands. Together they've cooked the books and doctored bank statements and are selling off the furniture and sending the profits to a numbered account at your branch in Oranjestad. We've hired lawyers and we're going to take civil action and try to have criminal charges brought. We're also in the process of notifying the bankruptcy trustee, but in the meantime a lot of our money is in Aruba. We just want to make sure it remains there while we resolve the legal issues."

"Do you have documentation to support your claim?"

"We do."

"Can you send it to me?"

"I'm working with an accountant in Amsterdam named Jacob Smits. I'll have him send you everything he has."

"Today?"

"Yes, I think that should be possible."

"Okay, I'll look at the information when it arrives and then I'll decide if I should get involved. As it happens, the Aruba branch is run by a colleague who is a very good friend, so it won't be entirely uncomfortable for me to call him on the matter. And you're correct, of course, that the bank is as sticky as ever when it comes to the ethics of our business."

"That's fantastic."

"I haven't made any promises, you understand. All I said was that I would look at the information."

"I wouldn't ask for any more than that."

"And to be clear, if I decide to make the call, all you're requesting is that the account be suspended pending —"

"Not suspended," Ava said quickly. "The account should remain active in terms of taking in deposits. What we're asking is that no money leave the account until the legal and bankruptcy issues are resolved."

"Understood."

She drew a deep breath. "Jeremy, I'm wondering, is there

any way you could take a peek into the account and tell me just how much of our money is already there?"

"Ava!"

"Please. We're close to thirty million U.S. dollars in the hole and they've been selling our inventory like mad for weeks. I just want to know how much money they've actually put away."

He hesitated, and she knew he was considering the request. "Please," she said again.

"You have the account number?"

She read it to him.

"Company name?"

"7793579 Aruba Inc."

His phone went to speaker and she heard the familiar clicks of a computer keyboard.

"The account has been open for only two months," he said. "The initial deposit was a hundred thousand euros, and since then... Well, over eleven million euros has been deposited — about fifteen million dollars."

"Any withdrawals?"

"Yes," he said. "It looks like close to five million dollars."

The number staggered Ava. This wasn't a commission deal — the money was probably being split three ways. The brothers were partners with the Dutch. "In a lump sum?"

"Bits and pieces."

"Wire transfers?"

"Yes."

"Sent where?"

"I don't think that's information I can share with you."

"Jeremy, the thing is, we believe that some former partners in our business here helped set up the fraud. We have no hard proof but we're working on getting it and have commenced legal action against them in the interim. All I need to know is the name of city — even the country — where the money was sent. It could help us eliminate them as suspects."

"This is rather irregular."

"But not precisely a meaningful breach of confidence. I mean, I haven't asked you what names are attached to the company or who has signing authority on the account."

"And please don't."

She heard the phone return to its normal mode and then the sound of Bates breathing. "The money went to Malaysia, to Kuala Lumpur," he said.

Those fucking brothers, she thought. "That's helpful to know. Thanks."

"Now the man who's going to send me the information, his name is Smits?" Jeremy said quickly. Ava guessed he was trying to deflect any more questions about the account.

"Jacob Smits. I'll contact him as soon as we're finished and give him your email address."

"Excellent. But as I said, no promises."

"Understood."

"And how do I reach you once I decide what to do?"

"Phone me," Ava said. "Or better, email me. I'll copy you on the note I send to Jacob so you'll have his address."

"And you have mine, of course."

"I do."

"How nice that you hung on to it. You know, if you're ever back in this part of the Caribbean..."

"You're the first person I'll call," she said.

Ava closed her phone, feeling quite pleased with herself.

She had sniffed out the money trail, and the connection to the brothers seemed to be clearer than ever.

She went into her email, found Bates's address in her contact list, and then wrote to Smits, copying Bates. Jacob, please send copies of everything you have with regard to the financial statements, bank accounts, and wire transfer, and an explanation of what you think occurred and how it occurred, to Jeremy Bates at Barrett's. He has kindly agreed to look at our documentation. If he thinks our position has merit, he's prepared to call Barrett's in Aruba to warn them that the account may be problematic. So please take the time to prepare a complete file. His email address is attached.

She sent the message and then leaned back in the chair. As she was giving her arms and back a good stretch, her room phone rang.

"Ava Lee."

"It's May."

"I was just about to call you."

"You sound livelier. Did your meeting go well?"

"Too soon to tell. I'm going to see them again in less than an hour. But we've had some very good news from the Netherlands."

"The trustee's changed his position?"

"No — we located the money. It's being sent to a bank in Aruba, a bank where I have some contacts. I'm working on making sure they can't withdraw any more funds until we tie down the legal side."

"That's great."

"About fifteen million dollars has been deposited, and five million has been wired in various amounts to a bank account in Kuala Lumpur. Looks like a three-way split."

"Profit-sharing?"

"What else could it be?"

"The money was sent to those brothers?"

"Probably, but I'm not completely certain. And before you get any more excited, you should know that I don't have an account number or a bank name to attach to the Malaysian account."

"It is those pricks. Who else could it be?"

"I think you should call our local lawyer; he needs to get onto this. There must be some way he can track the flow of money into that account. It would have originated from Barrett's Bank in Aruba. Here is the account number, and here is the company the account is registered to," Ava said.

"Repeat those numbers," May said. "I've just picked up a pen."

Ava recited them again and then said, "There has to be some kind of central record system in Malaysia for tracking incoming foreign currency."

"One would assume so, and if there is we'll get the information."

"So, not a bad day so far," Ava said

"No, not at my end either. The staff at the factory are quite capable and my young people have fit in very nicely. I'm optimistic about our chances of keeping the business intact, with or without the Dutch money. If we can get those funds back, then we're in really great shape. One good thing about a crisis like this is that it forces you to assess and re-evaluate every part of your business. I liked what I saw today."

"Any news from Hong Kong?"

"Not from my end."

"If I don't hear from Michael by tomorrow morning, I'm going to call. And I should probably talk to Jack Yee as well. By then I might have something constructive to say."

"Don't wait until then to call me. I'm going to stay up until you get back."

"Yes, Mummy," Ava said.

25

THE ESPLANADE WAS STILL BRIGHTLY LIT. MORE PEOPLE
were strolling along the boardwalk than earlier in the evening, the sea breeze pulling them there like a magnet.

Ava walked towards the statue of the swordfish, her mind cluttered with thoughts about Jacob Smits, Aruba, Jeremy Bates, Amanda, and the two brothers she was sure she would be confronting. In her old business, finding and collecting money that had gone astray was never personal unless the other party chose to make it so. Ava prided herself on her ability to be pragmatic, to focus on the job at hand and not be distracted by pettiness. She had been spat on, cursed at, and threatened with fists, knives, and guns more times than she could remember. Her initial response was always the same: *You stole the money. Now return the money and nothing else need happen.* She wasn't sure she could be so phlegmatic where Tambi and Mamat were concerned.

With the help of Jacob and Jeremy and May's lawyer, she knew she was going to find a path to the money. Every instinct she had honed over her ten years of working with

Uncle told her that the money in Kuala Lumpur was theirs, and that the brothers had earned it by undermining their sisters. Could she convince them to give it back? There wasn't much doubt about that. Could she convince them to implicate, in the clearest of terms, their Dutch co-conspirators? She could. She was, after all, dealing with cowards, with men who paid thugs to beat their own younger sister with a bat. But could she do all that without physically abusing them? She probably could, but the question was, did she want to?

She reached Fa Pang at just past eleven. The restaurant was dark. Ava looked down the esplanade in both directions. A few businesses had closed for the evening, but most were open. *They've run out on me*, she thought with a touch of panic.

She went to the door and peered inside. The owner was standing by the cash register, dimly lit by one overhead light. She rapped on the door. He looked towards her and waved. She relaxed.

"You close early," she said as he opened the door.

"My chief cook wasn't feeling that well," he said.

"Ah."

He turned and walked back towards the register. "They're waiting for you in the back room. Knock before you go in," he said over his shoulder.

She gathered herself at the door and then rapped three times. She heard a noise that sounded like feet shuffling. Then Wan's voice: "Come."

Ava opened the door and stepped inside. Wan sat at the table in the same chair, his aide Yu Fei by his side. She nodded and took two more steps. "Were you successful with your phone calls?" she asked.

"I have some information."

"And?"

He shrugged. "I also talked to some people about you."

"That couldn't have been too interesting."

"You have a reputation, huh?"

Ava glanced sideways. There were four other men in the room, two more than before. They stood in pairs on either side of her.

"Hey, pay attention, I'm talking to you," Wan said.

"I don't know what you mean by 'reputation.'"

"You're supposed to be a tough little bitch, handy with a gun and a knife, and some martial art."

"There have been times when I've needed to defend myself."

"Do you have a gun or knife on you now?"

"No."

He pushed his chair back, his feet dangling off the ground, his hands behind his head. "They told me the old man is ill."

"Who told you?"

"People who know. They say he has cancer and that you've been babysitting him."

"That's just gossip," she said. "Look, can we get back to the reason I'm here? Did you get my information?"

Yu Fei's eyes flickered to her left and Ava sensed movement from the men who stood there. She turned. A face leapt into focus. She thrust her elbow up and back, driving it into the tip of a nose. She heard it crack, and then a man screaming. The two men on her right had moved in close and were now almost on top of her. She took a step back and coiled, ready to strike.

"What is this —" she said to Wan.

She saw a smile cross his face as her right leg buckled. She collapsed onto the floor and then twisted to see a man with a bat, a bat whose end he had driven into the back of her knee. She struggled to get to her feet, but three men jumped on her, two of them pinning her arms as the third pressed a cloth against her mouth.

The last thing she remembered was hearing Wan say, "Make sure the bitch is out cold."

26

AVA WAS DREAMING OF HER FATHER. THEY WERE IN A
hotel and it was time to check out. He told her to collect
their bags while he paid the bill.

She saw him clearly, dressed in a suit, red Armani silk tie,
his hair slicked back, a wry smile on his face. She couldn't
exactly remember their room number but thought it was 3138.
When she got there, the door was open and the chambermaid
was vacuuming. She looked for their bags, then asked the
maid if she had seen them. The woman stared at her blankly.

The room was 1338, she thought as she rode the elevator
down. When she got to that room, the door was locked. She
tried the key she had and it didn't work. *Shit, he's going to
kill me*, she thought as she made her way back to the lobby.

She imagined he'd still be in line at the front desk, but
there was no line and there was no father. *He's getting our
taxi*, she thought as she approached the clerk.

"I've forgotten our room number and I need to get our
luggage," she said to the clerk.

"I need your name and some government identification,"
the clerk said.

"My name is Ava Lee."

"Identification?"

Ava reached for her bag but it wasn't there. She put her hand in her pants pockets. They were empty. "You don't know me? You don't remember me?" she asked.

"I need ID."

"Fuck you."

"Just one minute, miss, I think I need to call Security," the clerk said.

Ava looked through the glass walls and doors of the hotel entrance and saw her father outside. She yelled his name and began to walk towards him. Without looking back, he climbed into a taxi. She began to run. The taxi pulled away. The last thing she saw was his face in profile as the taxi turned left onto a street that looked like Hong Kong, but it could have been Bangkok, or Jakarta, or Manila.

She knew she was dreaming. These same events had visited her in the night countless times; the venues changed, the circumstances varied, but the dream always left her chasing her father. And they always seemed to come to her when she was travelling, when she was in a hotel room far from home. She tried to force herself to wake, to escape the sense of loss that was overwhelming her emotions. But this time her eyes couldn't open. Then she realized she wasn't in a hotel room, she wasn't in a bed, she wasn't lying under a down-filled duvet.

She was sitting on an armchair, her ankles taped to its legs and her wrists bound behind her back. She was blindfolded but not gagged. Her feet were bare and rested on a wooden floor. Then slowly she remembered how she'd got there: pain shooting down her leg as she fell to the floor, the cloth being pressed to her nose and mouth. Wan's last words came back to her, and she knew she wasn't in Fa Pang anymore.

There were voices in the background, mumbling, indistinct, and now she knew she wasn't alone. She strained to hear but her mind couldn't focus, distracted by the pain in her body. The chair was wood, and her tailbone felt as if it was balanced on a rock. Her leg muscles ached, her thighs were gripped in knots. And the back of her right knee throbbed, sending shocks down to her toes.

She began to shift her weight off her tailbone, flexing her glutes as gently as she could while still getting some kind of movement. When that discomfort eased, she started to work on her legs, moving her thighs from side to side not more than a millimetre at a time. Gradually the muscle knots began to unwind, but as they did, the pain in her knee became more intense. The bat had hit soft tissue, and she knew that at the least she had a deep bruise. She only hoped her ligaments and the kneecap itself hadn't been damaged. She slowly began to wiggle her toes, trying to tease muscle action up her calves.

"How long are we keeping her here?" she heard an unfamiliar, high-pitched voice say.

She took a slow breath. Either they were speaking more loudly or she was concentrating better.

"How the hell would I know?" another, a deep baritone, responded.

"The boss seemed excited."

"He thinks she's going to be a big payday."

"Shut up, you two," she heard Yu Fei say. At least she thought it was Yu Fei. She tried to picture him: close to six feet, lean, pockmarks on his cheeks, a wispy black beard, thin lips, and eyes that had looked at her as if she were a whore.

"We didn't hear you come in."

"How is the woman?"

"Hasn't moved."

"When she comes to, give her some water."

"Anything else?"

"What do you mean?"

"What if she has to piss?"

"She can piss where she is. You clean it up."

"Fuck."

"Just do what you're told. I'm going to meet Wan. He's been talking to the potential buyer. I'll be back this afternoon. Call me if there are any problems."

Ava heard a door close and she assumed Yu had left.

There was silence, as if the other two men were making sure he was truly gone. Then the higher of the two unknown voices said, "What buyer?" Ava decided to call him Squeaky.

"Whoever wanted the other two women fixed. Wan will want to see how much money he can get for getting rid of this one," the other one said. She named him Boom.

"And if there isn't any interest?"

"Wan has a way of making people interested."

"And if they don't want to pay enough?"

"Then he'll try to sell her back to her own people."

"And then?" Squeaky said.

"Then whatever. It isn't our decision. And these things usually end the same way."

"What a fucking waste."

"What is that supposed to mean?"

"She's pretty."

"You weren't saying that when she broke your brother's nose."

"She'll get hers."

A chair scraped across the floor. "I'm going to take a crap," Boom said. A door opened and closed.

Ava counted to thirty and then came alive. "Where am I?"

"Ah, wakey, wakey," Squeaky said.

"Where am I?"

"That is none of your business."

Ava moved around the chair and flexed her leg muscles as much as she could. "I don't need to be tied up like this."

"Not your choice, and not my choice."

"At least untie me a moment so I can stretch. My leg is killing me."

"No."

"The blindfold —"

"No, you're staying the way you are until I'm told to do something different."

She licked her lips. "I'm thirsty."

"Water I can do."

"Thank you."

She waited to hear him leave the room. Instead she heard the sound of water being poured from a Thermos into a glass.

"Here," he said, holding the glass to her lips.

His presence and voice jolted her. He had crossed the room without her being aware that he had moved.

She sipped, sliding water with her tongue over her lips. She took her time, and even then the water was gone too quickly. "Can I get some more?" she said.

"No."

"Please."

She heard what she thought was him placing the glass on the floor by her chair.

"Are those real?" he asked.

"What?" she said, feeling him close beside her.

His fingers began to unbutton her shirt. She twisted sideways. He grabbed her shoulder with his free hand to hold her in place. He reached into her shirt and down into her bra. "Nice," he said.

She spat in the direction of his voice.

"You bitch!" he shouted.

His hand left her chest and she collapsed back into the chair. Then she felt his hands coming over her shoulders — he had moved behind her. They shot down, grabbing both breasts and pulling them free from the bra. He cupped them at first, squeezing gently, but then his thumbs and index fingers moved to grip her nipples. He tugged at them and then rolled them between thumb and finger.

"I love big nipples," he said. "This is just a warm-up, sweetheart. You owe me. Actually, you owe my brother — he's the one you drove your elbow into. But he's not here, so I'm substituting. Keeping it in the family."

"Leave me alone or you'll be sorry."

"Not a fucking chance. I'm going to play with your tits, and then maybe I'll play with something else. The thing is, you're not going anywhere — at least, not for a while, and if I know Wan, probably never, so I'm not going to waste this chance."

Ava lowered her head, trying to calculate if she could drive it back into his chest with enough force to hurt him.

But then what? How would he react? It might make things worse. *No*, she thought as she coiled her neck, *I don't care how he reacts.*

Then she heard a voice yelling. "What the fuck do you think you're doing?" Boom was back in the room.

"She's awake."

"So I can see."

"She wanted water. I gave her a glass."

"And what? That gives you the right to fuck around like that?"

"I wanted to see if they were real. Look at them, they're fantastic."

"Do up her shirt."

"C'mon."

"Do it up or I'll do you up."

"Oh, what the hell," Squeaky said.

She felt him come around the chair to the front and gathered more spit in her mouth. She tried to gauge where his face might be.

"Do it," Boom said.

Ava felt his hands on her breasts again as he put them back inside her shirt but not in her bra. He closed two buttons, his face close enough to hers that she could smell breath that reeked of beer and cigarettes. She swallowed the spit.

"Your partner is a pig," she said to the air.

"I don't want you to talk," Boom said.

"But I need more water."

He went quiet and Ava thought he was ignoring her. Then he said, "How many glasses did you give her?"

"One."

"Give her another."

Squeaky stood over her and this time pressed the glass against her mouth, forcing her to gulp rather than sip.

"Now I need to pee," Ava said when he had moved away.

"Go ahead," said Boom.

"I want to go to the bathroom."

"No, if you pee, you pee there."

"I can't do that."

"That's your problem, not mine."

"What do think I'm going to do?"

"It doesn't matter what I think. I have my orders and I'm following them."

That's that, Ava thought, leaning back in the chair. *I should have known better than to go into that meeting room.* The dimly lit empty restaurant had been the first clue, the extra men the next, Wan's pointless conversation the third. She had made it so easy for them. Four months away from work and her instincts had deserted her. Now Wan and Yu were taking her to market. Until they closed a deal, they would keep her alive. After that — well, Boom and Squeaky had made that clear enough.

She had no illusions. She had been down this hostage/ransom path before, but on the negotiating side, trying to get her brother's partner released. The only reason he was still alive was that they had gone in after him and taken out the kidnappers. What had made that possible was that they knew where he was; they had time enough to get organized; and she had men she could call upon to help. If the brothers decided to pay to get rid of her, things would happen quickly. If they had to negotiate with May Ling, that at least would give her time, and if May Ling reached out to Uncle then they might have a chance of finding her. But then what?

One thing at a time, she thought. *Just think things through.* From what Yu had said about meeting Wan that afternoon, she guessed that it was morning and she had been missing for maybe twelve hours. May Ling would have looked for her at the hotel and, not finding her, would have taken some kind of action. Calling Uncle would be the most logical thing for her to do. And if she did — and she must have — then Uncle wouldn't have been idle. He knew the kind of man she was meeting with and would assume that things had gone badly.

He's already doing something, Ava thought. "Nothing is predestined," she murmured.

27

SOMETIME IN THE AFTERNOON — AT LEAST SHE SUP-posed it was the afternoon — she fell asleep. She wasn't sure how long she had been out, but when she woke, it was to the sound of Yu's voice telling the men they were going to be staying there at least overnight and that he was arranging to have some mattresses sent over.

The brothers didn't buy me, she thought instantly. May Ling was in play, or going to come into play, and that meant Ava had crossed her first hurdle.

"How about food?" Boom asked.

"It will come with the mattresses."

"What about her?"

"What do you mean?"

"Food."

"Give her some white rice and water."

"She hasn't pissed yet, and she keeps asking us to untie her so she can go...I mean, what can she do?"

"You saw what she can do when she took out your dumb shit of a brother. She stays there."

"Okay."

"Boss, do you have any idea how much longer this is going to take?" Squeaky asked.

"Why, do you have somewhere to go?"

"No."

"Another day maybe," Yu said. "The customer doesn't care what we do with her, so Wan contacted her partners this morning and started negotiating. It's going as fast as he can make it go, but the partners are asking for proof that she's still alive."

"How are you going to do that?"

"I'm sending a digital camera with the other stuff. Take some pictures and then give the camera back to the guy who brought it. We'll email the pix to them."

"Fine," Boom said.

"Hey, what happened to her shirt?" Yu asked. "Buttons are undone."

"Kang had a peek," Boom said.

"And?" Yu said.

"As good as I've ever seen," Kang said.

Ava heard chairs moving and then the shuffle of feet. She held her breath. She felt fingers loosen buttons and her shirt pulled back.

"They are nice," Yu said.

"Told you."

"But put them back in the bra and close the shirt. We want her to look tidy for the picture."

She felt clammy hands on her skin and tried not to react. Somehow the humiliation was lessened for her if they thought she was sleeping.

"Okay," Yu said. "Chin will be here in about two hours. I should be back here sometime tomorrow."

Ava heard the door open and close. She flexed her wrists. The tape was unyielding. Her legs had knotted again and her knee was throbbing. Her mouth was dry; she could feel her lips starting to crack.

"I would like some water," she said.

"She wakes," Kang said.

"Woman, did you hear Yu just now?" Boom asked.

"No."

"Well, there's some food on the way. Why don't you wait until it gets here? Then we can feed you and water you at the same time."

"I'm thirsty."

"And we don't want you pissing all over the floor."

"Then untie me and let me go the bathroom."

"You're a fucking pain in the ass with that. Don't ask again."

She had no driving urge to pee. There was some discomfort, but that was overpowered by her thirst. "I'm not going to wet myself. Some water, please."

This time it was Boom who brought the glass to her. "You're going to be here for a while, so get used to the idea."

"What's going on?"

"What do you mean?"

"Are they talking to my people about a ransom?"

"What do you think?"

"I think this is crazy."

"I'll be sure to tell my bosses."

"Look, I know you can't untie me, but could you at least take the blindfold off? It makes me feel claustrophobic... I can feel a panic attack coming on."

Boom paused. "Kang, what do you think?" he said.

"Makes no difference to me, but if Wan gets mad then it's on you."

"We'll take it off until the guy gets here with the camera. They'll want to see her full face anyway."

"Okay."

"Listen, woman, no promises after that."

"Thanks, and by the way, my name is Ava."

"I don't want to know your name," Boom said, slipping the blindfold over the top of her head.

She blinked, her eyes trying to adjust to what was nothing more than overhead tube lighting that struck her with the force of kliegs. She closed her eyes for a few seconds, opened them, and closed them again. She looked down at the floor, at her bare feet, not wanting to see her captors until she felt she had focus and control. She moved her right leg to one side and examined the back of her knee as well as she could. It was swollen, a mass of broken blood vessels visible through a patch of black and blue.

"Which of you hit me with the bat?" she asked, finally looking at them.

They were about thirty feet away, standing against a wall. They glanced at each other and said nothing.

Ava didn't recognize either of them from the night before. Boom was bulky and fleshy, probably in his thirties, a younger version of Wan. His face was round and small and his head looked freshly shaved, the skin slightly pink. He was five foot ten, Ava figured, and had at least two hundred pounds hidden under a roomy floral shirt and a pair of baggy jeans. She searched his arms for tattoos and to her surprise didn't find any. She looked up at his face again. He looked bored.

From his voice, she had pictured Kang to be small and scrawny, but he was at least as large as Boom, and where Boom was fat, he was all muscle. His upper body stretched a white T-shirt, and a pair of black jeans was tight around his thighs. His face was lean, and made to look even longer by his mohawk haircut. He had tattoos, and rings in both ears. He was smiling, his eyes flicking from her face to her chest.

She took in the room. It had a high ceiling, maybe sixteen feet, and formed a perfect square about forty feet on each side. It looked like a warehouse, and the furnishings — four wooden armchairs like hers, a card table with a radio on it, and an old brown leather couch that was slashed in places — looked lost in it. The walls were bare except for beige paint that was scraped and scarred as if pallets had been banged against them. The floor was covered with gouge marks, probably for the same reason, she thought. She looked down at it, trying to detect any signs of old blood.

"What's the time?" she asked.

"What does that matter?" Boom said.

"Does that radio work?"

"Stop fucking talking or the blindfold goes back on," Kang said.

"I'm going outside to make some phone calls," said Boom. "Do me a favour and stay away from her."

Kang shrugged and then reached into his back pocket and pulled out a pack of Marlboros. Ava watched Boom open the left side of the double door to leave. She looked past him and saw that the room she was in led into another that looked even larger and was equally as empty. It seemed they were in an abandoned warehouse.

Kang lit a cigarette, took a deep puff, and then started to walk towards Ava, a smile on his face. She turned her eyes away from him and tried to gather herself. He stopped ten paces short. Ava refused to acknowledge him.

He tossed the cigarette onto the ground and stepped on it. Ava sensed rather than saw his hand move towards his crotch and pull down his zipper. "Look at this," he said.

She shut her eyes.

"I'd like to give you some of it — in the cunt, in the ass, in the mouth. Maybe all three, one after another." He laughed. "But that's kind of hard the way you're tied, so I'll have to make do."

She felt him come near and shuddered. He was behind her before she realized it, and the now familiar sweaty hand reached down into her blouse. He pulled her left breast free from the bra and began to pinch the nipple with his left hand. She felt him pressing against her back, his other hand working his cock. She opened her eyes. His left arm lay across her chest. She twisted her head towards it. His wrist was beyond her reach, but the upper arm wasn't. She lunged, driving her teeth into him as deeply as she could. He screamed and tried to pull free, but Ava hung on until he struck her across the back of the head with his right hand. Her head slumped forward and she braced for another blow.

"You fucking bitch!" he yelled.

"Hey, I thought I told you to leave the woman alone," a voice roared from the doorway.

Ava looked up and saw Boom standing there.

Kang was still behind her. She heard him fumbling and guessed that he was putting things back where they belonged. "The bitch bit me," he said, and then he laughed.

He walked past Ava without a glance and went to the leather couch, where he lay down.

Behind Boom, the warehouse door opened and a third man came into the room. He wore jeans and a black T-shirt and had a shaved head. Ava recognized him from the restaurant the night before.

Kang sat up and went to join him at the card table, where he was emptying the contents of a paper bag. Even from that distance she could smell the food, and it triggered her appetite.

The new man opened a container of barbecued pork, another that held noodles, and a third that was filled with white rice, and finally he pulled a whole roasted chicken from a large sleeve. Boom walked over to the chairs and pushed them towards the table. The three men filled their plates and then sat and ate. None of them paid her any attention.

When they had finished, Boom and the new man left the room and returned a minute later, each carrying a mattress. They threw them on the floor near the couch. Kang lit a cigarette and said something to the newcomer. They both laughed and turned to look at Ava.

"You told me I would get some food and water," she said.

"In a minute. I want to get this picture out of the way," Boom said.

The three of them walked towards her, the newcomer holding the digital camera. They stopped only a few feet away.

"Look up at me and smile," he said.

Ava stared, her face impassive.

"Great," he said.

"Now one with those great tits front and centre," Kang said.

"No," Boom said.

"The boss won't mind. When did you get so fucking moral?" the newcomer said.

Ava closed her eyes and waited for Boom to assert himself.

Then she felt fingers on her shirt again, buttons coming undone, hands reaching inside her bra.

"Aren't they great?" Kang said.

She counted. At ten the newcomer said, "Look at that picture."

"Enough. You'd better get back to Wan, and back to business," Boom said.

"I'm done."

"Then go."

Her eyes still shut, she heard feet shuffle and the door open and close. Different hands slipped under her breasts and put them back in the bra.

"Sorry," Boom said.

28

THEY FED HER TWO PLATES OF WHITE RICE AND TWO glasses of water. Her appetite receded. Her thirst was slaked. The blindfold was pulled back over her eyes, and almost at once the need to pee began to occupy her mind.

"I have to go to the bathroom," she said.

"Then go," Kang said.

She did. The urine ran down the inside of both legs and poured over the middle of the seat onto the floor. She lifted her toes so they wouldn't have to rest in it. She was glad she wasn't wearing slacks.

"What a fucking mess," said Kang.

"There's a mop in the next room. Get it," said Boom. "I'll move her chair out of the way."

She heard Boom circle around her, trying to avoid the pool of urine. He grabbed the back of the chair and dragged it farther from the door. "You can put your feet down now," he said.

"Thanks. I'm not sure what I would have done without you."

"Don't make anything of it. I follow orders, just like Kang. I'm just not an animal."

She heard the mop swishing and Kang cursing.

"We're going to be lying down soon," Boom said. "We'll take turns so one of us will always have an eye on you. We're also going to leave the lights on, so don't think you can try any funny stuff in the dark."

"Like what?"

"Don't know. I'm just saying."

"What's the time?"

"Almost ten o'clock."

It was later than she had thought. In her mind, every hour out from the time she had been seized was a good thing. It had now been close to twenty-four hours. Somewhere, someone, somehow, was trying to get to her.

I should sleep, she thought. Emptying her bladder had actually relaxed her a bit, and the dampness between her legs and on her thighs was beginning to dry.

The radio crackled and she heard the softest hint of music. She strained to identify it but it was indistinct. Then, ever so slightly, the volume increased, and she heard the beautiful voice of Anita Mui singing the ballad "Drunken Dreams."

Mui was her mother's favourite Cantopop singer. Jennie Lee owned more than twenty of her CDs and listened to them endlessly, revelling in the ballads that mourned unrequited loves and bouncing around the house to her high-energy rock. Mui moved effortlessly between those genres, a complete singer, a complete entertainer, until her sudden death from cancer in 2003.

The song ended and was immediately followed by another Mui classic, "Bad Girl." The tune was incredibly catchy and Mui's voice was full of joy as she sang.

When it was over, the radio went quiet, and Ava thought they had turned it off. Instead, after a few seconds' break, she heard an announcer say that the evening's program was being dedicated to the work of the queen of Cantopop, Mui, and the king of Cantopop, Jacky Cheung. Mui was her mother's favourite; Cheung was Ava's.

The music began again and she heard the first bars of "Amour," an early and classic Cheung hit. Like Mui, he could switch back and forth between ballads and rock, and his voice was good enough that he sometimes ventured into operatic pop. "Amour" ended, giving way to "Smile," and then "In Love." Ava fell asleep somewhere in the middle of the song called "Goodbye Kiss."

She had no idea how long she slept, and for once she didn't dream. However much sleep she did get, though, ended in a shrill din of yelling voices and slamming doors. It startled her awake, and for a second she couldn't remember exactly where she was.

A lot of men were in the room and they were excited, talking over each other, more than a hint of fear in their voices.

Then Wan's voice cut through all the noise. "Shut the fuck up and wake her. And take off that blindfold. I need to talk to her."

She opened her eyes, the light piercing them as it had the day before. Seven men began to emerge out of the light. She saw Boom, the man she now knew as Kang, and Yu Fei sitting at the table talking on his cellphone.

"She's awake," Boom said.

Wan ran towards her, stopping when he was no more than three feet away. His face was distorted in anger, spittle gathered at the corners of his mouth. She leaned back, certain she was going to be struck.

"Why didn't you tell me you were connected to Xu?" Wan screamed, the spit flying in all directions.

Xu? Ava struggled to place the name and failed.

"Why the fuck didn't you tell me about Xu?"

"Why would I?" she said.

"If you had, none of this would have been happened," he shouted.

"I thought Uncle's name was enough."

"Get into this world," he said.

Wan stepped back and turned to look at Yu. All the other men in the room also seemed to have an interest in his conversation. Yu closed his phone and stared at Wan. "It's bad," he said.

"Hwang?"

"They caught five of our people at Fa Pang. Two died and the others talked, and that led them to Hwang. He was stupid enough to resist. They killed him and three more of our guys. They want to know where the woman is. They aren't taking 'I don't know' for an answer. We have to assume they know where we are, or will soon enough."

"How many of them?"

"A lot."

"What the fuck does that mean?"

"Two crews, maybe more. Twenty men, something like that."

"Fuck, fuck... Are you sure Hwang's people knew about this warehouse?"

"Even if they didn't, these guys aren't going to stop. They'll keep finding people, and soon enough they'll find someone who does."

"What a fucking mess," Wan said. He turned back to Ava. "You're the cause of all this, you bitch. Why didn't you tell me about Xu?"

"Does that matter now?" she said.

"What are we going to do?" Yu asked.

"I need to reach out to Xu, I need to negotiate some kind of truce," Wan said.

"We don't have much time."

"We'll go to Auntie Lin's house. That should buy us a few hours."

"Wan — hey, the woman is still alive."

"Thank God."

"And not hurt except for her knee."

"And being sexually assaulted by Kang," Ava said.

"What?" Wan said, spinning away from her, searching for Kang.

"I just looked at her tits," he said.

Yu grabbed Wan's elbow. "We can deal with that later. Right now we should be on the move."

Wan pointed to Boom and the man who had brought the food. "She's coming with us. Put her out again and then untie her. And be careful. We don't want to hurt her in any way."

Boom went to the couch and took a rag out of a paper bag that sat next to it. He poured a clear liquid into it.

"That isn't necessary," Ava said.

"Do it," Wan said.

Boom approached her with the rag. Her normal instinct was to resist, but this wasn't a normal situation. When he put the rag to her face, she breathed deeply. She felt a smile come to her face and a question pounding in her head: *Who is Xu?*

29

THE WOMAN'S HAIR WAS A MASS OF GREY CURLS framing a round, soft face. Her two hands held one of Ava's, stroking the back of it. She smiled. "You are such a pretty girl."

Ava was in a bed, the covers pulled up and one arm outside, in black silk. She sat up. She was wearing a black silk mandarin jacket, closed at the neck.

"I washed you myself," the woman said. "The jacket and pants are my daughter's. She's almost exactly your size."

"Thank you."

"And I put ointment and a light bandage on the back of your knee."

The room was big enough to hold a double bed, a dresser, and the chair that the old woman sat in. The door was no more than six feet from the foot of the bed. It was closed, but Ava could hear familiar voices on the other side.

"Are you Auntie Lin?"

"How did you know?"

"Wan said he was coming here."

"Yes, I am Auntie Lin."

"What time is it?"

"Eight."

"In the morning?"

"Yes."

"How long have I been here?"

"Four hours."

The voices rose. Wan seemed panicked. Yu was telling him that things were going to work out, but his voice was full of worry.

"What are those men to you?" Ava asked, pointing at the door.

"Yu is my sister's son. When she died, I looked after him until he found a job. It was for less than a year, but he never forgot and has looked after me ever since."

"You know what he does, right?"

"We can't always choose the paths our lives take."

Ava started to climb from the bed, but the old woman blocked her path with her body.

"I want to talk to them," Ava said.

"No, please don't try. They asked me to make sure you stayed here until the other men came."

"What other men?"

"The Shanghai men."

"Men are coming from Shanghai?"

"No, the men are here already, in KK. Wan told them just about ten minutes ago where my house is. They should be here soon."

Ava closed her eyes. She wanted to pray. She normally knelt when she prayed, but the old woman seemed determined to maintain her position, so she prayed sitting up in the bed. She prayed to Saint Jude, the patron saint of lost causes, to thank him. She had prayed to him many times when she needed help. This time, at the warehouse, she hadn't; she wasn't sure why. Perhaps she had thought it was too much to ask of him. But he had been there for her anyway, unbidden.

When she was finished, she looked at the old woman. Her head was lowered as if she was trying to give Ava privacy.

"Auntie, how do you know about the Shanghai men?"

"I heard them talking."

"When they did, did they mention the name Xu?"

She nodded.

"Is Xu here in KK?"

"I don't think so. I think he's in Shanghai," she said, and paused.

"What else?"

"Wan is afraid of him."

"How do you know that?"

"When Wan was talking to him, he was almost kowtowing."

"What did you think when you heard him?"

"That he was a man who was very afraid, a man who isn't ready to die."

A cellphone rang in the other room. Ava shushed the old woman and listened. Yu said, "Yes," three times and then, "You're only a few minutes away. The house is painted white with a red door. There's a black van parked outside."

"Your friends are almost here," Auntie Lin said.

"I don't know who they are."

The old woman looked at Ava. "Then who are you, for them to do this thing?"

"I think I'm a friend of a friend."

Someone knocked at the bedroom door. "Yes?" Auntie Lin said.

"Auntie, wake the woman now. We need to have her with us," Yu said.

"She's awake already."

"Bring her out."

The old woman moved to one side, motioning for Ava to climb down from the bed. Ava's left leg went first; her right followed, the knee stiff and aching. She winced.

"I'm not a doctor, but I don't think the damage is long-lasting," Auntie Lin said. "It's a very bad bruise but I was able to move your leg around when I washed you and put on the ointment."

Ava sat on the side of the bed, swinging the leg sideways and then back and forth. Gradually it began to loosen, the pain backing off or at least becoming bearable.

"Okay," she said, sliding to the floor. "Let's go see them."

The bedroom door opened into what Ava assumed was the living room. A couch, an easy chair, a coffee table, a hutch filled with photos, a large-screen television, and eight men filled it to capacity.

"You okay?" Wan said.

"My leg is sore," Ava replied.

"Sorry."

"I don't believe you."

"Xu's men will be here in a minute. You'll be going with them," Wan said, and then paused. "I don't want you to hold any grudges."

"Are you crazy?"

"It was just a mistake on my part, a bad judgement based on bad information."

"Just?"

"I'm sorry."

"You're only sorry because of Xu."

"I didn't know you were connected to him."

"So that's why you felt free to kidnap me?"

"I told you, it was a mistake."

She stared at the other men. Yu stood just behind his boss. Boom was leaning against a wall; Kang was next to him, trying to look invisible.

"Your man Kang, he molested me. Was that a mistake too?"

"We'll look after him when this is over."

"I'm not sure I believe you."

"What did he do except look at your tits?"

"His filthy hands were all over me while he was masturbating."

Wan looked at Kang. "We'll take off his right hand."

"That's all?"

"What else do you want?"

Kang went pale. He whispered something to Boom.

"I'm going to think about that," she said.

"Whatever else you want," Wan said. "I don't want you to hold any grudges."

"I'm not sure that's possible," Ava said.

Yu stepped alongside his boss. "I also want to apologize for any bad behaviour on the part of me or my other men."

Ava searched the room. "Where is the man who took the pictures?"

"He was with Hwang. He's dead," Yu said.

"And Ma said that he didn't approve and did what he could to stop him and Kang. If that isn't the case —" Wan said.

"Who is Ma?"

Yu pointed to the man whom Ava had called Boom.

"No, he was okay," she said. "I owe him my gratitude."

Boom turned his eyes to her and lowered his head in thanks.

"Is there anything else that we can do —" Wan began, and then stopped when the door crashed open.

Sonny Kwok filled its frame. In three steps he was in front of her. She looked up at him and said, "I'm all right."

Behind him, eight other men edged into the room. Sonny was dressed in his usual black suit, white shirt, and black tie. The others were in dress shirts and slacks. Several had shaved heads but none had a mohawk or an earring, and the only visible tattoos she could see were discreet.

"This is Suen," Sonny said, pointing to a man who had to be six foot six. "The others are his crew. There's another crew in the city, mopping up." He stared at Wan and his men. "Which is Wan?"

"I am," Wan said from the back of the room, where he was partially hidden by Yu.

Sonny moved so quickly that Yu was thrown against a wall as he was shoved aside. Wan retreated but Sonny caught him almost instantly, grabbed him by the throat, picked him up, and slammed him against a wall. He suspended him at eye level. "Ava, what do you want me to do with him?"

"Nothing right now. I need him," she said.

He continued to hold Wan against the wall, his hand squeezing. Wan gagged, his feet flailing in mid-air.

"Sonny, let him go," she said.

Yu took one step forward before coming to an abrupt

halt as Suen laid an arm across his chest. "Don't interfere," Suen said.

Sonny stared hard at Ava, then nodded and threw Wan to the ground.

"Xu said that if we returned the woman unharmed, this would end," Wan said through his gasps.

"Are you really okay?" Suen asked Ava.

"I'm fine."

"Then I'm going outside to call the boss to tell him," Suen said.

"What about our men here?" Yu said. "Are they free to go?"

"No one moves a muscle until I get back," Suen said.

Ava looked at Sonny. His mouth was drawn tightly, his jaw muscles clenched. Ava knew the signs. He wanted to hurt someone and was just waiting for an excuse. "I don't have a phone and we need to call Uncle to let him know that I'm safe," she said to him.

His eyes swung towards her, and she saw his rage turn into the same pain and confusion that had been there the last time they had met.

"Is he okay?" she asked quickly.

He shook his head.

"What's going on?" she said.

"He's in Hong Kong."

"So?"

"Going to Shanghai was too much for him. By the last day there I could tell he was worn out, weaker than I've ever seen him. Then, when he found about you, it was as if whatever was holding him together gave away."

"But you got him back to Hong Kong."

"Only because Xu arranged to fly him back by private jet, with a doctor and a nurse."

Ava froze. "He needs to know that I'm okay."

Sonny nodded. "We can phone the hospital."

"Do it. Do it now."

"Ava, he might not be able to take the call."

She felt her stomach contract. "If they won't let you talk to him, leave a message and tell them it's urgent that they give it to him."

"It would be better if you spoke to them."

"Call."

"Yeah," Sonny said, reaching into his jacket pocket.

"And we need to get there as fast as we can."

"We flew here from Shanghai on another private jet, a big one. Xu said we could use it to go to Hong Kong if things worked out here."

"What about these other men?"

"They'll drop us off and then go on to Shanghai."

"I might want some of them to stay here for a few days. I don't want to leave May Ling without support."

"I'm sure that can be arranged," he said, and then handed her his phone. "It's ringing."

Ava followed the prompts and reached patient information. She asked for Chow Tung.

"He's in the palliative care unit in R Block. There's no phone in his room," the operator said.

"Can you connect me with the nursing station?"

"Just a moment."

"Yes, I'm calling about Chow Tung," she said when the connection was made. "Can you tell me how he is, please?"

"He's resting."

"No, I need to know how he is."

"I'm sorry, Miss, but I'm not allowed to give out that kind of information over the phone. You need to speak to his doctor."

"Doctor Parker?"

"Yes, that's the one who's listed."

"Is he there?"

"No."

"Do you have a phone number for him?"

"I'm afraid not."

"Okay, thanks. I'll get it myself."

"Yes, you'll have to do that."

"One more thing, my name is Ava Lee and I'm his friend. He's been worried about me. I'm coming to Hong Kong later today to see him. Do you think someone could tell him that, that I'm coming, and that I'm well? It's important for him to know."

"I will do the best I can."

"What do you mean?"

"He's not communicative at present."

"What —"

"Miss, I can't discuss his condition in any more detail. Please call Doctor Parker."

She closed the phone. Sonny was staring at her. "Is it bad?" he asked.

"Yes, but I have to call Doctor Parker to find out how bad. Do you have his number?"

"No."

"Call Hong Kong information and get it for me."

"Okay."

Ava turned to Wan. "Where are my phone and my shoes?"

"They should be at the restaurant."

"Send one of your goons to get them."

"They won't get near the restaurant," one of Suen's men said.

"Why not?"

"We disposed of some of his men there. It was noisy, and messy. The cops are sure to have been called in. They'll have the place secured by now."

"Well, I need to get to my hotel and I need some shoes."

"My daughter wears a size close to yours," Auntie Lin said from the bedroom doorway. Ava wondered how long she had been standing there, what she had heard.

"Thanks," she said.

"I have Parker's number. I'm dialling it now," Sonny said.

She looked at Wan. "I want you to call the brothers."

He looked at Sonny and then finally turned to her with a mixture of confusion and fear crossing his face. "What brothers?"

"Tambi and Mamat, the brothers of Chi-Tze, one of the young women you arranged to have beaten up in the restaurant parking lot."

"I didn't arrange that," he said quickly. "It was done through my man Hwang. I knew nothing about it until it was over."

"I don't care what you knew or didn't know. Call the brothers."

"But why?"

"They paid your man Hwang."

He shook his head. "No, they didn't."

"Then who did?" Ava asked, searching his face for the lie.

"The woman."

"What woman?" Ava asked.

"The sister. The one named Ah-Pei."

30

THE SHOCK JOLTED AVA'S BODY, AND SHE KNEW THAT her face had to be registering the same surprise. "How do you know it was her? I mean, how do you know for certain?"

"Hwang told me."

"Hwang was killed, wasn't he?"

"Yes, he's dead, and probably so are the two men he sent to do the job," Wan said.

"So how am I to believe what I'm being told?"

Wan shrugged. "I talked to her yesterday; I talked to her about you. I asked her what she wanted us to do with you."

"And what did she say?"

"She wanted to know if we'd mentioned her name. When I said no, she said we could do whatever we wanted. You were no concern of hers."

"Ava, excuse me," Sonny said. "Parker's phone is ringing."

Ava took Sonny's cell from him and turned her back on Wan. The phone rang four times and went to voicemail. "Shit," she said, and left a message asking him to call her on Sonny's phone. "We'll be in Hong Kong later today. We'll go directly to the hospital."

Suen reappeared at the door. "The boss sends his regards."

"I'm sorry, but you might have to phone him again. Sonny and I need to get to Hong Kong today, and I don't want to leave my friend May Ling Wong alone here. Can you provide her with some men for a few days?" Ava said.

"Sure, and I don't have to call Xu. How many do you want?"

"Four?"

"Not a problem."

"Thanks."

"Now what about this bunch?"

"I need Wan and Yu."

"We made a deal with Xu," Wan said.

"Relax. All I want you to do is make a phone call and set up a meeting," Ava said.

"The woman?"

"Yes, the woman. Tell her to meet you in the lobby of the Méridien Hotel in an hour — no excuses for not being there. If she doesn't want to come, tell her you'll go to her office or her house. I want you to greet her when she arrives at the hotel, and then you can leave and get on with the rest of your life."

"Okay."

"Do it now," Ava said, and then turned back to Sonny. "Have you spoken to May Ling?"

"Not since we landed. She knows we're here, that's all."

"I'll call her from the bedroom."

As Ava turned to go, the pain in her knee flared and she stumbled. She pressed a hand against the wall and steadied herself. Common sense told her to see a doctor, but that would have to wait until she was in Hong Kong. She limped into the bedroom.

May's cell hadn't completed one ring before Ava heard her voice. "Sonny, is she all right?"

"May, it's me and I'm fine."

"Thank God, thank God, thank God. I've been so crazy with worry."

"When I got past twenty-four hours with those creeps, I thought I might be seeing Sonny, but I didn't expect him to arrive with an army."

"All I knew was that he's here—he called me when he arrived. I have no idea who's with him or what's been going on, though the hotel lobby was all abuzz this morning about gunfire in town. They made it sound like war had broken out."

"Close enough."

"I waited up for you the other night, as I said I would. By midnight I was starting to get concerned and I thought maybe you had forgotten to call me. I went to your room and then down to the lobby to ask if they had seen you come back. When they said no, I parked myself there to wait. By two I was seriously paranoid, so I called Uncle in Shanghai and told him what was going on. He tried to call the contact he'd given you here but couldn't get through. We kept in touch for the rest of the night. By seven he said he'd decided to send Sonny and was making arrangements. Then I got a call from the furniture factory saying that a guy had phoned looking for me. He said it had something to do with Ava Lee. He wouldn't leave a number, just said he'd call back in fifteen minutes. I told them to give him my cell number when he did. They did, and he called me."

"How did he know who you are? How did he know to ask specifically for you? I never gave them your name."

"I just assumed you had."

"No matter. What kind of deal did he try to cut?" Ava asked.

"He wanted a ransom. I told him that I thought we'd pay but I had to consult with my other partners. He gave me an hour to make a decision."

"How much did he ask for?"

"A million U.S. dollars."

"Which partners did you talk to?"

"Just Uncle."

"You didn't mention anything to Ah-Pei?"

May Ling paused, and Ava knew she had been caught off-guard. "No. Uncle was the only one I considered talking to."

"Of course."

"I have never heard him so upset. He could barely speak at first. He said the man he was meeting with — someone called Xu — had offered a plane to bring Sonny to KK and was organizing a squad of men to send with him. He told me to stall for as long as I could. He told me to ask for pictures, and when I got those, and if they were okay, to tell them it would take us some time to pull together that amount of cash."

"When did the men leave Shanghai?"

"After I got the pictures confirming that they had you and that you were still alive."

"How many pictures?"

"Two."

"Who saw them?"

"I had arranged to have them emailed directly to me. I sent only one to Shanghai."

"Thank you."

"Uncle seemed distraught enough already."

"He's in Hong Kong now. He's taken a bad turn."

"Ava, I'm so sorry."

"I want to get there today, but first we need to wrap up our business here."

"Don't think about business."

"No, we need to finish this thing in KK and with those thieves in Holland. I'm at a house somewhere in the city. I'm going to head to the Méridien in a few minutes. Can you meet me there?"

"I'm there already."

"May, did you get a chance to speak to the lawyer about the money that was sent from Aruba to Malaysia?"

"Yes, and his contacts have been able to track it. It was a very clear trail that led to a numbered account."

"Is there a name attached to the account?"

"Yes — Song, the brothers' family name."

"Was there a first name?"

"No, just the initials C.C. That surprised me a bit because the brothers' names are Mamat and Tambi, but when I asked the lawyer, he said the account had been in place for more than twenty years and until the past month had been dormant for about three years. I assume it was the parents who set it up."

"That seems logical. And as for the recent activity, I don't think it had anything to do with the brothers."

"What?"

"As hard as this may be to believe, I think Ah-Pei was responsible for the attack on the girls. And I think it's Ah-Pei who cut the deal with the Dutch."

May Ling gasped and then went silent.

"I know it sounds absurd," Ava said, "but the guy who told me has no reason to lie. In fact, he has every reason to tell me the truth."

"Why?" May said. "Why would she do something like that? *How* could she do something like that? It's... unthinkable."

"Those are questions we can ask her ourselves. I've arranged for her to be at the Méridien in about an hour."

"To meet with us?"

"No, she thinks she'll be meeting with the people she hired to act for her."

"Oh my God."

"May, I want to find out the truth and then I want our money back. That's where our day with her will start and end."

"If she doesn't co-operate?"

"She will," Ava said. "One more thing — call the lawyer again; he should be on standby for us. Once she comes clean, we'll want it in writing and videotaped. I want something we can use against the Dutch. I also don't want to give her any chance to change her story later when she has to face her sister."

"The police?"

"There's no need for them, except as a threat. Her life is going to be ruined — that's punishment enough."

"And the business? What do we do about that? We can't let her stay involved."

"That's a subject for another day. Can your Chiks hold the fort until we make a decision?"

"Of course they can."

"Good. Then let's leave it at that and take some time to consider our options. Now let me get myself sorted out here."

"I'll wait for you in the lobby."

"Just be discreet. I don't want Ah-Pei to see us until we're ready for her."

"I understand."

Ava came back into the living room. Wan and Yu were sitting on the couch and Sonny was leaning against the wall next to them.

"Did you talk to her?" asked Ava.

Wan nodded. "She'll be at the hotel."

"What did you say to her?"

"I told her there were big problems and that we had to meet."

"Did she have any questions? Did she ask about me? Did she ask if I had been ransomed, or shot?"

"No questions."

"So she readily agreed to meet with you."

"There was some resistance, until I stopped asking nicely. I scared her."

Ava turned to Suen. "How many cars do we have?"

"Two."

"Can I catch a ride to the Méridien Hotel with Sonny?"

"Sure, if someone tells me where it is and how to get there."

"Do you have a car outside?" she said to Wan.

"Yeah."

"Drive it to the Méridien. We'll follow."

"I'll send a couple of men with them, for company," Suen said.

"Thank you. Now there's one more thing I have to do before we leave," she said to Sonny. "See that scum over there with the mohawk? Put him against the wall."

Kang managed to take a step towards the door before Sonny reached him, picked him up, and slammed him against the wall where he had held Wan, his right hand gripping him by the throat.

"Lower him so his feet almost touch the ground, and then move to one side," Ava said.

Sonny let his hand slide down slowly.

Ava limped towards them. She put her right hand against Sonny's shoulder for balance and then drove her good left knee into Kang's groin. The groan turned into a gargle as Sonny squeezed his throat. Ava kneed him again.

She looked into his face. His eyes were half-open, and Ava thought she saw a hint of mockery in them. She stepped back, the memory of his hands on her breasts becoming more vivid. "Fuck you," she said, her right hand forming a phoenix-eye fist. "Now you can look exactly like your brother."

Sonny didn't let go of him even as blood from Kang's shattered nose spurted over the sleeve of his suit.

"We can leave now," said Ava.

Sonny loosened his grip and Kang fell to the floor, groaning and curling into a fetal position.

"You don't have any shoes," Sonny said.

Auntie Lin appeared at the kitchen doorway. She held a pair of pink flip-flops in one hand, a plastic shopping bag in the other. Ava walked over to her. "Your clothes are in the bag," the old woman said.

"Thanks for these, and for your kindness," she said. "I'll

return the shoes and the clothes you loaned me."

"There's no need. And besides, I want to ask for a favour."

"What?"

"My nephew, he isn't that bad a man."

"Then he should take on a different line of work. Nice guys aren't that good at it."

31

BY AVA'S RECKONING SHE HAD BEEN ABSENT FROM her world for about thirty-six hours. The last thing she had done before her second meeting with Wan at the restaurant was tell Jacob Smits to send the information he had to Jeremy Bates at Barrett's Bank. That seemed a long time ago.

She had given Sonny back his phone; now she asked for it again. She called her own number and accessed her voice messages. Three from May, each increasingly panicked; one from Maria, wondering she hadn't called; and one from Jeremy Bates saying he had received the information from Smits. He didn't say what he thought of it or what he had done with it. It was far too early to call to find out.

Ava and Sonny were in the back seat of the car. Suen and one of his men sat in the front. Ava had spoken only Mandarin since arriving in Kota Kinabalu, but now she switched to Cantonese. "Sonny, who is Xu?"

"He runs Shanghai."

"I assumed that, but how does Uncle know him? From the old days?"

"Xu's father was from Wuhan. He and Uncle were close when they were young."

"Ah."

"Xu came to Hong Kong about a year ago. I don't think Uncle had met him until then. He might have heard of him, but I don't think he had met him."

"What did Xu want?"

"I don't know. They always meet privately."

"Always?"

"After the first visit, Xu came to Hong Kong often. And twice — before you came back to look after him — Uncle went to Shanghai."

"What kind of man is he?"

"I don't know."

"Sonny, you have eyes and ears."

"I picked him up once at the airport in Hong Kong. I've seen him in Shanghai twice, and the only real time I've spent with him was when he and Uncle were discussing what to do about Wan."

"Describe him as best as you can."

Sonny looked doubtful and then said, "Well, he's young — still in his thirties, I think. He's quiet, respectful towards Uncle. He looks and behaves like a man who has an education."

"What do you mean by that?"

"He's very well-spoken. I've never heard him curse, and the only time I heard him raise his voice was when he saw how devastated Uncle was about your situation. He swore to Uncle that he'd get you back and that Wan would pay for his stupidity."

"His men don't look like typical triads."

"That's his doing. He likes them to look like regular citizens."

"And him?"

"The same. He looks quite ordinary, like a businessman, a professional of some kind."

"He can't be that ordinary."

"I mean the way he looks. He's obviously some kind of operator. His men worship him."

"Sonny, how many men died here today?"

"I'm not sure, maybe six or seven. I know Suen's crew took out three. Xu said that if you were harmed, all of them had to go. He said if you were well, Wan could live. But even then, only if that was your choice."

The Méridien appeared on their right and Wan's car turned into the driveway. Suen looked back at them. "Do you want us to come into the hotel with you?" His face was impassive, but Ava saw a gleam in his eye that hinted he might have understood the conversation she had just had with Sonny.

"Please. You need to meet May Ling Wong," she said. "And we should make sure that Wan continues to understand his position."

They pulled in behind Wan, who stopped his car in front of the hotel and tossed the keys to the valet.

"Do the same," Suen said to their driver.

Ava hadn't taken more than ten halting steps into the lobby before she saw May Ling hurrying across the floor. They hugged, Ava's head pressed against her friend's shoulder. "Don't make me cry," Ava said.

"Why not? I am," May said.

The men stood around them uncomfortably.

When the women finally separated, Ava said to Suen, "This is May Ling Wong."

He bowed his head.

"May, Suen is going to leave some men here for as long as you need them."

"Is that really necessary?"

"Until things settle."

"I guess there's some sense in that," May said, and then smiled at Sonny. "It's good to see you again."

"Yes. I only wish the circumstances were different."

"Me too."

"I'll be glad to get her back on the plane to Hong Kong."

Wan and Yu were off to one side, Suen's man standing next to them. "You wait here until Ah-Pei arrives," Ava said to Wan. "When she does, have Sonny call my room, and you sit with her until we're ready to talk to her."

"What should I say?"

"Whatever you want that doesn't include my name."

He nodded, without much conviction or enthusiasm.

"Now I'm going to go to my room to shower and change."

"Do you want me to go with you?" May asked.

"No, thanks. I think I could use fifteen minutes by myself. Why don't you wait in your room? I'll call you the moment she arrives," Ava said, and then remembered she didn't have her room key.

She was walking to the front desk when a sense of déjà vu enveloped her. She tried to place its source. And then the dream she'd had after they chloroformed her — the dream about her father — came rushing into her head. She reached the desk and smiled at the clerk. "Excuse me, my name is Ava Lee. I have a room here but no room key, and the bag containing my ID is upstairs," she said, just as she had in the dream.

"You're Ms. Lee?"

"I am."

"Do you want one key or two?" the desk clerk said.

I guess this isn't a dream, Ava thought. "One will be sufficient," she said.

The room was as she had left it, although it looked as if the orchid on her pillow had been replaced by a fresh one. She was completely naked under the black silk jacket and pants. As grateful as she was that Auntie Lin had cleaned her up, she felt almost nauseated at the idea of someone — anyone — washing her body while she was unconscious. Then there was Kang and his greasy hands. She shivered. *This isn't the time to think about what has been and what might have been*, she told herself.

She undressed and then removed the bandage around her knee. There was slight swelling on both sides. She pressed the kneecap and felt nothing. The back was a mess: a rainbow of black, blue, and yellow interspersed with broken blood vessels.

She climbed into the shower, turned the water pressure as high as it would go, and set the temperature close to scalding. As the water battered her, she imagined it removing every trace of Auntie Lin and Kang. She turned her body away from the water, letting it pour over the back of her knee.

She towelled herself off and then put on some ointment she had in her own case and wrapped the knee with a fresh bandage. Auntie Lin was probably right about the extent of the damage, but that didn't stop it from hurting like hell.

She dried her hair, pulled it back, and fixed it with the ivory chignon pin. She had worn the pin to the meeting with Wan, and somehow it had survived. She had left her other jewellery in the room, and now she put it on, finding security in its familiarity. The Cartier watch. Her crucifix. She put on a white Brooks Brothers shirt and secured the cuffs with her green jade links, and then she slid on a pair of black linen slacks and her black Cole Haan pumps. She was applying some mascara when her room phone rang.

"Ava, the woman is here. Wan is talking to her," Suen said.

"I'll be right down," she said. She phoned May's room. "She's here. I'll meet you downstairs at the elevators."

She started towards the door and then noticed her computer was on. She went to it, accessed her inbox, and found a long list of messages. One caught her eye: it was from Jeremy Bates. She opened it.

Ava, I received the information from your man Smits. It is all very compelling. I spoke to my colleague in Aruba, and though it does cause him concern, he isn't sure it gives him sufficient legal reason to deny a withdrawal request from the parties who control the account. He's asked us—you, actually—to provide him with something that has some binding legal teeth. In the meantime, he's promised that he'll inform me if any withdrawal requests are made. Sorry, that's the best I can do.

Ava replied, Thanks for the try. You should have what you need in the next few days. Tell your man it would be wise for him to stall if the account holders try to move a lot of money. She paused, reread her last sentence, and then deleted it. It sounded too much as if she was threatening the bank. Besides, she would have Ah-Pei under control soon enough, and the Dutch were probably happy enough to leave their money in what they thought was a secure location.

May was standing where the hotel lobby connected with the banks of elevators. The two women walked into the lobby side by side. It was more active than when they'd left. A line of people was now waiting to check out, and a knot of people at the door surrounded by luggage looked as if they were ready to check in.

Ava could see Sonny and Suen sitting together on a couch, staring off into the distance. She followed the direction of their eyes. In the farthest corner, in an alcove, Wan sat in a chair, his face visible. Across from him she saw the back of Ah-Pei's head, her straight black hair just reaching the nape of her neck.

"There they are," Ava said to May, pointing to the alcove. "Let's visit."

"I'm nervous," May said. "I don't know why, I just am."

"It will pass," Ava said.

Wan started to stand up as soon as he saw May and Ava crossing the lobby floor. Ah-Pei turned. When she saw her partners, her mouth gaped and then her hand flew over it.

"I meant to ask you, did you reach the lawyer?" Ava asked.

"He's on standby."

"Great."

As the women neared, Wan moved to one side as if he was getting ready to leave. "Wait a minute. You need to tell Ah-Pei what you told me," Ava said.

He shrugged and stared at Ah-Pei. "I told them that you hired our men to beat up those women," he said.

"Thank you. And now you can go."

Ava looked down at Ah-Pei. Her hands were trembling, her head was lowered, and there were tears streaming down her cheeks.

Wan left quickly, not looking back. He was halfway across the lobby when Suen stepped in front of him. He took Wan by the elbow and guided him towards the couch where he and Sonny were sitting. Ava knew they wouldn't let him leave until her business was done.

"I'm Ava Lee, and this is my partner May Ling Wong," she said. "We just wanted to introduce ourselves again."

Ah-Pei pressed her arms together, burrowed her chin into the top of her blouse, and sank deeply into the chair.

"Look at me," Ava said.

Ah-Pei shook her head. "I can't," she whispered.

Ava stood over her, reached down, and took hold of her chin with both hands. "You can't avoid this," she said, forcing the woman's head up.

Ah-Pei's eyes finally met Ava's. They were red, and the skin around them was puffy and etched with small lines.

Ava took the chair that Wan had vacated and May took the one next to it. Ava pulled hers closer to Ah-Pei until their knees almost touched.

"You were expecting something like this when Wan called?" Ava said.

"I didn't know what to expect. I just knew it wasn't going to be good," she said, lowering her eyes again.

"Look at me," Ava said.

"I didn't mean —" she began, and then the words were overtaken by deep, wrenching sobs.

Ava thought she had seen every response of thieves

and thugs to getting caught. Most of them — nearly all of them — started with denial, and then when the facts became clear, they would veer off into various combinations of bluster, threats, and elaborate justification. When those didn't work, the next stage was attempts at silence, which Ava always had ways of breaking, or violence, which she could manage as well. But as she looked at the woman across from her, she knew that none of those things was going to happen. Ah-Pei had already capitulated, collapsed, and the challenge would be how to calm her enough to tease the story from her. Talking about her sister was not the way to begin.

"We know about the money," Ava said softly. "We know about the bank account in Aruba, and we know about your bank account in Kuala Lumpur. What we don't know is whether your brothers were involved in this scheme. Were they?"

"No."

"We had assumed they were. It made sense that it would be them, grabbing a bit more money on their way out the door."

"They were happy with what they got. Why wouldn't they be?" Ah-Pei said, her voice wavering but clear.

"You mean they got all that money that they'd never really earned?"

"Yes."

"So they had no involvement at all, not even in putting together the sales contract?"

"Jan told them what he wanted. They were too obsessed with getting their buy-out money to care what it meant for the business."

"Jan de Groot?"

"Yes."

"You and he were...familiar?"

Ah-Pei lifted a finger to her mouth and chewed at the cuticle. Her eyes wandered. She seemed distracted, as if she was struggling to dig up a complicated memory. Then she shivered. "We had sex."

"You were lovers?"

"I wouldn't call it that."

"Then what would you call it?"

"We had sex. Whenever he was here, and the few times I went to the Netherlands. The rest of the time there was nothing going on between us."

"You weren't friends?"

"Maybe. I don't really know and I didn't really care. I had my needs. He was willing and able enough."

"I see."

"I'm thirty-four." Ah-Pei's voice was stronger now. "From the time I was seventeen I worked full-time in the business, six or seven days a week, ten to twelve hours a day. I don't remember having a holiday that was more than a long weekend. My sell-by date for finding a man here went past without me noticing," she said, and then passed her hand across her chest. "The first time, I forced myself on him."

"But he came back for more."

"He said he liked my enthusiasm."

"That's a strange word."

"It's the word he used. I didn't mind."

"Was it de Groot who suggested that you help him cheat your own company?" Ava asked.

Ah-Pei's head fell forward and Ava knew it was easier for

her to talk about sex than money.

"I want to know whose idea this was," Ava persisted.

"It was Jan's," she said, her voice cracking.

"How did that come about?"

"Do I have to?"

"Yes, you do. And I should tell you now that, after you're finished here with us, May will be taking you to our lawyer to repeat the entire story."

A look of panic came into her eyes and Ava realized she might be close to scaring her into silence.

"Ah-Pei, listen to me," Ava said, placing a hand on her knee. "We're going to get our money back from you, and from the Dutch. That is what this is about. We need to know why things happened. But as for what it means for you and your sister...well, I'm not sure that's for us to decide. So talk to me about the money."

"The police?"

"If we wanted to involve them, you would be talking to them right now, not us."

Ah-Pei drew a deep breath and then sighed. "The idea was Jan's, but I might have set it in motion," she said. "When Chi-Tze began to talk about buying out our brothers, I liked the idea at first. Then, as we got close to finalizing the deal, I began to think about how much money they would be getting and the kinds of lives they would have. I didn't think it was fair, that it was right."

"Because you built the business?"

"Me and my parents."

"And Chi-Tze?"

"I love my sister — even if it doesn't look that way — but she's the baby of the family and has always been treated differently. When I left high school, there was no talk about university; I went right into the business. For Chi-Tze it wasn't just university; it was a university abroad, and then it was graduate school abroad. My parents spent hundreds of thousands of dollars on her education. Her contribution to the business didn't come close to what had been spent. Maybe it would one day, but maybe not."

"The money spent on her was money you had earned?"

"Money I helped to earn."

"You resented them all? Your brothers and your sister?"

"Sometimes. Not always, but sometimes."

"So what was in it for you to sell us part of the business?"

"I'd be rid of my brothers, I'd be able to hire some capable people to replace them, and I'd have access to working capital. I can't tell you how many times we ran out of money over the years. Growing a business when you're undercapitalized isn't any fun."

"When did that plan change?"

"You mean when did I decide to keep some money for myself?"

"I mean when you decided to steal some money for yourself and Jan de Groot."

"And Meijer too. He was Jan's partner."

"Answer my question, please," Ava said.

"Jan was here in KK," she said. "We were at my house. I told him we were going to sell off part of the company. He asked me why and I told him I was fed up with my brothers, that I was tired of carrying the load for everyone. He didn't say much right away, but the next night he came back to the subject and started asking me a lot of questions."

"About the deal?"

"Yes, and about you and Ms. Wong."

"What did he want to know?"

"How much money you were putting in and how much you had behind you."

"Ah."

"Yes, he had things figured out quite well. He said it was a crime that my brothers should get such a big payday and that my sister, with her MBA and her connections with you, would probably end up running the company, while it was I who had made it all possible for everyone. He said it didn't have to be that way. He said there was a way I could be properly rewarded for what I had done."

"Aside from the illegality of it all, it didn't concern you that his scheme might put the company entirely out of business?"

"Jan said that because of all of the money you had already put in, you wouldn't let that happen...He was right."

"Yes, he was right," May Ling snapped.

May had been so quiet that Ava had almost forgotten she was there. Now she turned to her friend and saw in her firmly set jaw and steely eyes that Ah-Pei shouldn't expect even a shred of sympathy.

"The way he explained it to me, I thought it was a good plan. Everything would be done legally, he said, and we would be protected by the bankruptcy laws."

"What he didn't factor in is that Ava is very clever at finding money that has lost its way, and when she finds it, she doesn't let things like Dutch laws stop her from recovering it," May said.

Ah-Pei shook her head and slumped deeper into the chair. Ava, sensing that her confession had used up most of her emotional energy, quickly pressed another button. "Why did you hire those goons to attack your sister and Amanda?"

"I didn't."

"Bullshit."

"It's true. All I said was that I wanted to throw a scare into them. Hwang misunderstood me."

"How did you find a man like Hwang?"

"My father used him years ago to help collect bad debts. I remembered him and was surprised to find that he was still alive and in the same business."

"And why did you want to scare the girls?"

"Because of her," Ah-Pei said, looking at May.

"What do you mean?"

"She hired that lawyer to go after my brothers. I didn't want her to, but she wouldn't listen. They aren't even here; they're in Thailand with their wives. When they heard about what was going on, the charges that were being levelled against them, they freaked out. Mamat called me to find out what was behind it all, and I explained about de Groot declaring bankruptcy. That freaked him out even more, because he thought you might try to claw back the money you'd paid them. He said that I was the one responsible for the contract, and if anyone should be blamed it should be me. He also said he knew that de Groot and I were sleeping together, and that if I didn't call off the lawyer he'd make sure everyone knew."

"Did he know that you and de Groot pulled off this scam together?"

"Mamat may be lazy but he isn't stupid. I think he at least suspected something."

"And you didn't want him talking to May, or to our lawyer."

"That's right."

"And you thought that if you frightened the girls, they might go to May and ask her to back off?"

"That was the general idea. I thought that if the three of us went to her it would be hard for her to say no."

"So what went wrong?"

"I don't know," she said, her voice cracking again. "They were supposed to just yell at the girls and tell them that if they kept making false charges through lawyers, people would start getting hurt. I never wanted anyone to actually get hurt."

Ava sighed. "The trouble with using goons is that they're goons for a reason. They usually don't have the brains to hold down any other kind of job."

"I haven't slept since that night," Ah-Pei said in a rush. "I keep thinking about Amanda and Chi-Tze when I saw them for the first time at the hospital. I'd give anything to take all this back."

"Well, for starters, you're going to transfer the money that's sitting in Kuala Lumpur back into the company accounts," Ava said.

"I will."

"And then you're going to go with May to see the lawyer. You'll tell him everything you told us, and you'll answer any other questions he has."

"Yes, I will."

"Have you been in contact with de Groot?"

"No."

"Good. Keep it that way. I mean it — if he suspects there's

even the tiniest problem, everything I said about not involving the police will be reversed."

"I understand," Ah-Pei said.

"May, is there anything else you want to add?"

"Stay away from the office," she said, leaning forward and jabbing her index finger into Ah-Pei's knee.

Whatever composure Ah-Pei had left dissolved in a trail of tears.

"I'll have someone pack your things and send them to your house," May said, and then sat back. "Unfortunately there may be occasions when we need information or some help. When that need arises, one of my people will call you. I expect you to be one hundred percent co-operative. Otherwise I expect you to do nothing, absolutely nothing, that will interfere with the supply chain or the customer base."

"I would never do that."

"A week ago I'm quite sure you didn't think you'd cause so much damage to two young women," May said.

Ava stood up. Recrimination was pointless. At some point Ah-Pei would have to deal with her sister and brothers and Amanda, and it seemed obvious that the time between now and then would be painful enough. "May, when can the lawyer see you?" she asked.

"Whenever we want."

"I have to go upstairs. I'm going to email Jacob Smits, with a copy to you, and tell him what's going on here. When you finish with her at the lawyer's office, send everything you have to Jacob. He can take care of things on the Dutch side. Now I need to get to Hong Kong."

"I know. I'll look after things here."

"I'm so sorry," a small voice said.

Ava looked down at Ah-Pei. "What I don't understand is how you could tear your family apart like that. What else do we have in this world that we can rely on? If we don't have family, we have nothing. That's how I was raised, and I can't imagine you were raised any differently."

Ah-Pei stared at the ground.

Ava left the two women and limped towards Sonny and Suen. They leapt to their feet as soon as they saw her coming. "I'm finished here. I'm going upstairs to pack. How soon will the plane be ready to leave?"

"I'll call the pilot now," Suen said. "It shouldn't be more than an hour."

"May is taking Ah-Pei to the lawyer's office. Can you send someone with them?"

"Choo will go," Suen said, motioning to the man who had driven them to the hotel.

Ava made her way to the elevator. As the doors closed she looked back and saw that May and Ah-Pei had joined the men. Ah-Pei posed no threat of bolting, or of doing anything else, for that matter. She would do exactly what Ava had told her to do. So would May. So would Jacob. *Now*, she thought, *if only I had any control over what's going on in Hong Kong.*

32

THE PLANE WAS A TURBOPROP MODEL, A FAIRCHILD-
Dornier 328, that could seat thirty-two passengers. Ava,
Sonny, and sixteen men from Shanghai were on board. The
men sat together at the front. Ava sat alone in the back row.
She had kept Sonny's phone, and she checked it every ten
minutes for a call from Parker.

Ava turned on her laptop but couldn't get an Internet
connection. She pulled out her notebook and updated it
with the activities of the past three days. She was doing it
out of habit, as a way to kill time. When she finished, she
turned to the back of the book and, almost without thinking, began to make a list of things she had to do in Hong
Kong. Seeing Uncle's lawyer was a priority, if only because
Uncle had made such a pointed request.

She had a copy of his will. She hadn't wanted it but he
had been insistent, and then he had made her sit next to him
while they read it together. It was simple enough. Lourdes
inherited the Kowloon apartment and Sonny the car, and
both they and Uncle Fong were left some cash. Everything
else went to Ava.

"We're about half an hour out from Chek Lap Kok," she heard a voice say.

Suen stood several rows in front of her, as if afraid to invade her privacy.

"Thanks. I didn't know the airport took private planes."

"We'll land at the Business Aviation Centre; it's tucked into a corner of the airport. The immigration people will come on board to check our papers. When that's done, you can disembark. I had the pilot phone ahead and arrange for a limo to meet you at the plane."

"Thanks again."

"Give Uncle our best regards."

"I will."

"Our boss thinks the world of him."

"Yes," Ava said.

They began to descend just five minutes later. Ava looked out the window as they cleared the clouds and the South China Sea became visible. How many times had she looked out on that view? A hundred, maybe two hundred, maybe more? When Uncle was gone, what reason would she have to come back to Hong Kong? In her mind they were interlinked; she couldn't think of one without the other.

As they got closer to the airport, the sky ahead of them darkened. Rain began to pelt the windows and the plane began to rock in the wind. She saw some of the men shift uncomfortably in their seats. It was strange, the different things that generated fear in people.

They landed and then taxied for what seemed like ten minutes before stopping on the tarmac in front of a long, curved two-storey glass building. Ava saw a small group of people leave the building and run towards them, umbrellas pointed straight ahead. The pilot came out of the cockpit and opened the plane's door. Two immigration officers entered.

"Who's getting out here in Hong Kong?"

"We are," Ava said, pointing to Sonny.

"Follow my colleague here into the terminal. The rest of you, I need to see your papers."

Ava gathered her bags. Sonny took the heavier one from her and led her towards the exit. "Goodbye, and thanks," she said to Suen.

Holding a large umbrella, a young man in a raincoat waited at the foot of the stairs. He held it over Ava and then led the way into the terminal. Within minutes they were through Immigration and had entered the baggage area. They walked almost directly into a limo driver holding a sign that read MS. LEE. "Do you have any bags to collect?" he asked.

"No."

"So where am I taking you?"

"The Queen Elizabeth Hospital in Kowloon."

"The car is right outside."

Ava checked the phone again as soon as they were inside the limo. Still nothing from Parker. She tried his number again, and again it went to voicemail. She phoned Uncle Fong. He wasn't answering either. Then she phoned the Kowloon apartment, thinking that Lourdes was sure to be there. She let the phone ring until she heard Uncle's voice-message prompt.

It was verging on rush hour, and with the rain and the wind Ava was afraid they would be caught in a mess of traffic. But the limo coasted over the Tsing Ma suspension bridge and edged into Kowloon. Traffic in the city was slower; it took them another twenty minutes before the sprawling hospital complex came into view. By then it had stopped raining, and when the limo ran into a wall of traffic about two blocks from the hospital, Ava told the driver to pull over and let them out.

"Do you know which building we're supposed to go to?" Ava asked as she and Sonny started to walk.

"R Block."

"You're sure?"

"Yes."

They climbed the steps into R Block, Ava leading. She was starting to move towards the reception desk when she see saw a familiar figure leaving an elevator.

"Doctor Parker!" she shouted.

He took two steps to the side and stopped, searching the hall for the voice's origin. When he saw her, he lifted his chin ever so slightly. What she thought was surprise on his face turned into something that chilled her to the core.

"Ms. Lee," he said.

She felt her knees weaken.

Parker took several steps towards them. "Ms. Lee," he said.

She saw that his lips were moving but she couldn't hear him. Her legs buckled. She would have collapsed onto the floor if Sonny hadn't been gripping her arm.

33

THE FUNERAL HOME WAS IN FANLING, A NORTHERN suburb in the New Territories. Uncle had chosen it because it was only a kilometre from the cemetery in Wo Hop Shek, where he had chosen to be buried.

When he had explained the arrangements to her, Ava had asked, "Why Wo Hop Shek? Why Fanling?"

He had owned the plot, he said, for more than forty years. He was just starting his first gang then, in Fanling, and there had been a lot of opposition. He decided it would be prudent to plan for the worst, so he bought the plot. He had looked in Hong Kong and Kowloon, but even then land was being sold by the square inch and hardly anyone was buried anymore. Even finding places to put ashes was a challenge. And anyway, the idea of being cremated didn't appeal to him then, and it did so even less now. The plot at Wo Hop Shek Cemetery had given him peace of mind.

The funeral home came to collect his body late that Saturday night, after Dr. Parker had completed the paperwork. They placed Uncle in a silver-coloured basket-weave container that was to transport him to Fanling. He had bought a new suit—black, of course—and a new white shirt and new shoes a few months before. Lourdes sent them from the apartment to the funeral home so he could be dressed quickly in clothes that represented the start of his new life.

The reception at the funeral home would be brief, as Uncle had requested. It was scheduled for between eleven a.m. and three p.m. on the Tuesday. There was no embalming. Uncle had wanted a closed casket, so as soon as he arrived in Fanling he was dressed in his new suit and laid in a steel coffin with the traditional three humps.

Sonny, Lourdes, Uncle Fong, and Ava had decided that they would maintain a vigil at the funeral home. They split the time into six-hour shifts. Ava took the first and the last. Sonny drove her to Fanling on Saturday night so she would be there when his body arrived. She had been on the phone for most of the evening, talking to her mother, her sister, Maria, Mimi, her father, and May Ling. Both her mother and Maria wanted to come to Hong Kong. Ava discouraged them. The timing was tight, and the truth was that Ava wasn't sure she could handle the additional emotional pressure they would bring.

On Sunday morning she went back to the Queen Elizabeth Hospital to see Amanda. Her sister-in-law's room wasn't in R Block, but simply being at the hospital sent tremors through Ava's body.

She hadn't told them she was coming and didn't know what to expect, so it was with some trepidation that she walked into the private ward. There were two beds in the room. One was empty. In the other, Amanda lay on her back, a string of tubes running from her arm. Her head was bandaged diagonally, the right eye almost completely covered.

Ava approached the bed. Amanda's left eye and what she could see of the right were closed. Ava sat in a chair beside the bed and reached for her hand. She had been sitting quietly for five minutes, maybe longer, when she heard a sound at the door. She turned and saw Michael.

"Hey," he said.

"Maybe I should have called," she said.

"No, I'm glad you came."

He walked towards her. She stood, wincing as her knee reacted to the change of position, and reached up. They clung to each other.

"I heard about Uncle," he said when they finally separated.

"I knew it was just a matter of time, but it turned out that no time was ever going to be right."

"I'm sorry."

"And I'm sorry about Amanda. How is she?"

"Better — at least, better than she was. She fell asleep just about half an hour ago. She's been awake and alert, which is a blessing. She's concussed, but there doesn't seem to be any brain damage. The orbital bone will knit just fine, they think, although she'll probably have some kind of scar above the eye."

"Thank God."

"That's what Jack Yee keeps saying. You just missed him. We're taking turns sleeping in the other bed."

"He left a note for me in Borneo."

"I know."

"When you see him, tell him we got the person who did this."

Michael closed his eyes. "He'll be happy, but you know you can tell him yourself. He plans on going to Uncle's funeral."

"That won't be the place, or the time. Please do it for me."

"I will."

"And do me one more favour: don't come to the funeral yourself. You and Amanda have just got married. I don't want to bring any more bad luck into your lives by letting you attend a funeral. I know that's superstitious, but I believe it all the same."

"So does Jack, and so does my mother. So don't worry, I won't be going."

Ava turned towards Amanda. She leaned over and kissed her on the forehead. "Tell her that I was here. Tell her that May and I love her and worry about her and are praying for her."

"I will."

34

ON TUESDAY MORNING, THE DAY OF UNCLE'S FAREWELL,
Ava arrived at the funeral home at five a.m. for the final
vigil and for final inspection of the room they would be
using. It was long and narrow, and Uncle's coffin was
placed on a raised platform at the far end. It wasn't common for the coffin to be visible at a Chinese funeral, but
he wanted it that way and gave no reason. In front of it,
on an easel, was a large photo of him that was a particular favourite of Ava's. He was seated outside a restaurant,
wearing his black suit, his shirt done up to the collar. He
was leaning forward, a cigarette burning in one hand,
his eyes locked onto the person taking the picture. What
Ava loved about it was his eyes. They were so alive, so
alert, so full of intelligence — and, Ava thought, so full
of warning. He had been a complex man. The photo did
him justice.

Around the coffin were a circle of white candles and a
second circle of incense sticks. The candles would be lit
before people started arriving. The incense was for the
guests to light if they chose.

It was traditional for the family to sit on one side of the room and the guests to sit on the other. The funeral home director had suggested that, given the small size of Uncle's "family," they forego the tradition. Ava had to intervene before Sonny took the man's head off. So there were four chairs to the right of the coffin with Ava, as his closest "relative," sitting next to it to receive guests. A hundred chairs were set up to the left, though they doubted they would need that many. As it was, the four chairs would be only partly occupied, because Sonny and Uncle Fong would be standing at the door to welcome the guests and give each of them a white envelope that contained a small white towel, a candy, and a coin. The towel was to dab away tears. The candy represented something sweet in a time of bitterness. The coin was for the guests to take away, to buy something sweet when memories of the deceased came to them.

The guests themselves would bring white envelopes with money for the family. The amount in each packet would come to an odd single number, normally achieved by a bill plus a small coin. Just as the double number eight, so prevalent at Amanda's wedding, represented happiness, the single number was meant to represent a one-time occurrence.

The plan after the visitation ended was for the hearse to drive the kilometre or so to the cemetery. Ava, Sonny, Lourdes, and Uncle Fong would walk behind it, and any of the guests who chose to do so also were welcome.

At six o'clock Ava changed into her mourning clothes: a plain white skirt and a white tunic made from burlap. The top had a hood that she would wear from the time the first guest arrived until Uncle was buried. Sonny was already dressed in a thin surcoat of sackcloth over a white gown;

he had a white band tied around his forehead. Uncle Fong would be dressed identically.

During her vigil, Ava had avoided any close contact with the coffin; it still seemed unreal that it contained Uncle. It wasn't until she arrived that morning and saw the photograph and the chairs set in position that it began to take hold that he was gone.

"Sonny, do you think you could leave me alone for a little while?" she said.

"I'll go and talk to the funeral director about the wreaths. There are only three set up here, and I know more were sent."

"You do that," Ava said.

When she was alone, she took an orange and some money from her purse and approached the coffin. She knelt and placed both at its base. Then she lit an incense stick and pressed it between her palms. And then she prayed. She prayed to God, to every god, to any god who would listen. Her Catholic god, the Buddhist god, the Taoist god.

The man she had known was a gentle, generous, loving, and thoughtful man. Whatever deeds he had committed before she met him were unknown to her. All she knew was a man who had done immeasurable good, who had saved businesses, saved families, saved so many poor souls from ruin. *Please see him as I saw him*, she prayed. *Please accept him into whatever eternity there is.* Tears welled in her eyes and she found herself unable to continue. She remained there in front of the coffin, on her knees, silent, the incense stick burning down to its base between her palms.

She had no idea how long she had been there when she heard Sonny say, "Ava, I'm sorry to disturb you, but we have a problem."

She pushed herself to her feet. Sonny stood at the entrance of the room with the funeral director, who was looking alarmed. "What is it?"

"Wreaths. We have too many wreaths," Sonny said.

"They started arriving late in the day yesterday and they just kept coming," the director said. "We've filled our storage room and then some. I've never seen so many whie chrysanthemums."

"How many are we talking about?"

"At least eighty, and they're still arriving."

"They'll fill this room. We won't have space for a single chair," Sonny said.

"How many funerals do you have going on here today?" Ava asked the director.

"Only this one."

"And how many other rooms do you have?"

"Three."

"Put five more wreaths here; that will give us four on either side of the coffin. Then put some in the foyer — it's large enough — and the rest in one of the empty rooms. I'll pay for any extra space we're using."

"Do we need to transport them to the gravesite as well?" the director asked.

"Yes," Ava said. "Rent a truck, do whatever you have to do, but if people thought so well of Uncle as to send him flowers, the least we can do is make sure they're placed either on or somewhere near the gravesite."

"It will cost —" he began.

"Just do whatever you have to. I'll pay," Ava said.

When he left, Ava turned to Sonny. "Who is sending all these wreaths?"

"I looked at some of the cards. You have a lot of former clients."

"That's true enough. It's nice that they remembered."

"And many of the societies."

"What do you mean by 'many'?"

"I saw wreaths from at least nine or ten gangs in the 14K Group and a couple from the Wo Group. Also the Big Circle Gang, the Tung Group, and a huge one from one of the mainland Sun Yee On gangs. The only ones larger were from Changxing and May Ling Wong and Xu."

"How did they find out about Uncle's funeral?"

"I know he wanted it to be more private, but it was silly of him to think that word wouldn't get around in an instant."

Ava looked at the hundred chairs they had set up for guests. "Sonny, do you think we have enough seats? What if everyone who sent a wreath shows up?"

"That's not likely, especially with the triads."

"Still, we have to expect that some will come. And there might be more ex-clients than we imagined, so maybe we should ask for another hundred chairs. This room can hold two hundred."

"Okay, I'll go talk to the guy."

"Better to be prepared for more rather than not have enough."

"I know," he said, and then hesitated.

"What is it?" she asked.

"I forgot to tell you that Uncle Fong has hired a funeral band. He did it without asking me. They'll walk with us to the cemetery. That is, if you don't mind."

"Do I have a choice?"

"You could say no."

"Would Uncle have liked a band?"

Sonny smiled for the first time in days. "Yes, he would have liked a band."

"Then I guess we have a band."

While the funeral home staff came in to set up more chairs, Ava retreated to the foyer. Wreaths now covered every wall, and she thought it looked splendid. She opened her Chanel bag and took out her phone. She had turned it off the night before, when she went to bed. There had been a number of calls.

Her mother and Maria had left messages saying that she and Uncle were in their prayers.

Her father said he was coming to the funeral with Jack Yee.

May Ling had called to say that she and Changxing had arrived in Hong Kong. Then she had left a second message an hour later. Jacob Smits had taken Ah-Pei's confession, both written and on videotape, to Meijer, hoping to coerce him into voluntarily returning their money. Meijer had refused. So Smits, with May Ling's approval, had gone to his police contacts with the information he'd acquired earlier and the confession. He was quite confident that charges would be laid.

Smits had also given the entire package to the bankruptcy trustee and spent several hours going over it with him. May had just been informed that the trustee had contacted the bank in Aruba and asked them to freeze the account until the legal issues surrounding the bankruptcy were resolved. It was going to take some time, but meanwhile Ah-Pei had returned the money from the Kuala Lumpur account.

One way or another, their investment would be restored. But at that moment it couldn't have mattered less to Ava.

The door of the funeral home opened. Lourdes, dressed in a white skirt and blouse, with a white scarf tied around her head, stepped tentatively inside. Uncle Fong followed. Ava turned off her phone and put it back in her bag.

Lourdes had been crying almost nonstop since Uncle had died. The funeral director had said to Sonny that he had never heard louder wailing.

"She has a lot to grieve," he said.

She now seemed to have cried herself out, although her eyes were shot through with red. Ava said, "I prayed at the coffin by myself this morning. If you like, we can stay out here and you can have some quiet time with him as well."

"I can't pray anymore."

"Then let's go inside and sit. The guests will be here soon enough."

Lourdes stared at the wreaths. Sonny and Uncle Fong circled the foyer, looking at the condolence cards that accompanied them. Ava took Lourdes by the arm and joined the men. There were flowers from her father, Jack Yee, Simon and Jessie To, Tommy Ordonez and Uncle Chang in the Philippines, Soeprapto and his father in Indonesia, the Wo Group from Tsuen Wan, 14K from Guangzhou, and Chi Hsien Pang in Taiwan. And there was an immense wreath from Andrew Tam, a former client whose own uncle had been one of the men who swam from China with Uncle. As she read the card, she noticed Uncle Fong eyeing her.

"What is it?" she said to him.

"Sonny told me you approved the band. I'm very happy about that."

"I guess I am too. I should have thought of it myself and I didn't. Thank you for being so considerate."

Ava and Lourdes went back inside. The extra chairs on the guest side made the family side look even emptier. Ava didn't care. Uncle had always respected tradition, and she wasn't about to dishonour this one.

Lourdes sat with her eyes closed and her lips moving. Ava assumed she had found another prayer and sat quietly next to her, lost again in her own thoughts.

At ten o'clock Sonny and the funeral director barged into the room. "We have another problem," Sonny said.

"What is it this time?"

"People have already started to arrive. They're beginning to crowd the entrance."

"Crowd?"

"There must be fifty or sixty already, and they're nearly all triad. They're coming from all over. Uncle Fong says there are some very senior people among them, including the head men from Taiwan, Malaysia, and Los Angeles, he thinks, though he's less sure about that."

"Well, we did put in these extra hundred seats."

"It's just that we have a very small courtyard, and we can't have people standing in the street," the director said.

"What are you suggesting?"

"That we open our doors early."

"How early?"

"Now."

Ava looked at Sonny, who just shrugged. "Then let's do that," she said.

When they turned to leave, it occurred to her that there might be one more problem. "Tell me," she shouted after them, "do we have enough white envelopes if we have two hundred guests?"

"I have boxes of them," the director said.

It took them five minutes to lay out on the tables the first batch of white envelopes that Sonny and Uncle Fong would distribute. The candles around the coffin were lit, and Lourdes began to sniffle again.

Then the door to the room opened and the guests began to enter. Ava and Lourdes remained seated, their heads bent towards the floor. Then Ava heard the first man greet Sonny. His name was Wing, and he identified himself as being from 14K Sai Sing Ton. He approached the coffin solemnly and stopped directly in front of the Uncle's photograph. He bowed three times, his head reaching his knees, the tattoos on his neck visible as he lowered his body. Then he turned to where Ava and Lourdes sat. He bowed again, just as deeply, but only once. Ava lowered her head in acknowledgement.

For the next hour they walked in at a rate of about two a minute, bowing three times for Uncle and once for Ava and Lourdes. The early arrivals were nearly all triad, from major groups such as 14K, Wo, Sun Yee On, and Luen, but they also represented a broad spectrum of local gangs from places such as Mong Kok, Tai Po, Tsim Sha Tsui, Macau, Sheung Shui, Shenzhen, and Guangzhou. Some had worked for Uncle. Some had worked alongside Uncle. Some had been colleagues of equal rank, at least until he became chairman. As they identified themselves at the door, Sonny and Uncle Fong helped her classify them by addressing them by title or relationship.

Not many of them spoke to her, and those who did were the senior ones, the gang leaders. Most of them seemed uncomfortable around her and mumbled their condolences.

A few referred to her by name and let it be known that they had heard of her exploits with Uncle.

They were all hard men, rough around the edges and dangerous looking even when they had no visible scars, missing fingers, or tattoos. Still, with Ava they were unfailingly polite, and as they bowed to Uncle she saw in their faces a respect that verged on veneration. It was, in a way, unsettling. Her relationship with Uncle had existed mainly outside his previous life. Trying to connect the man she had known with the one who had been tough and ruthless and shrewd enough to make his way to the summit of the worldwide triad hierarchy seemed impossible and improbable, despite the fact that she knew it was true.

Partway through that first hour, with people lined up at the door all the way back through the foyer and into the courtyard, Uncle Fong came to Ava's side. "I thought this might happen, but I didn't want to say anything," he said. "Uncle was so respected..."

"By so many people," Ava said.

"And more to come, and more bands."

"How do you know that?"

"They're telling me. At least three of the societies have hired bands."

"You had better go and help Sonny at the door," Ava said, beginning to feel overwhelmed by this triad outpouring.

Ava had been holding up reasonably well emotionally. She didn't know the triads; they didn't represent any memories or emotional connections to Uncle. But she began to falter when Carlo and Andy walked into the room together just past eleven o'clock. They were triad too, but Ava had worked with them several times, including in Las Vegas and during the Macau raid. Both of them were friends who had shown extreme loyalty to her. They had been equally devoted to Uncle. She watched as they marched side by side up to the photo and bowed so low their heads almost touched the floor. When they turned towards Ava, she saw that Andy, who was small and wiry like Uncle, had tears running down his cheeks. She had to fight back her own.

Andy tried to speak. All he could get out was, "Boss..."

Carlo, the more confident and assertive of the two, said, "There will never be another man like him."

"Thank you," she said.

"And you know that whatever you need —"

"I know. Thanks to both of you," she said, her voice cracking.

Then the former clients began to arrive. Ava couldn't remember all of them clearly because Uncle had managed the direct contact part of the business, but as soon as she heard their names she was able to connect them to a case. And there were a lot to connect. She had forgotten just how many cases they'd taken on over the past ten years, and as they kept rolling in — interspersed with more triads — the immensity of what she and Uncle had been able to accomplish actually shocked her. He had always said, "We are in the business of getting their money back, but they come to us so desperate and lost that we are as much in the business of retrieving their souls." The clients seemed to understand that, as one by one they expressed respect and appreciation in terms that, outside the emotion-filled room, would have been excessive by any standard.

As Andrew Tam and his uncle came into the room, the older man clinging to his nephew's arm, Sonny left the envelope table and crossed the floor to Ava. "We've filled this room. The director is setting up chairs in the room next door. He thought people would pay their respects and then leave, but it seems that most of them are going to stay to walk to the cemetery with us. Do you want to keep any seats in here free for special guests?"

Ava looked at the other side of the room through a thick cloud of incense smoke — all of the joss sticks were now lit. The triads occupied the back rows, the clients sat in front. It was as if each group understood the natural order of things. "No, everyone is a special guest. Just make sure he keeps adding chairs until he has none left."

"And Ava, what will we do about the funeral dinner? We told the restaurant to expect about a hundred people."

"Call them and change the number."

"To what?"

"I don't know," Ava said. "Tell them three hundred."

"I just looked outside at the courtyard. It's still full. I think we should say five hundred, just to be on the safe side."

"Can they handle that many?"

"Even more, as long as we give them enough notice."

"Then book the whole restaurant and tell them to bring enough food to feed every seat in the place."

"I'll call them right away."

As Ava was finishing her conversation with Sonny, Andrew Tam caught her eye. He whispered something in his uncle's ear and the old man nodded at her. When they reached Uncle's picture, Tam bowed, but the old man fell to his knees and prostrated himself. "My brother, my brother," he wailed.

Tears exploded from Ava. It was so loud and sudden that Lourdes flinched and then, looking at Ava, she began to cry too.

The next hour was a blur. She was aware, vaguely, that her father and Amanda's father, Jack Yee, had arrived. Marcus Lee seemed alarmed by the intensity of his daughter's grief, but there was nothing that could be said or done to diminish it. Her head was filled with thoughts of Uncle as a young man swimming through cold, dark water towards Hong Kong, and the words he had spoken from his hospital bed the previous week kept repeating themselves. He had been a man with no family, no connections, no prospects. He had been a man with absolutely nothing, risking his life to get to a place he had never seen, with no idea what he would find or what he would do if he got there. Out of that nothingness he had created a life that had earned him the respect and admiration of all these businesspeople and all these hard men alike, people who had come from all over China, all over Asia, and even from North America to bow before his image.

At two o'clock Sonny came to her again. "Ava, the building is full. There isn't any more room, and out in the courtyard people are starting to back up onto the street. The director wants to know if we can leave for the cemetery now."

"We still have an hour to go."

"He's really worried."

"What about the monks? I don't want to go until I know the monks are there."

"Uncle Fong says they've been there since noon."

"And what about the people who haven't had a chance to pay their respects?"

"They can join the funeral procession and pay their respects at the cemetery."

"I'm not sure."

"Ava, there just isn't any more room."

She had done what he had asked and tried to keep the affair simple. She knew she couldn't be blamed for the fact that hordes of people came to pay their respects. But if the day devolved into chaos, she felt that she would be to blame.

She closed her eyes and thought about what Uncle would have wanted. Not chaos, certainly not chaos. "Yes, all right, tell him we'll leave for the cemetery now. But Sonny, I want you to go outside and explain to everyone why we're doing this, and I want you to tell them how much we appreciate their coming and that we want them to join us at the cemetery. And make sure everyone is invited to the funeral dinner."

Five minutes later, Sonny returned with the funeral director. "I think everyone understood," he said.

The funeral director addressed the people in the room. He told them there would be an early departure for the cemetery and asked them to leave the building by the front door. He said the coffin would be taken through a back door and then into the hearse for the journey to Wo Hop Shek Cemetery. The vehicle would be brought around to the front of the building and would leave from there. It would not leave without them, he promised.

As people began to file slowly out of the room, Ava, Lourdes, Sonny, and Uncle Fong were taken through a side door. Sonny took the picture of Uncle from the easel and carried it with him. As they stood outside waiting for the hearse, she heard a clash of cymbals, the banging of drums, and the high-pitched melody of flutes. The noise strengthened, filling the air around them. Ava said to Uncle Fong, "Four bands?"

Before he could answer, more drums began to play, and the cymbals became so loud it felt as if they were in the middle of a thunderstorm. "There are nine bands now," Sonny said. "Nearly every triad society has paid for one."

The hearse appeared and eased towards the door. The funeral director came up behind them and then motioned to the white ribbons strung from the back of the vehicle. Each of them grasped one, connecting themselves to Uncle for his last journey.

When they reached the street, the hearse had to stop while a path was cleared. The front courtyard was completely full, people spilling out onto the surrounding sidewalks and along the street for what had to be a hundred metres. Most of the guests were dressed in white or at least wore a white head covering of some kind.

The bands were also strung out along the street, their banners fluttering in the wind. They had stopped playing when the hearse appeared. The crowd had also gone still. As the hearse inched its way into the street to begin the kilometre-long drive, Ava heard a familiar voice. She turned and saw May Ling and Changxing standing at the edge of the crowd, just outside the courtyard. Ava had been too absorbed to realize she hadn't seen them inside.

She held out her hand. They came to her, May leading, her husband just behind. "They wouldn't let us inside," May said, her face tear-streaked and her white silk blouse stained with black mascara. She held out her arms. Ava walked into them, still holding on to the white ribbon. They hugged almost ferociously.

So began the longest funeral procession Fanling had

ever seen, and the first funeral within the memory of Hong Kong or the New Territories with as many bands.

The hearse began its ascent to Wo Hop Shek Cemetery. It was on a hillside, which was good feng shui — the higher the grave was located, the better the omens. Uncle's was at the top.

The guests marched in groups of about fifty, each followed by a band. The bands were playing at full volume, each in their own key. As discordant as it might have seemed, to Ava nothing could have more accurately reflected the range of emotions she was experiencing.

They had gone no more than fifty metres when a man came up from behind and began walking alongside Ava, startling her. "What are you doing?" she asked.

"I'm Xu," he said.

He was perhaps five foot ten, slim and elegant in a black suit, a white shirt, and a narrow white silk tie. He looked directly into her eyes. "Can I walk with you?" he said.

The hearse was moving, pulling Ava along with it. She focused on keeping her balance. Xu reached for a white ribbon between her and May. May glanced sideways at him and then at Ava. She said something, but the music made it impossible for Ava to hear her.

35

THE PROCESSION TOOK UP HALF OF THE FOUR-LANE
street that led to Wo Hop Shek Cemetery, leaving room
for vehicles to travel in both directions on the other side.
But the size and the noise of the funeral attracted so much
attention that traffic halted; people got out of their cars to
stand and watch. They were joined by onlookers from the
surrounding apartment buildings. By the time the procession had reached the midway point, the entire street was
gridlocked, with just enough room down the centre for the
hearse and the people following it. Sonny held Uncle's picture over his head as he walked, turning it this way and that
towards the encroaching crowd. As he did, they bowed one
by one.

It took them more than an hour to walk the kilometre.
Several times May Ling tried to speak to Ava, but the music
made it impossible to be heard. Xu was to Ava's right, his
eyes locked onto the hearse.

As the hearse cleared the cemetery gates, Ava could
see the monks in the distance, a cluster of orange robes.
Officials from the cemetery, a man from the funeral home,

and the five monks met them at the top of the rise. The hearse pulled off to one side and the funeral director led Ava and the others to the gravesite. They stood hand in hand while the procession worked its way into the cemetery and up the hill, circling the grave in rows that ran ten deep. It took close to twenty minutes for everyone to arrive and settle down.

Then they were all in place, and the only sound was the bands' banners flapping in the wind. Uncle Fong spoke to the head monk and the last rites began.

Ava had little experience with Taoism. She didn't understand the significance of the chanting, accompanied by the striking of bells and small brass singing bowls. It was heart-rending all the same, and she found that her tears had returned. May Ling and Lourdes cried with her.

When the monks finished, the hillside went eerily still. The funeral director nodded at Sonny and Sonny bowed his head. Four men from the funeral home went to the hearse and removed the coffin. Ava and the others turned their backs as it was carried to the grave and then lowered into the ground. Workmen slowly filled the hole. When it was almost done, Sonny tapped Ava lightly on the arm. She turned, picked up a handful of dirt, and threw it into the grave. Sonny, Uncle Fong, May Ling, Changxing, Lourdes, and Xu did the same.

When the grave was completely covered, Sonny lit two candles and gave one to Ava. They placed them at the head of the grave. Three incense sticks were lit, and Lourdes, May Ling, and Xu each placed one at the foot of the grave.

There was a heavy silence, and then the air erupted as firecrackers exploded all around them. Changxing smiled and said, "This is a good thing to do for a man from Wuhan." As firecrackers continued to erupt, the crowd became less sombre and one of the bands began to play.

Changxing stepped forward and took an orange from his pocket. He peeled it and placed it on the grave. From his other pocket he took out a Hong Kong thousand-dollar bill and put it next to the orange. Xu, Sonny, and Uncle Fong followed suit.

Emerging from the circle of onlookers, Jack Yee and Marcus Lee approached the grave and repeated the ritual. Then others followed, slowly and respectfully. Ava watched as the entire grave became a carpet of orange. Then Sonny once again tapped her lightly on the elbow and said, "It's time for us to go."

The crowd parted to let them pass. As they did, Ava heard Uncle's name being spoken, and then her own name. They seemed to her to be intertwined.

36

THEY BEGAN THE RETURN WALK TO THE FUNERAL HOME to change their clothes. Ava, Sonny, Uncle Fong, and Lourdes would give their funeral clothes to the director for burning. Ava would be putting on a white blouse; it was her intention to wear only white shirts, blouses, and T-shirts for the next month, following the tradition of mourning.

May Ling walked next to Ava, the rest of the funeral party trailing behind. They had gone about half the distance when Xu appeared at Ava's other side. This time she really looked at him. He was a bit taller than she had thought, close to six feet, and although he was slim, his body appeared wiry and athletic. His hair was cropped tight against his skull and he had a long, lean face, with a sharp chin and a rather pointed nose. His face would have been harsh if not for the large brown eyes that were full of concern.

"*Mei mei*," he said, "would you object if I kept in touch with you?"

"And why would you want to do that?" she asked, surprised by his question, and by his use of the familiar term *little sister*.

"We are united through Uncle," he said.

Eyes that had been almost soft now stared at her with a frankness that was intense. *What do you want with me?* she thought. "You know I have no interest in men?" she said.

"I have heard that."

"It's true."

"It makes no difference to me."

"And I never heard Uncle speak your name. I didn't know you existed until three days ago."

"Uncle was a man who led several lives, and he knew how to keep them apart."

"Then it's even stranger that my name would be mentioned and yours not."

Xu fell silent and Ava thought that their conversation had ended, but as they drew near the funeral home he said, "My father was from Wuhan."

"So I've been told."

"He went to Hong Kong one year after Uncle, and Uncle helped him start a new life. Sometime later my father went to Shanghai to begin his business, and Uncle supported him, always supported him. There wasn't a man in this world who my father trusted more than Uncle. I never met him until my father died, two years ago, when Uncle came to Shanghai and we connected. I was in the business then, and from time to time I would call Uncle to ask for advice.

"Six months ago I decided that changes must be made. I had been thinking about it for a long time but it was finally taking shape in my mind. It was a complicated situation, even sensitive, and if I made a large mistake I could destroy everything my father had built. So I called Uncle and told him what I had decided to try, and he counselled me. It became my habit to call him every day and to see him in Shanghai or Hong Kong when matters became particularly pressing. Like my father, I trusted him; I trusted him completely."

"I understand how that could be."

"And as for Uncle, there was no one on earth that he trusted more than you."

"He loved me," Ava said.

"Yes, he did," Xu said, touching her arm. "But his love had nothing to do with the trust he had in you. That came from the respect he had for your character. He was a dispassionate man: he had a remarkable ability to see people for exactly who they were. He told me — several times, many times — that if anything happened to him, I should keep you close."

"I don't understand."

"This thing I'm trying to do, the changes I'm trying to make . . . I need help."

"I don't see how I could possibly be of any use to you."

"Ava, Uncle talked to me about the business you and Madam Wong are starting. He thought it might provide an avenue for us to assist each other."

"Now I really don't understand."

"*Mei mei*, sometime in the near future, when things are settled here and when you and Madam Wong are ready to talk, I'd like you to visit Shanghai as my guests. I will explain to you then what I have in mind and how our interests intersect. I will be honest with you, completely honest. Uncle wouldn't have it any other way."

They had reached the courtyard of the funeral home. "Go inside. I'll join you in a minute," Ava said to May and the others. "I didn't thank you for what you did for me in Kota Kinabalu," she said, turning back to Xu.

"Uncle was responsible for that."

"You did it."

"For him as much as for you."

"Then tell me this, why did you send all those men? Why did you wreak such havoc? The moment Wan heard your name, he was terrified. Surely all you had to do was call him, contact him in some way. He would have released me, would he have not?"

"Probably."

"Then why?"

"I wanted to send a message, more to others than to him. I saw the opportunity and I took it. The timing was good and Wan was isolated. He has virtually no ties outside Borneo, no entanglements, no one who really cares if he lives or dies. So I could demonstrate my determination, my strength, and my loyalty to Uncle without having to worry about widespread repercussions."

"I'm not sure I should have heard that."

Xu pursed his lips. "This is a dangerous thing I'm trying to do. The stage has to be properly set. Poor Wan decided to be stupid and greedy at the wrong time."

"You spoke about business. What did that have to do with business?"

"There is an end to this that can meet many needs and can be a very good thing for a great many people. That is why Uncle agreed to counsel me. That is why I hope you will agree to play a role."

"I'm not sure that Madam Wong would ever agree to that kind of relationship."

Xu's eyes softened. "Whether or not you and Madam Wong visit me, and whether or not you accept my business proposition, I would still like to stay in touch with you on a personal basis."

"Why?"

"Uncle wanted it."

"And that's enough reason?"

"For me it is. So would you mind if I called you from time to time?"

"No, I guess I wouldn't," Ava said.

"Thank you, *mei mei*. When you find people worthy of your trust, you need to keep them close."

"You think too much of me."

He shrugged. "I think not. And perhaps there will be a day in the future when you think enough of me to call me *ge ge*."

"Big brother?"

"Yes."

Ava glanced up at his face. For a second she thought she was looking into Uncle's eyes.

COMING SOON
from House of Anansi Press
in February 2015

Read on for a preview of the next thrilling
Ava Lee novel, *The King of Shanghai*

(1)

AVA'S PLAN WAS TO GO BACK TO WORK AFTER FOUR months. She thought that would be enough time to get over the death of Chow Tung, the man she had called Uncle. For ten years he had been her business partner, her mentor, her friend — the most important man in her life. Then cancer took him. Ava was in her mid-thirties now; she was wealthy, had friends and family who loved her, and was a partner in a venture capital company called the Three Sisters. But she was emotionally adrift, still mourning the passing of Uncle.

She had left her downtown Toronto condo only once during the first month back from Hong Kong. She went to the neighbourhood bank, where she had a safety deposit box that contained Moleskine notebooks detailing every job she and Uncle had undertaken together. They had been debt collectors. Their clients were desperate people who had exhausted all legal and conventional means of recovering the money that had been stolen from them. It was a business fraught with peril: it was one thing to find the money, but it was entirely another to convince the thieves to return it. Over the years Ava had been kicked, knifed, shot, hit with a tire iron and a baseball bat, and kidnapped and held for ransom, as well as withstanding assassination attempts. Without Uncle she would never have survived. Now she had decided to relive every single case, every adventure.

She put away her computer and cellphone, closed the condo curtains, and spent her days sitting at the kitchen table, reading the notebooks and filling her head with memories. But she didn't disconnect her land line or cut herself off completely from the outside world. Her mother, Jennie, called and visited several times. Her girlfriend, Maria Gonzalez, came by with food. Maria wanted to stay but Ava wouldn't let her, and she refused to have sex.

"I'm not ready," Ava said.

Maria was forlorn. It wasn't until after two more rejections that she stopped asking and came to accept that Ava had to find herself again.

It is Chinese tradition to wear white for ten days after the death of a loved one. Ava wore white every day for the entire month. There was no plan; it just felt like the right thing to do, until one morning it wasn't. She had finished reading the last notebook the night before, and when she woke and went to her closet, she found herself reaching for an orange T-shirt. That afternoon she went for a long run.

The next day she ran again. When she got back to the condo, she phoned Maria. "I'd like to go out for dinner, and then maybe you can come back here and spend the night with me," she said.

Connecting with Maria was her first step back. A few days later she drove to Richmond Hill, a northern Toronto suburb, and had dim sum with her mother. Then she called her best friend, Mimi, and arranged to visit her and her baby.

After a week of running and when her energy level felt close to normal, she walked to the house of Grandmaster Tang. She hadn't seen her instructor in more than two months, but he welcomed her as if they'd been together just the day before. For two hours they practised bak mei, the martial art that he had been teaching her one-on-one — as was the custom — since she was a teenager. Her body ached when she got back to her apartment, and it did so every day for the next week, as she made repeat visits. When the aching stopped, another piece of her well-being fell into place.

In the middle of the second month, Ava began to chat with May Ling Wong and Amanda Yee, her friends and partners in the new business. Three Sisters had already taken ownership positions in a furniture-manufacturing business in Borneo and a warehouse and distribution company based in Shanghai, managed by Suki Chan, a long-time associate of May Ling. Ava knew that her partners were actively seeking other investments, but when she called them, she made it clear that she wanted to be the one to initiate contact, and that she had no interest in discussing business matters just yet.

Shortly thereafter she received her first phone call from Shanghai, from the man she knew as Xu. When she saw the Chinese country code, she assumed that it was May Ling. She answered at once, thinking that something terrible must have happened if May Ling was calling against her wishes. Instead she heard the soft, confident voice of Xu. He spoke to her in Mandarin, and she had never heard anyone speak it better, each word carefully pronounced as if it had a value that set it apart from the others.

"I hope you're well and I apologize if I'm inconveniencing you. I think often of Uncle, and whenever I do, you come to mind. No two people could have had a better mentor."

"I am well enough," was all Ava could say, flustered by the unexpectedness of his call and by the way he linked them through Uncle.

She hadn't known that Xu existed until the day before Uncle died, and she had met him exactly once — at Uncle's funeral. Any doubts she had about the depth of the relationship between the two men had been put to rest when she went through Uncle's papers. The men had been close. What alarmed her was that most of their correspondence concerned Xu's management of his triad gang in Shanghai.

During the course of their first conversation, Xu focused solely on his memories of Uncle, and Ava found herself sharing some of hers. It was cathartic for her, and when he asked if he could call again, she said yes. He became a regular contact. Xu was well-read and they shared an interest in Chinese films and good food. And then, of course, there was Uncle; every call involved at least one story about him.

One time Xu veered off into a discussion about his business, and Ava had to pull him back. "I don't want to talk about how you make your living," she said.

He retreated, but not without saying, "My business is in a constant state of flux. What it is today could turn into something entirely different tomorrow. When things are settled in your life, I would like you and Madam Wong to visit me in Shanghai. We may have some areas of shared interest, *mei mei*."

At Uncle's funeral he had made the same request. Ava had put it down to politeness. Now it had more import, but not enough that she wanted to pursue it. "Tell me more about that young female film director from Yantai you mentioned last week," she said, changing the subject.

In her third month at home, she felt the urge to travel. Maria took a week of leave from her job as assistant trade commissioner at the Colombian consulate in Toronto and they flew to Aruba. Four days into the trip, Ava felt the first touch of guilt about being idle. By the end of the week she'd had enough of beaches and eating out and was ready to go back to work.

She called May Ling as soon as she got back to Toronto. "I want to step into the business," she said.

"This is sooner than you thought," May said.

"I think I've worked through enough of the pain."

"Are you sure? We can wait."

"There will always be a hole in my heart where Uncle was, but I can't let it paralyze me. He wouldn't want that either."

"Well, in that case, how about meeting Amanda and me in Shanghai in a few days?"

"Shanghai?"

"It's year-end for Suki Chan. I'll be going over her numbers and looking at her plans for the coming year. She tells me she has some ideas she wants us to consider. I could use your input."

"How about Amanda?"

"She has her own project there, some mysterious investment proposal that she tells me has to be seen."

"Seen?"

"I've asked for the business plan. She says she'll give it to me when we're in Shanghai."

"That isn't like Amanda."

"I know, but she's quite giddy about it. I was going to go there anyway. She'll be even giddier knowing that you're coming."

"Yes," she said softly.

"Ava, is something wrong?"

"Why do you ask?"

"You don't sound particularly enthusiastic."

"It's Xu," Ava said.

"What about him?"

"He's been calling me."

"What does he want?"

"We share memories of Uncle. It's helped me get past some things."

"He lives in Shanghai," May said. "Is that the problem?"

"Yes. He asked me at the funeral, and again over the phone, if you and I could meet with him there."

"Both of us?"

"He hints that he has some business interests that could be mutually beneficial."

"Why on earth would we ever do business with a triad gang leader? I know he's sophisticated and doesn't look like your stereotypical gangster, but he didn't get to be as successful as he is without a very sharp cutting edge."

"I'm not suggesting we do business with him, May," Ava said. "I just don't think I can go to Shanghai and not meet with him. If you're uncomfortable with the idea, then I'll go alone."

"Is this about both of you being tied to Uncle?"

"It's partly that, of course, but I also can't forget that I owe Xu my life. We both know I would have been killed in Borneo without him," Ava said. The memory of being kidnapped and held for ransom by a local triad gang was still fresh. Uncle had been in Shanghai with Xu when it happened and had prevailed upon him to send men to rescue her. Ava was saved, but ten men died as Xu exacted revenge for reasons that had nothing with her.

"He did what he did for Uncle. I'm not sure you owe him anything."

"That could be true, but I can't deny that there's a connection that runs between us and that there's an obligation — if not a debt — that must be recognized. Meeting with Xu, especially socially over dinner or lunch, would be a trivial thing for us, and it's the only thing he's ever asked of me. So I can't go to Shanghai without telling him, and I can't be there and refuse to see him."

"All right, I'll go along," May sighed. "I'll ask Amanda to build a meeting with him into our schedule. Which do you prefer, dinner or lunch?"

"I think dinner shows more respect."

"Dinner it is."

"When Amanda forwards me the entire schedule, I'll call Xu and make sure the time works for him."

"From what you're telling me, I'll be surprised if he doesn't make any time work," May said.

"Perhaps, but regardless of when we end up meeting with him, I don't want Amanda there. He was quite specific about it being me and you. Will she be offended by that?"

"She isn't that sensitive, but in any event I'll tell her it's strictly a social thing."

"Okay."

"Ava, do you have any idea what he wants with us?"

"No."

"Really?" May said.

"I don't have a clue."

ACKNOWLEDGEMENTS

This is the sixth book in the Ava Lee series, and as Ava's life expands, so does the number of people who have made contributions.

As always, my family's support has been paramount as the first readers and editors of any Ava Lee book, and then as drum-beaters after the books have been released.

My thanks to Sarah MacLachlan and her team at House of Anansi Press.

Very special thanks — again — to my editor, the great Janie Yoon. In addition to being the custodian of Ava's and the book's style, in this case she also contributed a key plot change.

My agents, Bruce Westwood and Carolyn Forde, continue to keep my back covered. Their enthusiastic support has brightened many a bad writing day.

Last, I want to acknowledge the input I receive from readers, and in this instance, two of them in particular. As our readership has grown, so has the number of emails and letters I get. They arrive now on a daily basis from virtually all over the world and — complimentary or not — I answer them all. Some of them point out mistakes and offer advice.

Fawn Gao, who lives in Vancouver, has been especially helpful with her advice about the proper use of Chinese terms and phrases. So I thank her and hope she keeps passing along her knowledge.

Helena Ying, known professionally as Dr. Helena Lau, sent me an email that had quite an impact. She found an error in the *The Scottish Banker of Surabaya* that was contained in a single line. On the face of it, the error was quite minor. But the repercussions for *The Two Sisters of Borneo* were more telling, and I rewrote part of the book based on her comment.

A very special thanks, then, to Helena and to all the other readers who keep me on my toes. Please don't stop — I do pay attention.

IAN HAMILTON is the author of the Ava Lee series: *The Dragon Head of Hong Kong: The Ava Lee Prequel, The Water Rat of Wanchai, The Disciple of Las Vegas, The Wild Beasts of Wuhan, The Red Pole of Macau, The Scottish Banker of Surabaya,* and *The Two Sisters of Borneo. The Water Rat of Wanchai* was the winner of the Arthur Ellis Award for Best First Novel, an Amazon.ca Top 100 Book of the Year, an Amazon.ca Top 100 Editors' Pick, an Amazon.ca Canadian Pick, an Amazon.ca Mysteries and Thrillers Pick, a *Toronto Star* Top 5 Fiction Book of the Year, and a *Quill & Quire* Top 5 Fiction Book of the Year. The seventh book in the Ava Lee series, *The King of Shanghai,* will be published in February 2015.

NOW AVAILABLE
from House of Anansi Press
the first five books in the Ava Lee series.

Prequel and Book 1 **Book 2** **Book 3**

Book 4 **Book 5**

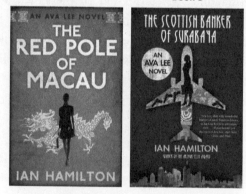